THE LORD GOD BIRD

THE LORD GOD BIRD

A novella by Russell Hill

New York

Caravel Books
a mystery imprint of
Pleasure Boat Studio: A Literary Press

The Lord God Bird
by Russell Hill

A Caravel Mystery
ISBN 978-1-929355-53-2
Library of Congress Control Number: 2008941329

Design by Laura Tolkow, Flush Left
Cover painting by Michael Suffield

Caravel Mystery Books is an imprint of Pleasure Boat Studio: A Literary Press
Our books are available through the following:
SPD (Small Press Distribution) Tel. 800-869-7553, Fax 510-524-0852
Partners/West Tel. 425-227-8486, Fax 425-204-2448
Baker & Taylor 800-775-1100, Fax 800-775-7480
Ingram Tel 615-793-5000, Fax 615-287-5429
Amazon.com and bn.com

and through
PLEASURE BOAT STUDIO: A LITERARY PRESS
www.pleasureboatstudio.com
201 West 89th Street
New York, NY 10024

Contact Jack Estes
Fax: 888-810-5308
Email: pleasboat@nyc.rr.com

Pleasure Boat Studio is a proud subscriber to the Green Press Initiative. This program
encourages the use of 100% post-consumer recycled paper with environmentally friendly
inks for all printing projects in an effort to reduce the book industry's economic and
social impact. With the cooperation of our printing company, we are pleased to offer this
book as a Green Press book.

MAN ARRESTED BY WEYMOUTH POLICE

A man arrested by Weymouth police was found preening himself on Chesil Beach, Sunday, clad only in a cape, shouting and gesturing at the sea. Police Constable White, the arresting officer, reported that the unidentified man was unable to speak, and could only utter shrill gull-like cries.

Dorset, England, *Western Gazette*, Nov. 21, 1972

I am like a pelican of the wilderness. I am like an owl of the desert.   Psalm 102

When the egret rose from the reeds I thought it was a woman rising from the green river.

Jean-Jacques Audubon, Florida, 1832

1.

It began with birds. It ended with a bird.

It was 1939 and we had a lawn in Arlington Heights. It was a scruffy lawn, and it sloped toward the lilacs. The scent of the lilac bush permeated the air and it was a perfume that women wore and it drew hummingbirds. Even now I can smell those bushes and see the fireflies in the Illinois summer darkness. The hummingbirds were iridescent, hovering jewels. Those are the first birds I can remember, but they were not the important birds.

On the other side of the house was a long driveway that led to a garage and behind the house, to the right, was a garden. Swiss chard. I remember the Swiss chard. Beyond that was an empty lot, somebody else's lot and I have no memory of neighbors. It was a rented house with a basement with a dirt floor and Paul and I slept in a second-floor room that looked out onto another vacant lot next to the driveway. It was mowed in the summer. I do not remember who mowed it. Perhaps my father did. In the winter it was covered with snow, a white expanse, and once I saw a scarlet tananger, like a clot of bright blood in the middle of the whiteness before it flew up into the bare branches of an elm tree. The sidewalks on both sides of S. Mitchell Street were buckled where the roots of elm trees had raised them.

If I went down the steps and turned left, I was aimed at the elementary school, a two-story brick building several blocks away. I must have been in fourth grade. I remember nothing about the school or the teachers. Only that we lived in Arlington Heights and my father taught at the high school on the other side of town and there was a race track nearby. Once Paul and I went out to Arlington Park on a November day, taking cheese sandwiches wrapped in wax paper with us, going past the lot where my father and mother had a victory garden and then across empty fields toward the track. We could see the grandstands in the distance but they loomed big enough so that it took far longer to reach them than we thought. The track was closed and the grandstand was cavernous and spooky. It turned cold and dark and we came back through muddy plowed fields with sharp spikes of corn stalk that cut our ankles.

There was an iceman who came on hot summer days and we waited until he went into the house and we went to the back of his truck and gathered slivers of ice from the wet wooden slats that covered the bed of the truck.

There were elm trees on S. Mitchell Street. There were elm trees on nearly every Midwestern street. Sometimes there were red-headed woodpeckers in those trees. I got a bird book for Christmas that year. Because my father was a teacher and my mother had taught school before she was married, they bought us books for birthdays and Christmas. They were usually books that had educational value, like a book about Abraham Lincoln growing up in a log cabin or young Audubon growing up in the West Indies. That book was one of my favorites, along with the Yankee Flier books. The Yankee Flier joined the RAF to fight the Nazis and he had incredible adventures, in books with boiled cardboard covers and pages that turned yellow if you left the book open in the sunshine.

But Audubon caught my fancy. He was my age and he
didn't go to school. His father was a French sea captain who
had a wife in the West Indies. Or at least that's what the book
intimated, although now I'm pretty sure she wasn't his wife.
Audubon spent his days in swamps and forests, shooting birds,
training himself to stuff them, buying the carcasses of exotic birds
in the market, and learning to draw them. My fascination with
Audubon is probably why my folks gave me the bird book. It was
Audubon's *Birds of America*, the "popular edition," 320 pages
of copies of Audubon's paintings. I found all of the birds that I
knew from the vacant lots around our house: the scarlet tananger,
the downy woodpecker, doves and pigeons, the purple martins
that lived in the eaves of an old barn near the victory garden, and
a meadowlark. I especially liked the picture of the ivory-billed
woodpecker which, the caption said, was nearly extinct. There
were three of them in the painting, clinging to a dead tree, and one
of them had a red crest that curved back over its neck, long and
shaped like a costume hat, framing a yellow eye with a brilliant
black dot in the center. It lived, according to the book, in primeval
timber of the southern states. I wasn't sure what primeval timber

was and when I looked it up in The World Book, there was a picture of huge trees with water surrounding them, a gloomy swamp-like scene.

2.

My mother took us to the Museum of Science and Industry in Chicago. It was an immense building, far bigger than a city block, surrounded by green lawn, Lake Michigan off in the distance, and inside was a room that seemed as big as a football field with model railroad trains. We stood on a mezzanine terrace and watched them rattle through papiér maché mountains and across mirrored lakes. There was a fake coal mine and we went down the dark elevator into the mine and later we went outside to climb into the captured Nazi submarine. But the part I liked best was a room with bird dioramas. Behind glass in little rooms that lined the walls were every bird I could imagine, stuffed, their glass eyes alert, woodpeckers attached to trees that came out of the floor and disappeared into the ceiling; herons and egrets that stood in plaster-of -Paris water, heads cocked; an eagle suspended

above a running rabbit, the rabbit in mid-jump, one foot attached
to the dirt floor, the eagle suspended by wires so thin, if you
squinted your eyes, they disappeared and the eagle seemed ready
to sink its extended claws into the frightened rabbit. My brother
got bored and wanted to see other things and my mother took him
off, leaving me to wander from window to window. There was a
pileated woodpecker, which is about as close as you can get to an
Ivory Bill, its red crest on the back of its head like an irrational
hairdo, something a madwoman would wear to a costume ball.

Like Audubon, I tried to draw birds, and like Audubon's
first efforts when he was my age, I wasn't successful. My birds
were, like his, lifeless and wooden. Even copying them from the
book of his paintings didn't work. I drew copies, flat things that
lay on the page, pressed to the paper so that they seemed never
to have lived at all. We moved to Elgin and lived in an apartment
building with four apartments and I went to fifth grade at a new
elementary school. Miss Higginbothan, the teacher, had us all
memorize a poem for a presentation to mothers one morning.
Most of the mothers didn't work, but my mother had taken a
job at the Elgin watch factory and my father had left his teaching

job to become a draftsman at the Kaiser shipyard in Seneca. He
stayed in Seneca during the week, coming home on weekends.
I remember that the poem I had to memorize began, "The
woodpecker pecked out a little round hole, and made him a house
in the telephone pole." I protested to Miss. H. that woodpeckers
didn't peck out holes. They looked for holes already in trees where
rotted limbs had dropped off, but she insisted that I was wrong.

"Certainly the man who wrote this poem knew more about
birds than an eleven-year-old," she said. She was, of course, wrong.

In one of the other apartments was an old lady who had
a parrot. Her apartment smelled musty, bird-like, and I never saw
her go out. A boy from the grocery store brought her groceries.
Sometimes I went to see her and she would give me a ginger snap
and I talked to the parrot, trying to make him talk back. He could
say things like," Hello, Jack!" and "Pipe down!" and sometimes he
whistled a song. Mrs. Kowalski said that her husband had taught it to
speak and there were other things it could say, but it chose not to say
them in the company of children. I asked how old the parrot was.

"Who knows?" she said. "Maybe older than me," which
I found hard to believe because she was a tiny, wrinkled woman

who spent her days crocheting lace doilies. They were everywhere, on the backs and arms of chairs, hanging off the mantle, draped over lamp shades.

I brought my paper and pencils and sketched the parrot, but about all I could do that seemed right were the beak and the eyes. My mother bought me a little watercolor set and I tried to capture the colors of the parrot, but the feathers were brilliant, iridescent red and yellow and a green that changed when the sunlight struck it.

I found a bird book in the library and read everything I could about parrots. There were more than three hundred species and despite the tiny size of their brains, they were rated among the smartest creatures in the animal kingdom. In that same book was more about the ivory-billed woodpecker and I found out that there was only a handful of them left, living in a forest on the border between Arkansas and Louisiana.

3.

We didn't stay long in Elgin. At the end of the school year, in June, we moved back to Arlington Heights and back into 123 S. Mitchell Street. My father mowed the lawn and my mother planted the garden in back. There would be more Swiss chard in the Fall.

I spent that summer finding dead birds. There was a big window at the end of a building downtown and apparently birds thought that it was still part of the sky, and when they banged into it, they sometimes broke their necks and I found them next to the foundation. Thrushes and sparrows and once a bluebird. I brought them home and following directions from a library book about taxidermy, I gutted them, took off the skin and tacked them to the wall of the garage to dry. But my bird skins were stiff and the eyes shrank into the skulls, leaving a hole. I knew that there were places where taxidermists bought glass eyes to insert in the holes, but I had no idea where they were or how to go about buying glass birds' eyes.

Sometimes my brother and I played baseball in the vacant lot next door, a complicated game in which we were all nine players on two teams, alternately pitching and hitting, sometimes throwing the ball up in the air and hitting it to the outfield, running the bases. Paul helped me look for dead birds and on one of our journeys to the outskirts of Arlington Heights we found several dead crows in a field of corn. When I took them apart I found tiny lead buckshot. A farmer had shot them. The back wall of the garage now had nearly a dozen feathered skins spread-eagled in the sun.

When school started in September, I was back in the same two-story brick building, but it held little interest for me. It would hold little interest for me for the next several years, much to the chagrin of my schoolteacher parents.

Two things of importance happened when I turned twelve. The war ended and Mrs. Kowalski died. I had forgotten about visiting her in the Elgin apartment, but one night my parents announced that she had died and she had left her African

Gray parrot, Oskar, to me. I remembered Mrs. Kowalski telling

me that his name was spelled with a K, not a C. He's a Polish

parrot, she said.

So on a Sunday we drove to Elgin and came back with

Oskar in his cage. My mother was reluctant to have the bird

in the house, fearing that it would smell, but I promised to

spread newspapers under the cage to catch spill-overs, to clean it

regularly, and it ended up in the room with Paul and me.

We spent hours talking to Oskar, although Paul soon

tired of it and I was left alone with the bird that cocked its head to

one side, fixed its eye on me and would finally say, "Pipe down!"

Eventually I found it could say, "Kill the Cat!" And "Oskar

wants a beer!" and "Good night!" and "Good morning!" and one

afternoon Oskar came out with a racking cough that sounded

just like a dying old man, followed by a series of "Fuck This!

Fuck This! Fuck this!" in a man's guttural voice. The voice had

an accent, and when Oskar shouted the words I had the startling

impression that someone else had entered my bedroom.

I read everything I could about African Grays. They were

the smartest and most expensive parrots. The most famous one

was named N'kisi and he had a vocabulary of a thousand words.

When I looked up his name I found it was an African word for a

wooden statue that people in a village drove nails into. Each nail

was meant to remember someone, like a grandfather or a child

who had died. There was a man in each village who was in charge

of the N'kisi and his job was to memorize each of the nails so that

people knew who they represented. It was a good name for a bird

who had memorized a thousand words

I got good at drawing pictures of Oskar, but the color of

his feathers continued to elude me.

My mother took me to a lecture at the public library.

A man named Albert Tanner talked about the Ivory-Billed

Woodpecker. There was a slide show, with photographs taken

in the 1930's of the Ivory Bill, and there was a sound recording

of the nasal KENK! KENK! of the Ivory Bill, recorded in 1944

by a man named Allan Wisdom. The last sighting had been in

1944, but Tanner said there were, possibly, more of the birds

somewhere in the dense forests of Arkansas, Louisiana, and Texas.

The forest had once covered eight million acres, but they were a fraction of that now, and Tanner said it was critical that we save

the forests where this magnificent bird lived. There was only

one woodpecker in the world bigger, and that was the Mexican

woodpecker. The Ivory Bill was, he said, a symbol of what

America had once been.

"A squirrel could have hopped from tree to tree from

Pennsylvania to Chicago," he said. "It could have started in

Tennessee and gone all the way across Arkansas into Oklahoma."

I had an image of a squirrel carrying a small suitcase,

traveling to Chicago to see a cousin.

When I got home, I practiced making the KENK! sound

of the Ivory Bill. It had sounded a bit like a cheap automobile

horn. It made two knocks when it pecked at trees, resounding

knocks that were more like two blocks of wood being struck

together. Tanner said that the bill was remarkable, long and stout.

"Whoever sees an Ivory Bill will be remembered," he said.

I resolved to be one of those people.

When I met Robin I was nineteen. It wasn't her name as much as the way she looked. Bird-like. Not delicate, but structurally she was like a bird, and the first time I saw her naked, she lifted her arms and there were the patagialus tendons, just the way they would have been on the delicate underside of a bird's wing, stretched between her pectoralis major and the levator caudae and there was a muscle that ran from the inside of her knee up to her pussy that was exactly like the pronators on a bird. I touched the hardness of that muscle when she stretched her leg out to the side and I fully expected her to hop off the bed, lift her wings, and dart off in fright.

I never finished high school. School bored me. My parents couldn't understand. I was an avid reader, and it wasn't that mathematics or science weren't interesting, but the teachers seemed dull, lifeless people who insisted in putting us in careful rows, the wooden desks bolted to the wooden floors of Arlington Heights High School. I wanted to take biology and find out as much as I could about birds. I had read everything I could find, had spent hours in the garage taking apart bird carcasses, and I had notebooks filled with sketches, some of them quite good. By now I had learned to stuff the bird skins, and had used my paper route money to buy glass eyes. I had a very life-like crow attached to a branch that stuck out from the garage wall and a diorama of chickadees at a mirrored puddle. But I was told that I would have to start with General Science and a stodgy man named Mr. Weiner lectured about the position of the planets and why it was colder in the winter, and chalked diagrams of volcanoes on the front board, white pimples with a pipe of red chalk coming up out of the center of the earth. I drew pictures of Mr. Weiner impaled on a stick, being held over a volcano by a group of laughing kids; and I had to explain them to the assistant principal, a stocky man with hair sprouting from his collar and the backs of his hands. I suspected he was Darwin's missing link.

After two years I simply stopped going, and my parents

gave up. I took a job in a hardware store sweeping up and unpacking nuts and bolts and stocking shelves and by the time I was seventeen I could tell customers how to wire the light fixture they had bought and could draw diagrams of framing and plumbing projects, knew how to drill a bolt out of an engine block and re-tap the threads. I continued to live at home, but Oskar and I moved into the garage where I was perfecting my taxidermy. My brother was happy to have the bedroom to himself and I think my parents were uncomfortable with my presence. The less they saw of me, the less they had to think about what I was becoming.

By the time I was nineteen I often ran the hardware store by myself while Jerry had coffee in the diner a block away or played cards with cronies in the storeroom in the back of the store. Then I met Robin.

The dime store was down the street from Jerry's Hardware. I went there for some shelf paper for a display of vases that Jerry had picked up second-hand and Robin was there. Something about her interested me. She wasn't pretty in the usual way; she was tiny, only about five feet tall, and she had no figure. She looked more like a slender boy, but when she looked at me, her eyes held mine, direct, not confrontational, but with that sort of look that says, I don't take any shit off anybody, even if I do work in a dime store. Her eyes were green and wide and I came back to the dime store to buy more shelf paper, even though we didn't need any.

Eventually I asked her to have lunch with me at the counter of the drugstore. When I found out she liked black licorice, I bought a box of it, and brought a new strand to the dime store every day. When I talked about birds, she listened, and when I loaned her my copy of Audubon's *Birds of America*, she brought it back the next day with pieces of paper marking a dozen birds.

"These are my favorites," she said. She had marked the Louisiana heron, the belted kingfisher, the snowy egret, the Ivory Bill, and of course an American robin.

Both of us wanted to get away from Arlington Heights. Robin lived with her parents, too, but she didn't have a separate place like my garage. She came over in the afternoons after the dime store and the hardware store closed and watched me work on birds and eventually she stayed for a night. My parents must have known. They said nothing. Robin stayed more often.

I sold Oskar. A pet store in Elgin paid a hundred and eighteen dollars for him. I sold my stuffed birds and got another fifteen dollars. I sold all of my taxidermy stuff for another ten dollars. I had four hundred dollars saved from Jerry's Hardware and I had a car, a 1939 Ford coupe, green, with a windshield that cranked out in front, and upholstery that sprouted tufts of stuffing. Robin had eighty-nine dollars saved from her job at the dime store and I cashed in the savings bond that my parents had bought when I turned twelve. They had visions of eventual wealth, but a bond bought for eighteen dollars was worth only twenty-five at maturity, so I cashed it in and got nineteen dollars. Paul bought my baseball mitt and my army surplus flashlight for two dollars. I collected my last week's pay from Jerry and we had six hundred and seventy-three dollars when we left Arlington Heights at the beginning of the summer. It would be enough to take us to the Arkansas-Louisiana border and live for several months. The Big Woods were there, and that was where Tanner had seen the Ivory Bill. When I told Robin that's what I wanted to do, she had said, "Me, too!"

"Me, too, what?" I said.

"If you want to see that bird, I want to see it, too."

"You know what it is?"

"You talk about it all the time."

"Not all the time."

"If it wasn't a bird, I would be jealous."

I reached out and touched her arm, slid my fingers down to her wrist, reached up and touched her face.

"You don't have feathers," I said.

"Is that good or bad?"

"It's good." I slipped my hand inside her shirt, touching the nipple of her breast.

"Woodpeckers don't have tits either."

"I don't have tits."

"You do. They just don't stick out like a sore thumb."

I squeezed her nipple between my thumb and forefinger.

"If you keep doing that, they're going to stick out like sore nipples," she said.

"We're going to find the Ivory-Billed Woodpecker," I said, "and we're going to tell the world what we saw and they're going to let up a fucking cheer like you never heard. You and me are going to be famous."

5.

We drove down through Illinois and crossed into Missouri and continued south until we came to Arkansas. The landscape changed from flat fields to rough hills and in the distance we could see the Ozarks. We stopped for that first night, exhausted, at a motor court that was made of stone, a long, low building with a sign in front of the office that said, NO WORKING ON CARS IN FRONT OF YOUR ROOM. There were swamp coolers in the window of every unit and they were wheezing, and it was hot, humid, and heat lightning played off the mountains to the west. I paid five dollars for a room and we left the door open. It smelled musty and damp and Robin and I sat outside sharing a cold beer that I bought in the little market down the street.

"This was a hot springs," the man behind the counter in the tiny office said. "Used to be quite the place. William Howard

Taft came here once."

I wasn't sure who William Howard Taft was.

"If you turn on the cold water, it won't run cold," he said. "Comes from the hot springs. Nice hot shower, though."

We watched the heat lightning touch down, outlining the mountains. Across from us someone sat in the shadow of a wall, smoking, and when he inhaled, the cigarette glowed and there was a brief outline of his face. Farther down the walk there was a cone of light on the ground and as insects hit the light and occasionally fried themselves and dropped, several large toads waited just outside the circle of light. They snatched the insect bodies before they hit the ground.

It was after midnight when we went to bed. It was still unbearably hot and we lay on the damp sheet and made love, our bodies sticking to each other, and then, as the night wore on, a wind came up, cooling our naked bodies until, at some point, we pulled the sheet over ourselves and lay, our bodies entwined. We woke with the barking of dogs. A rooster crowed and at first light we dressed and got into the car and drove until we came to the next town where a diner was open. A sign in front showed a man in a chef's hat flipping a pancake, and there was a single light bulb the glowed in the center of the pancake. Robin asked the waitress if she could have the child's breakfast.

"I'm not all that hungry," she said.

"Sweetheart," the waitress said, "if it's on the menu, you can have it." She turned to me. "Where'd you find this little bitty thing," she said. "She ought to eat more than a child's breakfast."

"She was the prize in a Crackerjack box."

"Well, aren't you the lucky one," the waitress said, with a wink at Robin.

That morning we drove until we were almost in Louisiana. Now the farms were small and there were woods here and there and the towns seemed scruffy. I had circled The Big Woods on the map and when we got near I stopped at a gas station and asked where The Big Woods began.

""You mean the deep woods?" the man said

"That's right."

"They's all over," he said. "You go on down to Crossett and they're just south of there but they run a ways into Louisiana." He pronounced it 'Lewzeeanna.'

"You go far enough," he said, "and you get into Despair Bayou."

We looked for a motor court in Crossett but there wasn't one. There was an old hotel in town, a two-story brick building that had seen better days, and we got a room for three dollars. It wasn't much better than the room we had the night before, but it was a place to stay and we found a diner where we had chicken fried steak and grits and greens and bread that must have been baked by someone's mother, soft and moist and warm. We put pats of butter on it and they melted and we wrapped the bread around pieces of the steak and ate them like sandwiches. Robin was ravenous.

I said, "You're not eating like a bird tonight," and she said, "Yes I am. I'm eating like a raptor."

"Which one?" I said.

"One of those big ones that eats stuff that's been killed. Rabbits and maybe even deer. There was a picture in the Audubon book of a bunch of them sitting down around a deer and eating, just like it was a family dinner."

"Those weren't raptors," I said.

6.

She wore a black tee shirt with a torn neck, and a
necklace. I remembered the necklace from the dime store. One
afternoon, waiting for her to get off work, I had bought it. We
went for a coke at the drugstore and she put it on, admiring
herself in the mirror behind the counter. It was a silver chain with
tin hearts alternating with black beads. The hearts were so tiny
that you had to look closely to see that they were hearts. As I
paid for the cokes, she stood, thumbing through a magazine from
the rack next to the cash register and I noticed a man watching
her carefully, and at first I wondered what his interest in her
was and then it came to me that she looked quite beautiful, the
white of her throat and the freckled plane of skin below it, the
tiny necklace and the black cloth. She wore no bra—she rarely
did—and her nipples were faint bumps where the roundness of her

small breasts showed. Her small hands turned the pages idly.

It was oppressively hot. Humid. When I left the car I could feel my shirt peel from the car seat. We walked down the road and there were puddles in the ruts and clouds of mosquitoes, so many that we pulled up clumps of grass and used them to wave away the mosquitoes as we walked. The road skirted the edge of the trees and suddenly entered the woods, ending abruptly at the water. Ahead of us was a dark expanse of green, still, almost like the mirrored lakes in the toy train diorama in the museum in Chicago. But this water smelled of decay and there were immense cypress trees rising from it. We could feel the heat. It shimmered in the air. There was a foreboding, a heaviness that pressed against my chest, stilled my heartbeat. It was a place of snakes and ancient creatures, things that the rest of the world thought no longer existed, but I knew that somewhere in that permanent dusk there were Ivory Bills, a female in a nest hole, the black crest at the back of her head curving forward, and the long gliding flight of the male, his red jester's cap and his ebony wings floating toward the nest, wings suddenly turned up to brake his flight, talons hooked into the cypress, his sharp tail holding him erect against the trunk.

There were bird calls somewhere and the constant whine of insects. Robin turned to me, her face shining with sweat.

"It's too fucking hot," she said. She pulled the neck of her tee shirt away from her chest and blew down into it.

"It's perfect for the Ivory Bill," I said.

"Is this where we look?"

"This is it. We'll need a boat"

"How do you know where to start?"

"Tanner said they find dead or dying trees and they peel off the bark and eat the insect grubs beneath them. So they have to keep looking for dead trees. That's what we'll look for."

"We could get lost in there."

"We'll take a compass. We'll mark trees."

"Everything feels old," she said. "Really old."

"It is."

7.

We looked for a place to stay. We asked in Crossett and the woman at the chamber of commerce gave us a list of rentals but nothing seemed right. We drove back toward The Big Springs and as we passed a farm, I noticed a house off to one side, at the edge of the woods, and it seemed empty. I stopped the car and we walked through the field to the house. It was small, a single room with a sink on one wall and a hand pump at the end of the sink. A small wood stove was in the center of the room. There was an empty iron bed frame in the room and a sagging set of empty shelves. There was an outhouse behind it.

"What do you think?" I said.

Robin looked around. The screen door sagged on one hinge and she pulled it toward her.

"I could fix that," I said, pulling the door closed.

"We'd be all by ourselves," she said.

"Nobody would bother us."

"I like it," she said.

We went back to the car and I drove back to the entrance to the farm. There was a solid farmhouse, brick, with a big front porch, and two barns off to one side. A stock tank was at the edge of the lawn that stretched behind the house. I knocked on the door and eventually a woman opened it, wiping her hands on her apron.

I asked about the house. It wasn't for rent, she said. Her husband appeared at her side and asked who we were and why did we want to live in a shack on the edge of the woods.

"I'm an ornithologist," I lied. "I'm studying the Ivory-Billed Woodpecker and there may be some still in The Big Woods. My wife and I need a place to stay that's close enough to the bayou so we can go into it regularly."

""Nobody goes in there except hunters and the Singer people."

"Who are the Singer people?" I asked.

"Singer Sewing machine. They own most of it. They're

busy draining it and cutting down the trees."

"We'd pay a fair rent," I said.

"There's no running water. There's a hand pump but there's no toilet. Only an outhouse."

"That's OK with us," I said.

He looked at me. "There's no furniture," he said.

"We can find something."

"I'm not sure what an ornithologist is," he said, "but you kids can have it if you want. Five dollars a week too much?"

We stood in the single room and looked at each other and Robin began to giggle.

"We have a house," she said.

"Yes."

She took the edge of her tee shirt in both hands, raising them to strip it off over her head, shaking her hair out of the neck and tossing it on the counter next to the sink.

"Let's fuck," she said. "Right now. Here. In our own house." She reached up and pressed her nipples to her chest. "Come here," she said. "Show me how birds fuck. Show me how they make love."

"They don't make love. They just do it so there will be more birds. I don't think they feel about it the way I feel about you."

"You said geese mate for life. They must have some feeling for each other. You said if a hunter shoots one of a pair the other one hangs around and cries."

"Maybe," I said.

She was stepping out of her Levis. She stripped her panties off and stood naked in the afternoon light that filtered through the dirty kitchen window. She raised her arms and stretched until she was on tiptoe. Her tiny breasts were flattened against her chest and the bones of her hips formed a vee rising from her legs.

"Imagine I'm a bird," she said. "What kind of a bird do you want me to be?"

"Right now you look like an egret," I said. Her skin was white, almost porcelain, and her neck seemed longer, and as I looked at her, I imagined the egret, wings outstretched, rising to leave the water in the ditch by the roadside, lifting its wings gracefully, catching the air.

"What does the egret sound like?" she asked.

"Not pretty. It's a croak. As if you startled a big frog."

She let out a hoarse belching sound and lowered her arms, lifting them again.

"Fuck me," she said. "Now."

8.

In the evening the fireflies came out. They winked in the edge of the field, in the dark of the woods, and if I caught one in my hand, the tiny end of it glowed briefly, enough to reveal the lines on my palm. It was a sexual attractor, that much I knew, and there was even another insect that mimicked the firefly, turning on its little light so that when the male firefly came calling, it ate him.

Moths whirled up into the light above the door, a single bulb that brought mayflies and cicadas and moths, some almost as big as my hand. The cicadas were fierce looking creatures, armored insects that gave off a constant buzzing that filled the night, rising and falling, something we learned to sleep with.

We needed a boat. The Woods were permanently under water and we would have to use a boat to get deep into them and if we went farther into the bayou, it would be a necessity. I asked at the gas station in Crossett and at the grocery store and went to

the weekly newspaper and eventually I found a man who wanted

to get rid of a boat. It was a skiff, shallow drafted, with oars, and it

was tight.

"You got a truck?" he asked.

"No."

"How you going to get this to where you're going

fishing?"

"There's no trailer with it?"

"No." He looked at me as if I had asked if there was a

magic carpet.

"Could I put it on top of the car?"

"I suspect you could. Wouldn't be easy."

I found two pieces of two-by four behind the house,

borrowed a drill from the farmer, drilled holes in them and in the

car roof and bolted them to the top of the car. When I went back,

the man looked at what I had done and shook his head.

"You might get some leaks in them bolt holes when it

rains," he said.

"I might. I can live with that."

We hoisted the boat onto the makeshift rack and I paid him fifteen dollars for it.

"That's a fine boat," he said. "I caught many a bass out of that boat. It's a good luck boat."

I hoped he was right.

The mosquitoes were fierce. They came in clouds, and our arms and faces darkened with them. We only stayed in the bayou an hour before we were forced out. I left the boat chained to a tree, and I piled branches over it so we wouldn't have to load it back onto the car. Back at the house we rubbed alcohol onto the welts and tried to figure out how we could go back into the woods and stay without being eaten alive.

"We could wear long-sleeved shirts and pants with legs," Robin said.

"Yes, but what about our faces and hands?"

"We could wear masks and gloves."

"And die in the heat."

We drove back into Crossett and went to the drugstore where a white-coated man in a cubbyhole at the back of a little store filled with creams and bottles and stretchy bandages for trick knees asked what he could do for us. I told him we lived in a little house on the edge of some woods and at night the mosquitoes were fierce.

"You could use oil of eucalyptus," he said. "Some people swear by it. It smells like Vicks Vaporub, and that's because Vicks has eucalyptus oil in it, too. Some people rub garlic on themselves. That seems to keep them off, but you smell something awful. Never did like the smell of garlic."

"How much is oil of eucalyptus?" I asked.

He came out from behind his counter and searched along a shelf.

"Good-sized bottle for a buck," he said, holding up a brown bottle with a kangaroo on it. "It's not cheap."

"Why the kangaroo?" I asked.

"Comes from Australia."

We bought a bottle of eucalyptus oil and the next day smeared ourselves with it. It worked fairly well but there were still welts when we left the woods about noon, so we added garlic. I bought several big bulbs at the little grocery store in Crossett and we mashed them against a board, rubbing the juice all over each other before applying the eucalyptus oil. That day we worked our way far back into the woods, rowing silently through columns of great cypress trees. We saw a snake swimming, its head just above the water, leaving a sinuous wake. It was a cottonmouth. There were herons, great blues and whites, and we could hear their loud croak before they lifted off. They were easily disturbed and no matter how silently I rowed, I could never get close to them. We lay back in the boat and looked up into the trees but, of course, there was no sign of an Ivory Bill.

"It's going to take awhile," I said.

"I could dress up like an Ivory Bill," Robin said.

"Why?"

"I would be a kind of decoy and if one flew through the trees and saw me, it might pause, come closer so we could see it."

"What makes you think you could look like an ivory-billed woodpecker?"

"They're big," she said.

"Not that big."

"No, but I'm small and if they saw me from far away they might think I was one of them."

"How could you make yourself look like an Ivory Bill?"

"I could cut my hair and dye it red and comb it back in a crest. We could make a cape out of black and white feathers." She reached out to touch my face, trace her fingers down my nose. "Your nose isn't big enough," she said. She traced her nose with the tip of her forefinger.

"Yours isn't either," I said.

"But I'm small and skinny and I have little tits and you always say I'm like a bird."

"You could wear white tights on your legs."

"No, I would have to be naked."

"Why?"

"Just because. If I'm going to be a bird I can't have anything human on me."

"Jesus, Robin, even if you smear yourself with oil and garlic, you'll still get eaten alive by mosquitoes!"

"No. We'll smear mud on me. On my whole body. If we mix it with chalk, it will be white, like the underside of the Ivory Bill."

"You're serious."

"Yes," she said. "You could stay in the boat near the

bottom of the tree and make your knocking noise."

I think at that moment I loved her more than anything in the world. It was a crazy idea and there was no evidence that it would work, but it was a testimony that she shared my madness for the Ivory Bill.

9.

We talked about how we could find black feathers. Sometimes there were crow feathers in the field next to the house, but it would take years to collect enough to make a cape big enough to cover Robin's back and legs. A farmer who kept turkeys might be the answer but we didn't know such a farmer and, besides, turkey feathers weren't the rich black that we needed. It was apparent that I would have to kill some crows and we would have to pluck their feathers. Flocks of crows came over the house each morning headed east, and then, again, at dusk they returned. Robin called it the Crow Show. The cacophony of their raucous cries filled the air and they went on to the woods at the far edge of the pasture where they settled in for the night.

"I could shoot some," I said.

"I don't want you to shoot them," Robin said.

"There's no other way. If we get twenty or thirty big feathers from each crow, I shouldn't have to shoot more than six or seven."

"I don't want to hear about it," she said. "I don't want anything to do with it."

I went into Wilmot in search of a gun. There was a little grocery store that sold fishing and hunting licenses but the man said he didn't have anything like what I seemed to want. I told him I wanted something I could kill rats with. "They're running all over the place," I said. "They come out of the fields and they get in the basement and my wife is going nuts."

"I know what you mean," he said. "What you need is a .22. You say you want something cheap. Maybe a bolt action, something real simple, one shell at a time. You go on over to Crossett," he said. "Try the pawn shop there. He might just have what you're looking for."

So I drove to Crossett and found the pawnshop, a narrow cave-like store filled with guitars and old power drills and fishing reels. There was a case in the back with rifles and another locked case with handguns and yet another with watches and jewelry. All of it was crammed into a dark space with counters on both sides,

clothes and musical instruments hanging from the ceiling like

shadowy stalactites.

I was shown a bolt-action .22 with a scarred butt and the

blue worn down to dull metal.

"Don't look like much," he said, "but it shoots straight."

"It's for rats," I said.

"That'll do."

We haggled until he agreed to ten dollars with a carton of

shells thrown in. I put the rifle on the floor behind the seat and

wondered if I could actually kill a bird. But ornithologists did

it all the time, that much I knew. The study skins that lay by the

thousands in drawers in museums were testimony to dead birds.

Audubon killed birds so he could study their feathers, get the

precise shape of a beak, the curve of talons.

I took the gun, the box of shells, and a paper bag with

hard-shelled corn across the field in late afternoon. The corn field

was waist high, and I threaded my way through it until I came to

the opening at the edge of the woods. There was a narrow strip

along the fence where it wasn't plowed and I took some of the corn and spread it, throwing a handful out onto the dirt along the fence, some into the grass that grew around the posts. Then I went to the edge of the woods and sat against a tree with the rifle in my lap. I opened the box of shells and put it next to my leg. I put one of the shells into the chamber, closed the bolt, and turned it down. I pulled back the knurled cock until it clicked. I was ready. If I remained motionless long enough, I knew, birds would ignore me.

Eventually birds came, but they weren't crows. Some doves came out of the woods behind me and they were soon joined by a thrush. But no crows. I tried to remember where I had seen crows foraging and I had the image of crows in a newly plowed field, a flock of them strutting up and down the furrows, new arrivals coming in, wings spread as they braked, feet outstretched. I waited for nearly an hour. Birds came and went. No crows. Eventually the Crow Show began, their scolding shouts announcing their approach, a cloud of them going overhead into the woods behind me. I thought about looking for the rookery but I knew it would be dark by the time I found them, too dark to aim. Finally, I tore off a piece off the cartridge box and stuck it in a crack in a fence post. I chambered a shell and rested the barrel of the gun on my upraised knee, carefully squeezing the trigger. The .22 made a loud pop and when I went to look at the piece of cardboard there was no hole. But the post was torn just below it so I tried again, raising the barrel so the little vee of the sight was above the cardboard. This time there was a neat hole in the cardboard. When it began to get dark I went back to the house.

Robin had dinner ready. Robin only knew how to make one kind of dinner. Boiled hot dogs and canned beans. She opened a can of beans, put it in a pot and heated it until it was bubbling. She boiled the hot dogs and cut them into pieces using a pair of scissors, dropping them into the beans and stirring the mixture with the point of the scissors. A slice of white bread went with it. So I mostly cooked.

"You shot a crow?" she asked. "I heard."

"None came. I practiced hitting a piece of cardboard. I need to find another place where crows congregate."

"I don't want to know," she said.

10.

I found a field near Louanne where a farmer had planted late corn. Louanne was not much more than a post office and a few buildings that leaned on each other. The field was isolated and there were crows picking their way across the newly furrowed field.

The crows lifted into the air, yelling in irritation at me as I went across the field to the far side. I settled in against the fence as I had done before. It wasn't long before the crows came back, dropping, one by one, into the field. I waited as they came closer, and then pulled one leg up so that my knee was in front of me, rested the .22 on my kneecap and carefully sighted in on the nearest crow. I waited until it lifted its head, raised the sight just above it, and squeezed the trigger. The .22 popped, not loud enough to be heard at any distance, I hoped, and the crow cartwheeled over. The other crows whirled up again and I waited.

Apparently a dead crow was no deterrent, for they soon settled back in. By the time the sun had heated things up and I began to bake, I had killed four crows. I retrieved them from the field and pulled out the biggest feathers. I kicked a hole in the soft earth under the fence where I knew it wouldn't get plowed up and buried the bodies. I gathered the feathers into a bundle, took off my shirt and wrapped them up. There were forty or fifty shiny black feathers.

I hunted crows while we worked on the cape. I hunted wood pigeons, too, since we needed white feathers for the two bands that fell from the shoulders. I lied about how many crows it took to make a bundle of feathers. Robin and I tied the feathers in bunches. We laid three feathers together and, using heavy black thread, tied them into a small fan. We laid the next fan on top of the first and tied the two together, linking the central feathers. We continued until we had a long band of black that went from Robin's neck to her feet. Then we made another band and another and eventually laid them side-by-side, stitching them together to make a feathered cloak. The white pigeon feathers were stitched in between two black bands and the contrast was startling. Pieces of Robin's black tee shirt became the arm holes and once the thing was complete, it hung down like a long black and white cloak, shimmering in the sun.

"It's perfect." I said, "but the leading edge of the wing has to be white."

"My arms will have white mud on them," she said. She lifted her arms so that the cloak spread, almost as if wings were lifting out, and her thin white arms were like a part of the wings.

"Lord God," I said.

"What's that mean?"

"That's what they used to say when the saw the Ivory Bill. Lord God. Like it was something so spectacular that was all they could say."

"You think I'm spectacular?"

"Lord God," I repeated.

Robin cut her hair, leaving only a fuzzy covering on the sides of her head, the center combed back into a crest. She dyed it bright red and combed it up with pomade so that it came to a sharp point, smoothing it with her hands, teasing it into the shape of the crest of the Ivory Bill, and she preened, stepping around the room, naked, approaching a wall, pressing up against it with her

arms down at her sides, pretending to whack her nose at the wood.

"KENK!" she cried out and then looked at me with a grin.

"Want to fuck a woodpecker?" she asked.

"If the crest is red, then it's a male," I said.

"So?"

"You're something else," I said.

"Yes. I'm the Lord God Bird."

11.

We took the boat farther back into the woods, and Robin practiced climbing the big cypress trees. We found a dead one, the kind that an Ivory Bill might favor, only there were no handholds or footholds. I brought a long length of rope, tied knots in it every few feet, and weighted one end with a stone. I threw it over the lowest branch, nearly thirty feet above the boat. It took repeated tries before it looped over the branch. I held one end while Robin climbed the rope, pulling herself onto the branch, pulling the rope up after her and throwing it over the next branch, only a few feet over her head. She climbed until I called out for her to stop.

"You're high enough," I said.

"I can go higher," she said.

But I was nervous, seeing her small body perched on a branch sixty feet above the water. There were stumps and bracken below her and I could see her falling and I told her it was enough, she should come down.

She laughed and raised her arms, like wings, moved them up and down, pushing her body up against the trunk. I heard the nasal KENK! echo in the rank air and she made the sound several more times before she began to descend.

We finished the cape and she practiced climbing with it, discovering that she had to climb first, then raise the cape with the rope, putting it on when she got as high as she wanted to be. I was still nervous when I saw her so high above the surface of the water, but she seemed at ease.

"I feel like a bird up there," she said.

"You're not a bird. You can't fly."

"I know that. You don't have to tell me that," she said

"I'm not sure I want you to keep doing this," I said.

"Tomorrow we put the mud on me and we find a tree so far back in the woods that there will be a bird." Her voice was prickly, and I knew that if I objected again, there would be a fight. We would cover her body with white mud and she would climb a tree and put on the cloak and she would become the Lord God Bird. At least once.

12.

That morning I went to the little creek at the edge of the woods and filled a bucket with clay from the bank. It was a viscous gray, like grease, and I brought it back up to the house where Robin waited. We had a bucket of chalk, chunks picked up from plowed fields. I pulverized them into dust and we mixed it with the clay until it was a pale white.

"This stuff is going to dry and then it will come off," I said.

"I'll take some with me when I go up. I can smear it on whenever I need to." She had a determined look on her face.

She stood, naked, in the center of the room while I smeared the mud under her arms, on her back, between her legs, her feet and her toes, her arms, fingers, her face. I touched my muddy fingers to her small breasts and traced the whiteness over

and over again, coating them until her ruby nipples disappeared.
When I rubbed it into the hair at the base of her belly, the skin
turned white but the hair remained a rich black in contrast. I
dipped my fingers into the mud and smoothed it until that, too,
was no longer visible. When I was finished she looked ghostly,
a pale blue figure, like some kind of African goddess, or a stone
figure from the museum in Chicago.

I draped the feather cloak over her and we drove to the
woods. By now the sun was higher and when she walked, the mud
cracked, but it stuck to her skin and she lay back in the boat while I
rowed. We went for nearly two hours, farther back into the woods
than we had ever been, pausing now and then to blaze a mark on a
tree. It was like Audubon's painting, the flat, still water, small shafts
of sunlight filtering into the gloom, and all we could hear were the
creaking of the oars in the oarlocks and the softness of the water
with each stroke. We stopped at noon and drank from the canteen
and ate some cheese and bread. I had my back to where we were
going and Robin looked past me until she said, "There. That tree."

It was a huge dead cypress and the bark hung in strips,
like scabs that had been picked loose from an old wound. Robin

waited while I threw the rope, and then she climbed to the first branch, and waited while I attached the cape and a can of mud to it. She pulled them up and I watched her climb to the next branch and the next and the next.

"Stop now," I called out, but there was no answer.

I backed off with the oars, retreating from the trunk until I could see up into the canopy of the trees and she was there, the cloak over her back, her pale arms at her sides, her head against the tree. The bright flash of her hair caught the sun and there was a black and white pattern to her body, mottled, the crow feathers oily and iridescent; and she was the bird, no beak, but it didn't matter, she had become the Ivory-Billed Woodpecker, the Lord God Bird, and I let the boat drift while I watched and then came the sound, the KENK! Like an old car horn, and another cry. I took out the two blocks of wood from beneath the thwart and hit them together, making the sharp two-stroke bang of an Ivory Bill, and I did it again and again. And then Robin and I were silent for a long time. But I could feel her silence in her still presence high above me, and I waited. Surely the Lord God Bird would come. How could it not come.

13.

We kept going farther back into the woods. I bought a sheet of mosquito netting that fit over the boat so we could spend the night there. Robin came down out of the tree and slipped over the side of the boat, soaking until the mud came off, washing herself and climbing back in, waiting in the late evening heat to dry off before she put on a tee shirt and shorts. We stretched the mosquito netting over the boat and lay below it, listening to the night noises of the woods. There were strange cries, a chorus of frogs that was deafening, and the constant whine of insects. In the morning we ate cold sandwiches I had made of fried eggs and bacon between slices of bread. Robin coated herself with mud from the bucket we brought and climbed again. I made repeated knocks with my blocks of wood. Several times pileated woodpeckers came to investigate, but there was no sign of the Ivory Bill.

A week later, I was in Crossett buying shells for the .22 when I overheard two men talking to the clerk.

"I'm not shitting you, Earl. We was in the Woods and we was back in there, maybe a mile or two, looking for coons and I thought I saw one of them Lord God Birds, and I put the glasses on it, and I swear it was a girl all dressed up like a woodpecker."

"No," Earl said. "You got to be bullshitting me."

"No," the man said. He was a stocky guy in his thirties, a buzz cut and a growing belly that hung just over his belt. "I swear to you on my mother's grave. It was a girl, only she was all white, I mean a spooky white, and she had some kind of a coat over her, looked like feathers, and there she was. Her hair was stuck up like that birds' head shows in them pictures, and at first I thought, holy shit, I seen one of them birds. But when I looked at her through the glasses, she had little tits and there was her pussy, only it was all caked with something, but it was a female, no doubt about it."

He turned to his companion. "Junior saw her too, didn't you?"

Junior nodded.

"I give him the glasses and he took a look, but she was coming down out of the tree and by the time we got there, she was gone."

""You been drinking that 'shine your uncle makes?"

"I'm telling you, God's truth," and he raised his hand, as if he were taking an oath.

The clerk turned to me. "How can I help you, sir?" he asked.

"I need a box of .22 longs."

He put the box on the counter, turned again to the two men. "Are you telling me," he said, "that there's some girl who's dressing up like a Lord God Bird and climbing trees in the Big Woods?"

"Swear to God," Buzz Cut said.

I laid two dollars on the counter. I could feel my chest tighten and I wanted them not to notice me, to forget that I had been next to them in the store. I wanted to get back to the house and make Robin cut off the red crest on her head. I was as terrified at that moment as I have ever been.

14.

We went much farther back into the woods the next day, a half day of rowing; and then it changed and I knew we had come into Despair Bayou. The trees were farther apart and there were patches of sun on the surface. We found a likely tree, half-dead, strips of bark hanging, and Robin climbed higher and higher until she was a tiny thing, the black and white feathers and her red crest visible when I rowed away from the tree. I worked my way through cypress and tupelo until I was fifty yards off, but could still see Robin through a gap in the trees. I heard her KENK! KENK! and I replied with several double-knocks on my wood blocks. It was early afternoon and the heat was like a thick blanket, making it hard to breathe, and at first I didn't recognize the outboard motor. It sounded like the whine of insects, fading, then growing louder and suddenly I knew that it was a boat and I started toward Robin's tree.

But the low skiff with two men appeared and one of the men shouted, "There!" pointing up toward Robin, and I froze, letting the oars drift on the water. They cut the motor and the boat drifted toward the base of her tree.

In the sudden silence, I could hear their words clearly, skipping across the still surface of the water.

"Come on, Billy, she's some kind of a nut. Let it alone."

"How many times you get to fuck a bird, cousin? Hey! Little bird," he called up.

I saw him raise his shotgun and I raised the .22, balanced it on my knee, just as if I were aiming at a crow.

"Jesus, Billy, you ain't going to shoot her are you?"

"No, just a little something to let her know we mean business."

At that moment, out of the corner of my eye, I saw it. It came in a long floating arc toward the tree, down out of the canopy, and it was the Ivory Bill, a female with the black crest that curved forward, the wings outspread, as big as a man's arms, and it came straight toward Robin, tilting a bit as it slipped between the trees. It was just as Tanner had described it, so magnificent that my heart stopped. It slid through a shaft of light, and Robin called out KENK! KENK! And it flared up, the wings black and white; and I thought, there it is, all the pictures of my childhood wrapped into one instant, swimming in the air. Audubon never saw it. He painted it from study skins of dead birds. And now I was seeing it, rising, curling away from Robin. The men in the boat looked up and I heard one of them, I don't know which one, say "Holy shit! It's one of them birds," and the one with the shotgun swung the gun toward the bird, tracking it, and there was an explosion and the bird crumpled in the air, as if it had hit a wall, just tumbled, and it seemed to take a long time to fall, pinwheeling, the wings half folded, and I aimed the .22 at the man's ear, raised the barrel until it was just at the edge of his buzz cut hair and pulled the trigger. There was a pop! He reached up to swat the side of his head, a gesture that he might have made if he had been bitten by an insect, and he pitched forward into the bow of the boat.

The other man shouted, "Holy Jesus, Billy!" And looked wildly about and crouched down. He reached back, yanked the cord on the outboard and it came to life, shattering the silence of the woods. The boat jerked, went forward and then lay on its side as he bent the motor in an arc. He never looked back. I listened as the motor receded, and then began to row as fast as I could toward Robin's tree.

The Ivory Bill was on the surface of the water, turning slowly, and there was no sign of a wound, but it was dead, and I scooped it up, laid it in the boat and went to the tree. Robin came down the rope, not bothering to take off the cape and when she collapsed into the boat I began to row, the boat surging with every stroke, listening for the motor of the other boat, hearing nothing but the whine of mosquitoes and the echo of Robin's KENK! KENK! in my head.

15.

Neither of us said much. I parked the car, Robin went down to the creek to wash off the mud and when she came back we wrapped the body of the Ivory Bill in the feather cape and put it under the bed. Then we waited. I don't know what it was that we waited for.

"Do you think you killed him?" Robin asked.

"I don't know. It's a .22. It doesn't pack much punch. It's okay for killing crows. It depends on where it hit. What it hit."

"What did you aim for?"

"His head. His ear. It could easily have gone into his skull. People are like birds. That part of the skull is thin."

"You think they could connect us to it?"

"I bought a .22. I bought ammunition. We told the farmer we were here to find the Ivory Bill. We bought a boat. Look at you."

"What do you mean?"

"Your hair. That red crest. They saw you up in a tree."

"So what do we do?"

"We should go away. Tomorrow. Go back to Arlington Heights."

"And the Ivory Bill?"

"Take it with us."

"What will we do with it?"

"I don't know."

We finally went to bed. The house was stifling so we laid blankets on the ground behind the house and I stretched the mosquito netting over us. An owl called persistently from the woods.

I woke in the light, but it wasn't daylight, only the moon. It hung above the tree line, huge and yellow and it illuminated Robin, who lay next to me under the mosquito net. She was naked and her arms were at her sides and the moon had turned her a soft, chalky white. How do I save the silver of moonlight on skin, I thought. The light on the grass. I might as well try to save touch or the owl's song or the smell of the damp earth. Or love, for that matter.

She stirred, brought one arm across her stomach. It can't

be done, I thought. We will fumble on, knowing we cannot save any of this.

The Sheriff's car rolled to the front of the house, the tires crunching on the gravel. I came to the door and stood, waiting, while a portly man got out of the car, adjusted his trooper's hat and came toward me.

"How can I help you, sir?" I called out.

He came to the steps, stepped up slowly until he was on the porch in front of me. He reached out a hand.

"I'm Sheriff Culpepper. Big Woods County."

"Good to meet you, sheriff. What can I do for you?" I repeated.

"Buster tells me that you're an ornithologist."

"Who's Buster?"

"I'm sorry," he said. "Mr. Brieser. Owner of the farm who's renting you the house."

"I'm not exactly an ornithologist."

"That's what he said you told him."

"I'm an amateur ornithologist. I know a lot about birds."

"That so? He says you came down here to find the Lord

God Bird."

"The Ivory-Billed Woodpecker. I think there may still be some alive."

"So folks say. You've got a wife here someplace, I believe."

"No, my wife went back up to Chicago. Her mother is sick."

"That so?"

"Yes, sir. She left about a week ago."

"Well, Buster said he didn't see much of her these past few weeks. He says she's a little bitty woman."

"I guess you could say that. She's not very big."

"You go back into the Big Woods much, mister"—he paused. "I'm afraid I don't know your name."

"Hamrick. Jacob Hamrick. Jake."

"Well, Mr. Hamrick, Buster says you got yourself a boat and you spend a lot of time back in the bayou. That so?"

"Mr. Breiser seems to know a lot about what I do."

"It's a small community, Mr. Hamrick. There's not much that goes unnoticed around here."

"That's why I came here. To try to find that bird. Yes, I go back into the woods in a boat. Is there some reason I shouldn't be doing that?"

"No. Lots of folks go into the woods. Hunt, Fish. Your wife ever dress up like a Lord God Vird?"

"Why in the world would she do that?"

"That wasn't my question, Mr. Hamrick. My question was, does she ever dress up like one of them birds?"

"Good God, no."

"Were you back in the bayou on Thursday, Mr. Hamrick?"

"Yes."

"You own a gun, do you?"

I thought for a moment. If he knew as much about us as he seemed to, it would do no good to lie. The man who had sold me the gun had, no doubt, told him.

"Yes. I use it to shoot rats."

"You mind showing me that gun, Mr. Hamrick?"

"I would if I could. I had it with me in the bayou a couple of weeks ago and it got lost over the side of the boat."

"Well now, that's a shame. Nobody likes to lose a firearm, that's for sure. You see anybody else when you were back in the bayou on Thursday, Mr. Hamrick."

"No."

"You didn't happen to see one of them birds, did you?"

"If I had, I'd be telling the whole world about it."

"My problem is," he said, pausing to look at the crows that were going overhead, "I've got a fellow over to Crossett who got shot in the head last Thursday while he was in the Big Woods, and his cousin says they saw one of them birds, and Billy shot it. Billy is the fellow who got shot. By somebody who had a small caliber rifle, which, coincidentally, is pretty much what you bought from Ray Lewis about a month ago."

"Are you saying I shot somebody?"

"I'm not saying you did. I'm not saying you didn't. I'm just asking questions, Mr. Hamrick. I certainly wish you hadn't lost that rifle."

"So am I."

"You planning on staying here for a while longer, Mr. Hamrick?"

"I don't see why not. I haven't found the bird I've been looking for, although they say it's been seen in Texas near the border and I may go on down there if this doesn't pan out."

"Well, I'd appreciate it if you'd let me know before you go anyplace," he said.

"This fellow who got shot, is he okay?"

"You take a bullet to the head and you aren't okay, Mr. Hamrick."

"Is he dead?"

"No, but he might as well be. Bullet went right in through his left ear hole, mixed up his brains a bit. He ain't never going to be the same."

"I'm sorry to hear that."

"Well, be that as it may. Somebody shot him and my job is to find out who did it."

"And they say he shot an Ivory Bill?"

"That's what his cousin says. We didn't find it. Could have been some other kind of woodpecker, though."

"Be hard to mistake one of those for something else."

"His cousin, Junior, isn't the brightest bulb in the package. I wouldn't get your hopes up." He paused. "You got an address for your wife's folks up in Chicago, Mr. Hamrick?"

"She's staying with an aunt. I'm afraid I don't have the aunt's address, but she said she'd be back in a week. When she comes back I'll let you know. Although I'm not sure what you need with her."

"You never can tell, Mr. Hamrick. You mind telling me where you keep your boat?"

"At the end of the county road that goes into Big Woods just past Louanne. It's chained to a tree, covered with brush."

"You Chicago folks aren't the trusting kind, are you?"

"I didn't want somebody to steal it."

He smiled. "Down here, somebody might borrow your boat, but it would get put back where he found it."

I tried to remember if I had cleaned out the boat, taken the bucket of mud, any feathers from the cloak.

"I'd appreciate it if you didn't say anything to anybody about Billy and his cousin seeing that bird. It would just bring all kinds of folks down here and things might get confused. And if you were to ask me, I'm not all that sure they saw a Lord God Bird."

He turned and looked off toward the woods at the far end of the corn field.

"What makes you so interested in a bird that just maybe don't even exist any more?" he said.

"I'm not sure."

"If I was to drive all the way down here from Chicago and live in a house like this and go out into them woods and get half-eaten by mosquitoes, I think I'd be sure."

"Maybe it's because everybody says there aren't any of them left. You ever see a picture of the Ivory Bill, Sheriff?"

"I guess everybody down around here has, at one time or another."

"Audubon painted a picture with three of them in it. You know who Audubon was, don't you?"

"Yes."

"I saw that picture when I was ten. Ever since then, I've wanted to see one alive"

"And how old are you now, Mr. Hamrick?"

"Nineteen."

"You're a young man." He paused, turned to look back at me. "Sometimes young men do rash things. I hope you haven't done anything rash, Mr. Hamrick."

16.

I needed to do something with the body of the bird.
There was no point in trying to stuff it. I didn't have the right
tools or the right materials. But I could make a study skin,
preserve it, only I needed borax and a sharp tool for cutting into
small places and some tweezers. In the drugstore in Crossett I
found a box of Twenty Mule Team Borax, and I knew that it was
the kind used for washing clothes, and wasn't as strong as the
borax used in taxidermy, but it would have to do. I would buy
some salt and use that to help cure the skin. I bought a box of
cotton balls, a pair of stout scissors, and I searched until I found
a pair of tweezers that were long and narrow, and a straight razor
with a bone handle.

The town was, as usual in midday, almost deserted, but
I had the feeling that people were watching me. That I was the

stranger from the north who looked for the Lord God Bird and I
had pulled the trigger that had scrambled Billy's brains.

Back at the house I laid the bird on the wooden counter
next to the tiny metal sink. I filled the sink with water. Robin
said she wanted to watch but when I made the first incision, she
disappeared.

"Don't go out where anyone can see you," I called out,
but there was no answer. I knew she would go into the corn field,
which was now head-high.

I inserted the point of the scissors into the incision at
the base of the tail and began to cut up toward the base of the
bill. The bill was white and long and the end was worn and the
eyes were still yellow, staring at me in reproach. Using my hand
as a measurement, it was perhaps twenty inches long and the
wingspread was almost as much as my own outspread arms.
I opened the bird and began to peel the skin from the flesh,
using the razor, careful not to cut into the skin or dislodge the
feathers. It was already hot and I was sweating and I took off
my shirt and then my pants until I stood naked at the sink,
dipping my hand into the water in the sink so that I could keep

the flesh damp and flexible.

When I had cleaned out the body cavity, I took the neck, peeled the skin away, and using the razor and the scissors, hacked it off as close to the skull as I could. Using the tip of my pocketknife I picked out the remains of the stump and I used the knife and the tweezers to empty the skull cavity.

What did your little brain hold, I wondered. Did you know that there were so few of you left? They kept cutting down the woods where you live, and your world got smaller and smaller. Leave or die, they kept saying, but you stayed.

I scraped the skin carefully, cleaning off the shreds of flesh, soaking up the moisture with cotton balls. I mixed the borax with corn meal and shoved it into the skull, soaking up whatever was left of the brains, emptying it out, pressing more borax and corn meal into the body cavity.

When I was finished, I peeled several boards from the back of the house and stretched the skin on them. It looked like a great feathery crucifix.

We decided that we would wait until dark to leave. Hopefully the Sheriff wouldn't be watching although I suspected that he wouldn't let us go off without trying to stop us. Still, we seemed to have no choice. Robin took the straight razor and shaved off the rest of her hair. Her small head was smooth and I rubbed my hands over it and held it, kissing the top of it and I told her things would be all right.

But that evening, as it grew dark, I heard cars coming into the field in front of the house and when I looked out, there were several pickup trucks, a beat-up sedan and two motorcycles between our car and the main road. Men were climbing out, coming toward the house. I grabbed the .22 and chambered a round.

They stopped when they got to my car, and they gathered around it and began to rock it from side to side, Eventually, it teetered on two wheels and tipped over, rolling on one side with the crunch of breaking glass.

"Hey! Birdman!" yelled one of the men.

I didn't reply.

"Birdman! We know you're in there. You and that fucking cunt who dresses up like a bird. We know you're in there!"

The heat was thick, pressing down, an oven that had been left open. Sweat ran down my arms and my face. Robin was beside me, her naked head shining, but she said nothing, just watched out the window next to me.

"Hey birdman!" he shouted again. The other men were fanning out, going around the house. Two of them disappeared from sight. They had what looked like axe handles in their hands. Another man was taking more axe handles from the back of one of the pickups, tossing them to those who caught them, like baseball players who were waiting their turn at bat.

"You put a bullet in my cousin's head, you Yankee son of a bitch." He started toward the house. The others began to move as he did.

"You take one more step and I'll put a bullet in your head," I called out, and he stopped.

"Well, how about that?" He turned to the man next to him. ""Sounds like we got ourselves a birdman in a cage."

Beyond him I could see the plume of dust as another car came down the county road. I leveled the .22 at his head. The dust settled and the white police car turned across the field, coming to a

stop behind the line of trucks and cars. The portly sheriff stepped
out as they turned toward him.

"Emmet Johnson, you better have yourself a good excuse
for this party or there's going to be hell to pay," he called out.

The line of men faced the voice and the ringleader said,
"Sheriff, we come out here to say hello to the son of a bitch who
put a bullet in Billy's head. It's just a social call."

"I got a dog that's smarter than you, Emmett. He knows
better than to piss on himself. Which is what you were about to do."

"There's ten of us and but one of you, sheriff."

"Like I said, Emmett, my dog is smarter than that. The
rest of you!" He called out to the others. "You know me. If that
man in there had anything to do with that bullet in Billy's head,
you know I'll take care of him. Emmett's got himself carried away
in the heat of the moment and probably you all got a little help
from what you been drinking. If you get back in your vehicles and
go on back home I don't believe I'll be able to remember who was
here. But if you don't, then I got a memory like an elephant and it
will go down hard."

There was a shifting of bodies. It was darker now, the

headlights of the Sheriff's car illuminating the outlines of the men

and they began to drift off. I heard trucks start and headlights

came on.

"You, too, Emmett," the Sheriff said.

Emmett turned back toward the house and shouted,

"Birdman! You ain't seen the last of me!"

The Sheriff's car remained where it was, headlights on,

while the others left. Suddenly all I could hear was the rising and

falling of the cicadas. The solitary dark figure of the Sheriff was

outlined in the headlights.

"Mr. Hamrick," he called out. "I'd appreciate it if you

would come out onto the porch where I can see you."

I leaned the .22 against the wall, opened the screen door

and stepped out into the light. The Sheriff came to the bottom of

the steps. I couldn't see his face.

"I don't have any direct evidence to connect you with

the shooting of Billy Galloway, but a whole lot of things point

a finger at you. However, I don't cotton to a bunch of drunken

men beating you to death. They won't be back this evening, you

can put money on that. But I can't babysit you around the clock, so if you have something you want to tell me, it might make a difference in your well-being."

"What do you want me to say, Sheriff? That I shot him?"

"If you was to say that, I would take you into the County seat and put you in jail, and a bunch of drunks with axe handles would not show up at your door. And your wife would be able to go up to Chicago to see her sick mother."

"I told you, that's where she is."

"Well, I know you told me that, but unless she's walking to Chicago, I doubt if you told me the truth."

"And you'd charge me with trying to kill that man?"

"That would be about it."

"And some of those men who stood here would sit on the jury?"

"That's possible."

"I didn't shoot anybody."

"I'll be back out tomorrow, Mr. Hamrick. You and your missus talk it over." He turned and went back to his car. The lights went off, the engine started and the lights came on again. I watched as he turned the car toward the road, and then there were only the cicadas, their constant chorus rising and falling. Robin came out and put her arms around me . Her body was hot, as if she had a fever.

17.

We slept outside again, but I took the mosquito net down to the woods and we made a bed away from the house. I took the rifle and the box of cartridges, the wrapped-up skin of the Ivory Bill, two bottles of water, and a flashlight. We lay awake listening to the night noises, the cicadas that never seemed to cease, owls, sometimes a far-off dog. Eventually we slept, waking only when the sun touched us. It was well past sunrise.

I heard the car approaching and we stayed in the woods until I was sure that it belonged to the Sheriff. He parked next to the porch, opened the car door, but stayed behind the wheel, waiting. Robin and I came up through corner of the corn field to the back of the house, and then came around the side nearest the car. She took my hand, gripping it tightly.

The Sheriff heaved himself out of the seat and stood,

resting one arm on the open door of the car.

"This must be Mrs. Hamrick?"

"Not exactly.

"Exactly who is she?"

"She might as well be my wife. We live together."

He smiled. "There's a whole lot of folks in the same boat, young man. Nothing to be ashamed about."

"We're not ashamed. Of anything."

"You thought over what I said last night?"

"We have."

"And what did you decide?"

"I didn't shoot anybody."

"I'm sorry to hear that."

"You're sorry I didn't shoot him?"

"No, I think you did shoot him. I'm sorry to hear you deny it."

He shifted his weight. There were already dark sweat circles on his brown shirt under his arms and a patch on his belly.

"You deny that your lady dressed up like a Lord God Bird and climbed into a tree in the Big Woods?"

"Yes."

"You mind telling me, miss, why you got your head shaved like that?"

"I got nits. My hair was long and I tried kerosene but in this heat it was awful, so I just shaved it off. You ever see kids in school with their heads shaved, sheriff? I'll bet you had nits when you were a kid."

"No need to get uppity, miss." He looked at me. "You find that rifle of yours, Mr. Hamrick?"

"No. Like I said, it's somewhere in the water out in the woods."

"Last night you told Emmett that you'd put a bullet in his head if he came closer to the house. Were you going to throw it at him?"

"It was a bluff."

"Mr. Hamrick, I'm beginning to lose patience with you. I got folks in town who want me to find the person who put a bullet in Billy Galloway's head. I think you're the right one. All I have to do is make a little trip after dark over to the other side of the county on some errand and you'll get that same bunch of drunks with axe handles only I won't be coming down the road in time to save you. You'll save the county the cost of a trial and the worst part is that your little bitty friend here would be at the mercy of a bunch of drunks with blood on the brain, and that's not something I think you want to happen."

"You want me to confess to something I didn't do or you'll let them beat me to death and then sic them on Robin?"

"I got enough to charge you and in this county it wouldn't take but about ten minutes for a jury to say yes. You had a gun, same caliber as what scrambled Billy's brains; you got a wife the size of the woman up in that tree; she's got her head shaved so we can't see how she had it all red like a woodpecker. You admitted you were out in the bayou the same day; you got some vested interest in the Lord God Bird and Billy killed one. Might be something to get your back up, that's for sure. And I'll bet if I look long enough and hard enough, I'll find that dead bird."

"It's all circumstantial."

"You practicing law now, boy? You're an outsider in this county. Folks here tend to close ranks when one of their own gets hurt."

I said nothing. I think that if Robin had not been gripping my hand so hard, I would have given in.

He looked at my car, lying on its side a few yards off.

"It would appear that you aren't going to drive off any time soon, boy."

I was no longer Mr. Hamrick. There was coarseness to his voice and I wondered if he would arrest me, but he continued to look at my car and then he settled back into the seat behind the wheel, closing the door. He gripped the steering wheel with both hands.

"You change your mind, you go on up to Buster's farmhouse. He's got a telephone. I'll come and collect you. Your lady can stay with them. Nobody will do anything if she's there, you can count on that."

18.

Robin said there was no way she would let me admit to
shooting Billy Galloway.

"If you do, they'll put you in jail for years."

We couldn't drive off. The car remained on its side
and although Robin and I tried to rock it up, it was, of course,
hopeless. The only answer was to try to make a run for it on foot.
We decided that we would go through the neighboring woods
at dark, come out the other side and go across the fields until we
came to Louanne, four miles off. It was a short hike from there
to where the boat was and we would go into the Big Woods in the
dark, go as far as we could, and then the next day try to work our
way through, hoping to find some way to exit the woods closer to
Louisiana. The Sheriff would look for us, and he would, no doubt,
look for the boat. And they would have boats with outboard

motors and they would know the woods well, having hunted and fished in them. We would be blindly feeling our way, but there seemed to be no other way out.

I tied the legs of a pair of pants together and stuffed one with two cans of beans, four hardboiled eggs, two jars of water, the mosquito net, the rest of the kangaroo juice for mosquitoes, an extra shirt for Robin and one for me. I folded the feather cape as best as I could, and shoved it, along with the skin of the Ivory Bill, down the other leg. We would carry the .22 and the flashlight.

There was a haze at dusk, and the sun became a red ball, like the door of a furnace left open when we went into the woods. We kept the sun at our right so that we would continue south. I knew these woods were shallow in a low swale between fields and we would come out into corn fields. We could follow the long aisles of corn from field to field and not be seen. We sweated in the heat and I thought of cottonmouths in the brush at our feet . We were only about a half hour into the woods when the light began to fail. That was when we heard voices. We stopped, listening. Behind us were shouts, faint, and then rising above the trees was a black column of smoke, sparks spiraling in the evening air. They had come and they had set the house on fire. Whether or not they had thought we were in it made no difference. They would know, eventually, if not at that moment, that we had gone, and they would be looking for us.

When we broke out of the woods it was dark. We went into the first cornfield, and the sharp leaves cut at us as we walked. The light of a farmhouse was a beacon that we followed, going into a field, coming out, making sure we were still moving south. Soon the lights of Louanne were to our left, only a few yellow windows and then we came to the road that led into the Big Woods.

"Do you think they went to the boat?" Robin asked.

"Maybe. That bunch of drunks probably doesn't know where it is. If the Sheriff knows by now that we've hightailed it, then he might."

But there was no one there when we reached the end of the road and it dipped down into the water.

The woods at night were another world. We pushed off into the dark and almost immediately it was a velvet black, the darkness so complete that I could not see Robin opposite me, nor could I see anything. I held my hand in front of my face and blew on it and I could feel my breath, but when I did not blow, only held my hand upright inches from my eyes, there was no sensation of anything there, only emptiness. Robin climbed past me into the bow and turned the flashlight ahead and I rowed, slowly, each stroke a careful push as she guided us between trees, the water as black as tar. Occasionally she said, "Look," and aimed the flashlight at a blaze I had made on a tree.

I thought, God must be close to us in this place. He will not let them find us. There were serpents in the swamp and strange birds that could see us even though we could not see them. I imagined them sleeping in trees above us, their heads tucked under their wings, but aware that we were passing beneath them, ready to fly at the least movement. We slathered the kangaroo juice on our exposed skin but mosquitoes flew up my nostrils and if I breathed with my mouth open, I felt them on my tongue and against the roof of my mouth.

I rowed silently until we began to hear birds and I knew we would soon have light. Behind us the faint wake of the boat became visible, and then the shadowy grey of tree trunks and more birdsong, trills and yells and squawks. There was the constant drumming of a woodpecker, not an Ivory Bill, but a smaller bird, its throbbing beat echoing among the now visible trees.

I stopped rowing and we drifted.

"We should keep going," Robin said.

"I need to rest."

"I can row."

It seemed like we were close to where the Ivory Bill had been shot, or at least it looked like it, but every long drift between the trees resembled the others. We could easily have gone in a circle in the night. Perhaps the road to Louanne was only a few hundred yards away. But the light in the tree canopy ahead of us told me that was the east and if we paid attention to the light as it rose overhead, then we could keep ourselves in a straight line. South, I thought, toward Louisiana.

Robin rowed and I sat in the back of the boat facing her, watching her thin shoulders bend to the oars. Her naked head shone and I wanted to touch it, hold it in my hands, feel the smoothness of her skin, trace the bones of her face with my fingers.

We wandered through long avenues of water between the trees, turning first one way and then another, but always toward the south. The sun lit the canopy overhead and the heat became

fierce and Robin rowed, slowly, leaning forward, catching the oars

in the water, leaning back with each stroke, and then I took over,

rowing steadily while she told me, "turn this way," pointing over

my shoulder. "Turn there," and we threaded our way between

moss-covered three stumps.

The water courses narrowed, and we searched for channels

that might take us farther, but there were none and we came to

places where the oars caught on the grasses and heavy growth on

either side. We were running out of water. But there had been no

sound of pursuit, no outboard motors, no voices, nothing but the

incessant whine of mosquitoes and the chatter of birds.

We stopped in the early afternoon, ate a hard boiled egg,

drank the last of the water, and then Robin began to row again,

but it was almost useless. The boat kept bogging down in masses

of submerged grass and roots and finally we gave up. We took

off our clothes and tied them into bundles. I looped the legs of

the stuffed trousers over my shoulders and we went over the

side into the green water. It was waist deep and we waded and it

became deeper, the soft mud on the bottom sucking at our feet.

I was almost chest deep when I realized that Robin was nearly submerged, the water coming to her chin, and I hoisted her onto my back, with her arms clasped tightly around my neck, our clothes and shoes stuffed into the legs of our pants, along with the trousers that held the Ivory Bill skin looped over Robin's neck.

We worked our way to an island, and when we climbed onto it, there was spongy ground covered with grass and it was dappled with light. The canopy was thinner and ahead we could see more ground, the water courses dwindling. In another hour we were among huge stumps and spindly trees. It had been logged, and the dark avenues of water were gone, the clouds of mosquitoes had disappeared, and the only sounds were crows somewhere ahead of us, and, once, a barking dog. We froze at the sound, waiting, but it was an intermittent bark, and it stopped. We put our clothes back on, and our shoes, and we walked again until the woods gave away to a field, and there was maize and scraggly cotton, and a shack of a house at one edge. A dirt road ran along the field.

There seemed to be no one near the house but when we had passed it and I looked back, there was a small black child behind the house and the child was looking at us.

We followed the road until it came to another small clump of woods and we went into the woods and there was a creek, only a trickle, but it was enough.

We drank from it and we took off our clothes and lay in the shallow water, washing off the mud and sweat and we washed our pants and shirts and laid them out in the sun to dry. We lay on the leaves in the shade and I took the Ivory Bill skin out and stretched it in the sun. It was damp and I knew that I would have to find more borax or at least some salt. As I watched, ants began to collect on it, tearing away tiny bits of flesh and that was good. They were bright red ants that glowed in the sun.

Robin and I lay on the leaves and we fell asleep, and when I awoke, the sun was low through the trees.

I watched Robin's body rise and fall as she breathed and I reached out and ran my hand down her back, caressing the smooth curve of her thigh. She turned so that she faced me and murmured, "My shoulders and my arms—they hurt."

My fingers touched the gently curved bone of her skull, above her eyes, and felt the shape of her skull and found the flat bone that was her clavicle and the sinew that stretched on the inside of her leg, how hard it was, stretched tight; and I pressed the edge of her shoulder blades and the ridges of her backbone. I could feel them just under the skin and I searched for the muscle that ran across from shoulder to shoulder, and when I found it she cried out and I lifted it with my fingers, kneaded it gently, tried to imagine what it looked like beneath her skin, where it was tied to the bone, how it wrapped around under her arms; and I worked my fingers across her jaw, sliding them up under her chin, trying to pull the muscles taut, stretch them so that when I let go they would relax and the tension would dissolve.

I thought of skinning the Ivory Bill, how the muscles and flesh had peeled away from the tough membrane that held the feathers tight, how I had lifted the mass of it out, the heart and the lungs and its gut, and how somewhere in that inert mass there had been a voice that called out in a nasal shout for another Ivory Bill.

When it began to get dark, we dressed and rubbed the last of the kangaroo juice on our hands and faces. I opened the can of beans and we ate it and the other two hard-boiled eggs and then I stretched the mosquito net over us and we waited in the woods.

No one came.

At first light we packed up. I shook the ants off the Ivory Bill skin and wrapped it in the feather cloak, stowing it in the pants legs along with the mosquito net, our change of shirts and the .22. We came out of the woods as the sun rose above the field, and followed the road, keeping the sun on our left so that we knew we were still going south. I don't know what made me so sure that a southerly direction would be safer. Perhaps it was the idea that if we could get into Louisiana the Sheriff would lose his jurisdiction, but I knew that he wouldn't be terribly concerned over the formality of a state border. We passed another shack, but saw no one, and then we came to a clearing where there was a church.

It was a small wooden church, unpainted, and when we stepped inside it smelled of oiled floors. Dust motes floated in the band of light that came from a single window behind the altar. There were no pews, only wooden chairs, a mismatched collection, some painted, others sturdy kitchen chairs.

Robin turned to me. "I was raised Catholic," she said.

"This isn't a Catholic church."

"I know that." She turned and went toward the altar and

I stayed, watching her walk slowly to the front of the church. When she got to the altar, a table with a cloth draped over it, an open Bible, and two unlit candles, she paused, crossed herself and dipped her shoulders ever so slightly, as if she knew that I was watching and didn't want me to think she was doing something in this church that wasn't right. She stood there for a few moments, looked back at me, then turned again to the altar. There was a small box of kitchen matches next to one of the candles, and she struck a match, lighting the candle. She blew out the match, stepped back, and knelt. I waited.

She rose, blew out the candle, and came back toward me.

"We light candles in the Catholic church," she said, "when we say a prayer for someone."

"Who did you say a prayer for?"

"Not you. Not me," she said.

"Why did you blow out the candle?"

"Because it's a wooden church."

"We could stay here," I said.

"They would find us."

"In the old days, a church was a sanctuary. The king's

soldiers couldn't touch you if you were in a church."

"These aren't the king's soldiers," Robin said. "If they found us they would drag us out and they would lock you up if they didn't beat you to death." She waited at the church door, opening it a crack to look outside.

"There's someone there," she whispered.

"The Sheriff?"

"No, it's a black man. He's standing in the road, looking at the church."

"We'll wait," I said. "He'll go on."

"What if he saw us come in here?"

"We'll wait."

Robin left the door open a crack, and when she looked again, the man was still standing in the road.

"He hasn't moved," she said.

Then we heard the voice. "Y'all in the church," the voice called. "No need to hide. I'se not going to harm you. I'se all by myself."

Robin opened the door a crack wider. A tall black man wearing bib overalls stood in the middle of the road, facing the church. He had no shoes on, and his hands were clasped in front of him. His black skin shone in the hot sun.

"What do we do?" Robin asked.

"Open the door. See what he does."

She opened the door and we stepped back into the shadow of the church.

"Is you the lady what dresses like the Lord God Bird?" the man called out. "And her man what shot the cracker up to Woods County?"

I stepped into the doorway. "What if we are?" I said.

"Y'all need to know the Sheriff be here yesterday and he put a price on your heads."

"A fat sheriff from north of the woods?"

"Him and the Sheriff of Union Parish."

"And he put a price on us?"

"A hundred dollars on each of your heads. Alive."

Robin and I were worth one hundred dollars each. Which would be a king's ransom to the poor blacks of Union parish. Apparently we were in Union Parish in Louisiana and now we knew they were looking for us here. The Sheriff must have gone to the boat, found it missing, and now he was looking for where we might come out.

The black man remained where he was, motionless in the hot sun.

"My name be Robert," he said. "You can't stay in the church. They find you there."

"We weren't going to stay here," I said.

"And where do you s'pose you goin' to go?" he asked.

"We don't know."

"That cracker sheriff wants your blood."

"We know that."

"You saw the Lord God Bird. He knows you seed it."

I held out the stuffed trousers and said, "It's here. I've got the skin."

"Lord God," he said. "Them white folks been lookin' for that bird. Used to be they was lots of them, but not no more."

"I'se Choctaw," he said. "My people be half black and half Choctaw. When they marched those folks to Oklahoma, my grandmother be one of them. She run off and marry a free slave over to Mississippi. The Choctaws, they held that bird in high esteem. They make a crown of the head and the bill. My grandma

use to tell me 'bout it. When I be a boy if we seed a woodpecker

she say Lord God ever time. Even if it weren't no Lord God Bird.

They's some peckers what looks like it." He laughed. "I mean

some woodpeckers, not folks like the one what you put a bullet in."

"Then you're not going to turn us in for the money?"

"Lord, no. They promise the money but one of us black

folk tells them, the money just don't show up. And that's a fack.

More we keep outta their way, the easier it be for all."

"Is there some place we can hide?"

"You mean hide 'til they stops lookin' for you?"

"Yes."

"Hardly."

"We could go back to our boat and go back into the

bayou."

"No. You ain't got a boat no more."

"What happened to it?"

"A cousin take it down river. Then he cut it loose. Mebbe

it'll fetch up on the gulf."

Robin stepped into the doorway so that the black man

could see her.

"Can you help us?" she asked.

"You the girl what dress like the Lord God Bird?"

"Yes."

"They say you look just like the bird."

"I had my hair cut like the bird. I dyed it red."

"Even so, you a bitty thing."

"Can you help us?"

"Not for long. They gonna come back and they probly bring some dogs. Mebbe you might could go in the night to a cousin. You might go to Texas. They's goin' to look for you to go south. Ever'body go south."

"Why would you help us?" I asked.

"That cracker shot a Lord God Bird. You shot the cracker. That strike me as justice. Ain't no justice in you getting' kilt."

"I put a bullet in his brain. He won't ever be the same."

"I suspect they's all a bit crazy. Some of them crackers just as soon set fire to a black man as go to church."

"Where can we go now?"

"You foller me," he said. He walked across the weedy

yard of the church and disappeared around the corner. Robin and I came out into the sun and followed. He was several yards ahead of us and didn't look back.

"Should we catch up?" Robin asked.

"I'm not sure."

So we stayed behind Robert as he stepped into a cotton field, and we kept twenty paces behind him, sweating now, until we came to another woods, this one with thinly standing trees. Once in the shade, he stopped. When we caught up with him, he said, "I wants to see the Lord God Bird."

I laid the trousers on the ground and pulled the feather cloak out, unrolling it. I stretched the skin out so that the wings were like arms and the body and wings formed a crucifix.

Robert kneeled and stroked the feathers at the back of the head with a finger. "It's not red," he said.

"It's a female. The crest on the male is red; the females are black."

He fingered the long stout bill. "I ain't seed one of these since I was a boy," he said. "What you gonna do with it?"

"I don't know. It's proof they're still alive. It ought to

go to somebody who cares about them. Maybe a museum or a

college. But I don't know how to do that."

"You suppose they's another one up there in the bayou,

with a red head, lookin' for this lady bird?"

"I don't know."

"You was up the tree when it come?" he asked Robin.

"Yes."

"You think it come to you 'cause you had your hair red?"

"I called out to it."

"What you say?"

Robin lifted her head and suddenly there was the nasal

KENK! KENK! so like the sound I had heard years ago in the

high school auditorium, as if Robin had swallowed that sound

and it came belching out; and Robert pressed his hands to the bird

skin and said, "Oh, Lord God, I hear that voice when I be just a

boy. My grandma, she say, Robert, listen. That the Lord God Bird.

How come you know that voice?"

"Jake gave it to me," she said.

"A man named Tanner gave it to me," I said. "He lived for

a while in the woods. He was the last man to see them."

"Maybe he the last white man to see them. Sometime you all think there be nobody else in the world but folks with white skin. Some black man come to you and say, I seed the Lord God Bird, and people say, no, how could we trust a old black man. If you gives me this Lord God Bird, I see you gets away from that sheriff."

"What would you do with it?"

"I keep it where nobody can steal it. I tell people the Lord God Bird still be here."

Robin bent and picked up the feather cloak. She slipped her arms into the arm holes, and drew it around her, lifting her head again, and I could imagine the ivory beak and the yellow eyes. Robert, too, watched as she took a step and then another, and she opened her arms, the cloak spreading like wings, and her thin arms were the leading edges of the wings, pale white, glowing with sweat, like the exposed bones of the bird. She was no longer a nineteen-year-old girl, but an old creature, something so old that I felt childlike in her presence. She turned to us and said, "If I had dyed my hair black, a different bird would have come," and I knew that the bird whose skin and feathers were in Robert's hands had come to the tree because Robin had willed it to do so. She had

willed it to do so because I wanted to see it and she had brought it

to me as a gift.

Robert stood, the bird skin in his hands.

"If you gives this to me to keep safe, we see 'bout keeping

you safe from that sheriff."

We had no choice. Robert told us to continue on through

the woods.

"Listen for dogs," he said. "You get close enough to my

cousin, you hear his dogs. He got a whole bunch of hounds and

they makes a racket like nothin' else. When you hear the dogs, go

slow. You come to the edge of the woods, you see his house. You

make sure there ain't no white folks there. You waits a bit. Ezra,

he come to see what his dogs is raisin' a fuss 'bout. But you waits

in the trees. Don't go out in the clear. When he gits close, you call

out, tell him Robert send you. Tell him Robert say for him to keep

you this night.."

He rolled the Ivory Bill skin tightly.

"The skin isn't cured," I said. "You'll need borax or salt,

Don't let it get too hot or it will dry and crack and the feathers will come out. Try to pick off any little bits of flesh."

"I been curin' animal skins since before you was born, young man. I knows how to do it. You go on now. Ezra, he take you in. You tell him I be sendin' him word by one of the childern." He looked at Robin. "What you gonna do, child, with them wings?"

Robin raised the cloak again and it looked as if she were about to fly.

"Take it with me,"

"No, child, that won't work. Anybody sees it, they knows who you be. You gots to grow your hair out and that takes time, but they's folks what shaves their heads in the summer so maybe you get away with that, but them black and white feathers, they a sign. You leave it with me, too. I takes care of it."

19.

We did as Robert told us, picking our way through the wood until we heard the dogs. We could see a clearing and another crude house and a half dozen mangy dogs milled in front of it, facing us, their barking mixed with yelps, and then a man's voice.

"Shut up! Stop that racket!" But the dogs kept up and a black man came out onto the lean-to porch and stood looking at the woods. I was sure he could see us. He took a few steps off the porch and I called out, "Ezra! Robert sent us!"

He stopped. The dogs swirled around him and he reached out and cuffed the nearest one on the side of its head. It yelped and scurried under the house.

"Show yourself," he called out.

Robin and I stepped to the edge of the wood.

"What you white folks want with me?" he called out.

"Robert said to tell you he sent us. He said he would send a child later."

"I knows who you be. You be the white folks what the Sheriff wants. You can't stay here."

`"Robert said you would take us for the night."

"Robert a crazy nigger if he want me to take you in. That sheriff come here and find you, and me and my whole family goin' to end up in the bayou."

"There's a price on our heads. If he finds us here, you could collect it."

"If you think that, you as crazy as Robert."

The dogs had stopped barking. But they stayed at his side, their heads fixed on the two of us at the edge of the trees. We waited. Robin turned to me and said, "What if he won't hide us?"

"Then we keep on running."

Ezra called out again.

"Y'all come out."

We crossed the clearing toward the house and as we got closer he said, "I'se probly as crazy as Robert, but I heerd what you done up to the other side of Despair Bayou and I'se just dumb enough to do what Robert say to do. You be lucky Robert take to you. He got hoodoo charms what can fix things that go wrong, so I ain't about to cross him. You stays one night. Then you be gone."

The house was one room, oppressively hot. There were no windows, only two openings on either side of the door. There was a metal sink and a hand pump at the end of it and a small wood stove in the center of the room. It was, I realized, a copy of the house Robin and I had rented. Muslin curtains covered the window openings.

A woman stood at the sink, snapping beans, and four children stood, wide-eyed at the appearance of two white people, one a girl with a shiny bald head.

"This here's Naomi," Ezra said. "These our childerns."

The woman looked at us and then at Ezra.

"You lose your mind?" she said. "You bring them two in here? You mought just as well bring a bucket of cottonmouths and spill 'em on the floor."

"Robert sent them."

"Robert ain't here. We is. That sheriff come here, you gonna tell him to go find Robert and hang him from the nearest tree?"

"It just for tonight."

"That what Jesus say 'fore they come for him."

Ezra motioned to the children to move and they fluttered to the side of the room, like black birds, backing against the wall, still staring at us.

"We don't have to stay," I said.

"You leave, you find white folks lookin' for you. You gots a price on your heads." He turned to his wife.

"They stays."

Eventually the children went outside and came back only when Naomi called them to supper. We ate at a simple table with homemade stools. Because Robin and I were there, two of the children took their plates outside. Dinner consisted of cold johnnycakes with sorghum, sweet tea, and the snap beans that Naomi had cooked in bacon drippings on the little stove. It was growing dark and suddenly the children outside came bursting into the house.

"They's white mens comin'!" they said, and Ezra looked outside.

"Where?" he said.

"They's over to the woods," the tall child said.

He looked across the clearing and then said to us, "Quick! Foller me," and we went outside and around the house.

"In there," he said, pointing to the outhouse, a small square lean-to at the edge of the clearing.

"But they'll look in there for us," I said.

"Ain't no choice. Not likely, though. White mans rather shit in the woods than go where some black man put his ass."

It stank in the outhouse, and there were flies. There were two holes in the plank seat and Robin and I sat on them, waiting. We heard voices and then nothing, and the light in the cracks in the boards faded as the sun set.

"It's my fault," Robin finally whispered.

"You didn't shoot anybody."

"No, but if I hadn't dressed like the Ivory Bill and gone up that tree, they wouldn't have come and none of this would have happened."

"The Ivory Bill wouldn't have come, either. We saw the Lord God Bird."

"It would still be alive if I hadn't gone up that tree."

"It would still be alive if that ignorant son of a bitch hadn't shot it."

I held her, and felt her hot skin, ran my hands over the smooth wetness of her sweaty arms and belly, and I wanted only to be far away from the hot stink of the south. I thought about the snow in the vacant lot next to the house on Mitchell Street and I told Robin about the scarlet tananger and we waited.

It seemed like hours before Ezra opened the door of the outhouse. It was dark outside, fireflies winking in the trees and the house was a dark blot in the clearing.

"Y'all goin' to have to sleep on the floor and 'fore first light you best be goin' back to Robert. The mens what come say they know you somewhere 'round here. I say to let them use my dogs, but they say they gots their own dogs and they goin' to use them."

"Was it the Sheriff?"

"No. But they a price on your head and they's lots a white folks what could use that so ain't no use in you runnin' south. I don't know what Robert goin' do with you but you be gone first light. I sends a chile to Robert so he know you comin'."

We spent the night on the floor of the house, half-awake, listening to the movement of the dogs under the house, and the restless sounds of children sleeping on straw mats in the hot room. A rumble of thunder came and lightning flashed, lighting up the window openings; and the rain came in a sudden rush, accompanied by loud cracks of thunder, and then the rain fell off and the rumblings faded and there was the steady dripping of water from the roof.

It was still dark when Ezra told us to gather ourselves and follow him.

We went across the wet clearing, followed by two of the dogs, and when we got to the edge of the woods, he said, "Moon be just about down." He pointed to a sliver of moon hanging beyond the woods. "It goin' to set just about where the church be. You follows this path. It the one we use when we goes to church. You keep the moon ahead of you, you comes out just about where you goes in. Robert be there. If he ain't, then you waits. Sun come up behind you if you in the right place."

And then he and the dogs were gone.

20.

Robert was there. He stood at the edge of the woods, his hands at his sides, wearing the same bib overalls,, his face impassive.

"Y'all gots to go back into the bayou," he said.

"We haven't got a boat."

"I'se got a pirogue," Robert said.

"What's a pirogue?"

"Boat for the bayou. Go places no other boat can go. I take you to a place where you can hole up 'til that sheriff tires of lookin'."

We followed Robert through the fields, skirting the clearings, and by noon when the sun was at its hottest we were at the edge of the bayou. A small flat-bottomed boat was drawn onto the bank among the reeds. Made of a single piece of wood, it floated barely above water. Robert had a bundle wrapped in a cloth that he took out of the crotch of a small tree.

`   "This here's some vittles," he said. "They's grits and johnnycakes and some fatback what my daughter cook up for you. It last you a few days."

Robert pushed the boat into the water and we climbed into it. It seemed as if it would sink under our weight but Robert assured us it wouldn't. He used a long pole to push us into the deeper water and we spent the next two hours threading our way through cypress and tupelo. Once we came on a stump where a water moccasin was waiting, coiled like a carelessly dropped length of rope. Robert brought the pirogue close to it and it didn't move.

"You can eat them," Robert said. "They stinks when you cleans 'em, but you wash 'em good and cut 'em up and they okay to eat."

We moved on and the bayou became dense, so little water that it seemed the boat wouldn't float, but it glided over weeds and muddy shallows and then we came to a shack on stilts, a box made of old planks with a ladder hanging below a narrow doorway.

"You stays here," he said. "I come back day after tomorrer. Bring you something more to eat. Some more water for you to drink. Nobody find you here. They's a little stove in there, but don't make no fire."

"Why are you doing this, Robert?" I asked.

"You seed the Lord God Bird. Your lady, she call the bird. She gots a charm and that's a fack. I knows a lot about charms, but that one special. Ain't no way I gonna let them crackers touch her." He reached out and stroked Robin's forehead, then cupped her shiny skull in his large hand. "You special, chile," he said.

21.

We spent the night in the shack, wrapped in the mosquito netting, listening to the sounds of the bayou: the croak of herons, owls, once a shriek of some animal caught, and then the far-off barking of dogs and a rooster near dawn, so faint we wondered if we had heard them at all.

The day went slowly. Several times we slipped into the water to cool ourselves and we spent another night wrapped in the netting and on the third morning Robert came. He came so silently we were startled when he appeared in the doorway.

He had more johnnycakes and some pigs feet, a canvas bag with water, and an oily liquid that he said we should rub on ourselves to ward off the mosquitoes.

"They don't bother some but they's some what gets bit awful bad. This here keep them off."

"What is it?" I asked.

"Roots and things. Some roots you make a tea and you mix with some oil what comes from green shoots and it work pretty good."

We stayed two weeks in the bayou. Robert brought us food and replenished the canvas bag with drinking water. The water beneath the shack was only a few feet deep and we waded until we came to a tangle of cypress roots and brush a hundred yards away. That was our toilet so we wouldn't foul the water beneath the shack.

Sometimes at night we made love when it cooled and all we could hear were the call of owls. There was never a sign of a boat. Rain came in the midafternoon, thunderheads building over us and then the rush of rain on the water, the clap of thunder and when it passed everything was suddenly cool.

Robert came the last time. It was evening when the pirogue silently nosed under the shack.

"They brings dogs but they don't find no smell," he said. "They gone south to look for you."

He took us in the pirogue to another shack, this one on

the edge of a clearing where the stumps were raw.

"They's cuttin' down the woods," he said, "They won't be nothin' left but boll weevils and sharecroppers."

So we moved into the abandoned shack. I fashioned a table from scraps of wood and Robert brought a sack we could stuff with grass for sleeping. At first Robert brought us things to eat, but I was handy with a hammer and I knew how to build and fix things so I had a value to the scattered families and I was paid in food, a chicken or sorghum molasses or corn meal. It was Fall now and the days were cooler. We had been a month in the abandoned shack and it was clean and the holes in the walls were patched. We had a spring nearby for water and I dug a pit for an outhouse. Robert came by every few days. Once he brought the black feather cape and he asked Robin to put it on and she did.

"You with chile," he said. He reached out and touched her belly.

"How do you know that?" she said.

"I knows such things."

"You're pregnant?" I said.

"Yes."

"When?"

"I think it's been since we left Arlington Heights."

"You've been pregnant all this time?"

"I think so," she said. "At first I wasn't sure. But now I am." She raised her arms and the feather cloak lifted like black and white wings and Robert said, under his breath, "Lord God."

"We have to leave," I said to Robert. "We have to go back north."

"Not yet. They's still folks what looks for you. The Sheriff ain't comin' 'round, but it ain't safe for you to go out on your own. You waits 'til the weather changes, folks turn in on theyselfs. Then they not so likely to be lookin' out for someone else."

We stayed. But now I watched Robin carefully, made sure she didn't lift things, insisted that she rest, even though she said she didn't need to. Her belly began to grow round and Robert said we should stay longer, that his daughter was good with childbirth, she had five children of her own, that we shouldn't risk exposing ourselves to the white world. I think, looking back, that he only wanted Robin to stay. That he wanted her to have her child there.

The days were no longer oppressively hot. I caught fish in the bayou now, and neither Robin nor I looked the way we had looked when we fled the house north of the bayou. Robin's skin was fair and she was thickly freckled. Her hair was long again, usually tied in a pigtail down her back and her breasts were fuller, her belly extended. My skin had turned dark brown from the sun, my hair was long, and I, too, wore it in a braid. But I was more muscular, I could pole a pirogue deep into the bayou and walk ten miles and do a day's work with ease. A logging crew from the north came into the tract and I got work with them. Robert was nervous about it, but they were outsiders and lived in a camp in the woods north of where we were and there seemed little chance that they would have any contact with the white world that Robert said still wanted me.

One afternoon when I came home from the logging camp, Robin was sitting in the shack, leaning against the wall, her hands in her lap. She had been wringing out clothes and she looked exhausted.

"My hands hurt," she said.

"Here." I reached out and took one of her hands in

mine. It was small, and my fingers closed easily around it. I took some of the oil that Robert had given us for the mosquitoes and dribbled a bit on her palm and began to massage the palm of her hand, the heel where the callous was, slipping my fingers around hers and stretching them. Her hand became oily and smooth and when I pressed hard against the palm I could feel the bones of her hand, as if they were the bones of a bird's feet, delicate and held together by a thin web of muscle.

"That feels good," she said, and I slid my hand up her wrist, massaging the muscle of her forearm, coming back to close her fingers into a fist, squeeze it and then open it again, stretching the muscles while she lay against the wall of the shack, eyes closed.

"I can do this forever," I said.

"I know."

"Your hands are beautiful."

"Don't be silly."

"No. They're the hands of a bird."

"Birds don't have hands."

"If they did, they would have hands like yours."

We counted the days, reckoning that in another month

we would be able to leave. Robin's belly was more pronounced although Robert was insistent that we couldn't leave without endangering ourselves. But when we were alone we talked about going back north, about Arlington Heights and how we would make a life for ourselves far away from the south.

Robin was more beautiful now, a radiance that was hard to define. One afternoon I watched her as she stood at the clothes line, reaching up to hang a towel, clothespins in her mouth. She wore one of my shirts, a white shirt with a ragged collar, but it was newly washed and it shone in the sun. When she reached up to put a clothespin on the line, the shirt rose, and her round belly was exposed, and the fabric of the shirt pressed against her breasts. The neck was open and there was a vee of skin that I could see as well, and she said, "Jake, help me with this," holding up a sheet, and I stood behind her, placing one hand on her shoulder and felt the skin and bones and muscle beneath the fabric of the shirt, and I did not trust myself to do anything more than rest my hand there while my other hand reached into the bag for a clothespin and I held the end of the sheet while she went to the other end and it hung there in the sun, so white it hurt my eyes.

There was the smell of fresh laundry, the smell of hot cotton and soap, and it was a smell that I remembered when my mother had hung clothes on the line in Arlington Heights. Robin turned and lifted her arms again so that her belly glowed in the sun, glazed with sweat, and she said, "This is for you," and she grinned and I thought of the roundness of her belly when she bent over, naked, above me, and the hardness of her belly when she said, "Here, feel this," and I touched her rigid belly, taut with child.

She bent to lift the empty basket and I looked beyond her at the bayou and I imagined that she was rising, naked, from the water and the water dripped from her shoulders and her breasts and her thighs and her round belly and she stood, toes pressing into the mud at the edge, and far into the bayou a cormorant disappeared, cleaving the water as if there were a wet opening in the water and the bird had slipped inside the opening and would not reappear until she was gone.

One leg was in front of the other and as she lifted the basket, the muscle on the inside of her leg grew rigid and then relaxed, and my fingers touched the memory of the tendon that rose on the inside of her thigh and I waited for the cormorant to

reappear, but it was still throbbing inside the bayou, somewhere

just under the surface, touching secret places among the grasses.

22.

It was the next day when I went back to the logging camp that things changed. The foreman stopped me as we gathered to start the day's work.

"Some fellow come to camp yesterday asking about you," he said.

I had a sudden chill.

"What did he look like?"

"Ordinary looking."

"White or black."

"White man. He asked if we seen a white guy who lived in the bayou and I told him the only white guy we seen was you. He wanted to know if you were somebody named Hamrick, but I said no, not the name I know you by. Is there a problem?"

"No. Probably he's looking for somebody to do a job."

But it was a problem and when I finished that day I told the foreman I wouldn't be back for several days. That I had to take my wife into town to see a doctor.

When I told Robin a man had been asking for me at the logging camp, she said we had to leave. "We have to take our chances. If they find us, that's the end. We'll talk to Robert."

We didn't get a chance to talk to Robert.

I went fishing the next afternoon and it was dark when I came back to the house. There was a faint light in the windows, a candle, I thought, but I didn't call out. A few yards from the house I heard the man's voice. It was low and threatening. I stopped, laid the catfish carefully on the ground and stepped closer. I had, in those few months, learned to move as quietly as Robert and when I was next to the window I could hear the words.

"He's out there some place. He ain't going to leave no woman with child all alone."

"You got the wrong people," Robin said. Her voice was even.

"I ain't got the wrong people," the voice said.

"Everybody else give up on you but I say to myself, they's two hunnert dollars somewhere out there where them niggers live. I get a bone between my teeth, I don't let it go. Now you can tell me when he's coming back or maybe I cut it out of you."

"You wouldn't do that" she said.

"Ain't nothing said about you being worth a hunnert dollars with a whole skin. How you like it if I cut that baby out? You think maybe that will change your mind?"

"You wouldn't do that," she repeated.

"I do it quick as you can blink," the voice said.

I carefully looked around the edge of the window and Robin was facing me, holding her belly with both hands. The bulk of a man was between us and I could see the glint of a knife in the light from the candle that burned on the table. I slid along the wall to the screen door. I knew that he would whirl when I opened it but he would be only a couple of steps away and I would have the advantage of surprise. Grab the hand with the knife first, I thought, then deal with him. I took a breath. He had the point of the knife at her belly. Robin's eyes widened and I knew she could see my shape in the darkness beyond the screen. Everything was still.

I tore open the door and leaped at him, and as I expected, he half-turned to face me and I grabbed his wrist, felt the point of the knife cut me and I slammed his hand against the edge of the table as hard as I could. The knife clattered to the floor and I raised my other arm, ramming it into his throat and he gagged, stumbling back. I drove him back against the wall, past Robin, and the strength I had gained in months of work rolling logs and walking for miles and poling the pirogue deep into the bayou was concentrated in crushing his neck against the wood. He struggled, tried to kick me, but I put both hands against his throat and he gurgled, pulled at my arms with his hands. He was strong, but I could only see Robin holding her belly and the knife pointing at it, and I threw all my weight against my arms and he sagged, no breath coming from his open mouth, his hands losing their grip on my arms.

I heard Robin's voice and paid no attention to it and then I realized she was shouting at me.

"Don't kill him!" were the words, and I let up on the pressure. He sagged to the floor, gasping, and I turned him over on his face and knelt on his back, my knees pressing all my weight on his spine.

"Give me a towel," I said, and Robin handed me a worn dishtowel. I wrapped it around his wrists, knotting it hard twice and then I turned, took off my belt and wrapped it around his ankles, cinching it so that his legs were tight together.

"Jesus," came the hoarse whisper. "Don't kill me. I didn't mean nothing. I wasn't going to hurt her."

"Shut up you piece of shit," I said. I rolled him on his side. His eyes were wide with fright and blood came from his nose, dribbling down the side of his face. He was a wiry man, with a hawk face.

"Who knows you're here?" I said.

"Nobody."

I slid across the floor, grabbed the knife and held it poised above his mouth.

"Who knows you're here?" I repeated.

"Sweet Jesus, I'm telling you the truth. Nobody knows I'm here."

" I could run this in your gullet and pin your head to the floor," I said. "Just like sticking a toad to a log. How do I know you're telling me the truth?"

"'Cause you worth a hunnert dollars apiece and I wasn't going to share it with nobody."

"And you thought you could come in here and I'd go with you like some fucking sheep?"

"They says you some scrawny white boy from up north and his little bitty wife. I don't guess it would be all that hard."

"You guessed wrong, didn't you?"

"You let me go and I won't say nothing and that's the God's truth."

"You lying sack of shit. I let you go and that cracker sheriff will be here as fast as you can run."

"What you gonna do?"

"I might just kill you, bury you back in the woods so deep nobody ever finds your body."

"You wouldn't do that."

I touched the point of the knife to his eyelid.

"I do it quick as you can blink," I said.

We left him lying on the floor of the shack and went outside where Robin took deep breaths, holding her belly with both hands.

"You all right?" I asked. "He didn't do anything to you, did he?"

"No. He grabbed me from behind while I was washing some things in the sink. I didn't hear him. I thought it was you, trying to surprise me, but he was rough and he stinks and when he let go I had to hold on to the table to keep from falling."

"The son of a bitch. If he's found us, there's going to be others. We need to find Robert. We need to get out."

"What will you do with him?" she asked.

"I don't know. I'm going to tie him up good and leave him in the outhouse. I'll find Robert and see what we should do."

I took the .22 down and chambered a cartridge.

"Take this," I said. "Sit outside where you can see the door of the outhouse. If he comes out, shoot him. But wait until he's close so you don't miss."

"I'm not sure I can do that," she said.

"He won't come out," I said. "I'll wrap him in baling wire. It will take me an hour to get to Robert's. Another hour back."

I hoisted the man to his feet and dragged him to the outhouse. I took baling wire and wrapped it around him a dozen times, twisting the ends tightly.

"You struggle, you cut yourself on the wire," I said. "You do what I tell you, and you can keep on breathing. You try to fuck with me and it's the last breath you'll ever take. You hear me?"

He pulled his knees up so that his chest rested against them. "I got friends. They going to be looking for me."

"They ain't going to find you tonight," I said.

I set out in the dark, but I knew the way and I made good time. Robert's house still had lantern light when I got there and when I told him what had happened, he said, "You gots to bring him here."

"Why here?"

"You bring your lady here and you bring him. We figure out what to do with him when he's here. But we can't leave him out there. Somebody come lookin' for him, we gots to have a plan. Ever since you work for them loggers, I'se afraid of this."

"Should I bring him back tonight?"

"Yes. But hobble him so's he can't run. And tie a rope 'round his mouth so he can't yell out. He probly make some noise, but I don't want to wake up the whole woods."

When I got back to the shack, Robin was still sitting at the back facing the outhouse, leaning against the wall, the .22 across her legs.

"He yelled at me some," she said. "But he's quiet now."

"We're taking him back to Robert," I said.

"Now? In the dark?"

"Yes."

I found some rope and, using a short length, tied his legs together, leaving a foot-long piece loose so that he could take short steps. When I pulled him to his feet he cursed again. "You cain't get away with this," he said. "They gonna find you and cut off your balls and stuff 'em in your mouth."

We set out, Robin going ahead with a lantern, the hobbled man between us. It was slow going and we weren't half way there when Robin stopped and slid to the ground.

"What's the matter?" I said.

She had the lantern between her legs and she said, "Cramps. I've got pains in my belly and my legs. Oh Jake," and she began to cry.

"Can you walk?" I said.

"No." She rested her hands on her swollen belly. "It's all wrong," she said.

I dragged the white man to a tree and kicked his legs out from under him. He collapsed heavily at the base of the tree. I untied his hands, pulled them around the tree and tied them again. I took off my belt and wrapped it around his legs, cinching it up, and then I took off my shirt, tore it into strips and gagged him. I tied another strip around his neck and around the tree and when I was finished he was immobile, unable to move anything.

I picked up Robin and carried her toward Robert's house while she held the lantern. She was heavier now, but it made no difference. There was a strength in me that was quite remarkable, and I moved quickly, sliding my feet so that I could feel the uneven ground, careful that I didn't trip. She buried her head in my shoulder and her body was clammy and hot and I prayed and I wished I had candles to light for her and I cursed the white man who had sliced his way into our lives.

At Robert's house I found him waiting outside and he opened the door so that I could stumble in.

I laid Robin on a bed and Robert's daughter, Esther, knelt

beside her. She wiped Robin's face with a wet cloth. She turned and said, "Y'all go outside. Leave us be."

Her children gathered against the wall, their faces shining in the lantern light. They looked like startled animals, the eyes of possum or deer, not moving, until Esther said again sharply, "Out! Leave us be. You, too," she added, looking at me.

Outside, Robert asked me where the white man was.

"He's tied to a tree half an hour from here," I said.

"We go get him before first light," Robert said.

We stood in the dark, Robert smoking his pipe, the children somewhere in the darkness. Finally Esther came out, wiping her hands on a towel.

"What she be doin' this past day?" she asked.

"Nothing different. But the white man came sometime this afternoon and he threatened her. Did he touch her?"

"Ain't no sign of that," she said. "She say nothing happen, but I gots to tell you she done lost her chile."

It was silent and then Robert said, "Sweet Jesus, is the chile goin' to be all right?"

"I think she be all right, but the chile inside her be

halfway out and it not alive."

I started for the house but she caught my arm.

"That no place for you," she said. "Not yet. I go back in and tend to her. I call you when it be right for you to come back." She reached up and stroked the side of my face. "You both such children," she said. "This ain't right, but they's nothin' we can do."

She went back into the house and Robert and I sat at the edge of the clearing, listening to the night sounds, not speaking. I wanted to cry but I couldn't. All I could think of was finding the man at the base of the tree and taking his knife and cutting his gut out, pulling him apart while he still lived.

It was beginning to get light when Esther came out again. The children had rolled up in blankets along the side of the house and she bent to touch each of them before she found Robert and me.

"She goin' to be all right," she said. "She miss-carried her child and that's a fack. She sleepin' now."

I went into the house and in the dim lantern light I could see Robin on the bed, wrapped in a blanket. Her clothes were in a pile, bloody, and there was a shallow pan with a cloth over it and I knew what it was but I didn't dare lift the cloth. I bent to touch her face, lifted her hair with my fingers, and she stirred. When I went outside, Robert was waiting.

"We best go find your white man," he said. "She be all right. Esther take good care of her. Now we gots business to take care of."

A false dawn had lit the sky for a few minutes, but by the time we were on the trail, it was dark again.

23.

Robert carried two sacks. There was a rope tied around the neck of one of them and he had it on the end of a stick over his shoulder. As he walked, the sack swayed and as it did so, whatever was in the sack moved so that it seemed like a skin with something throbbing in it. He carried the other sack at his side.

"What you carrying over your shoulder?" I asked.

"I'se got a poke full a death," he said.

"What is it?"

"You find out soon enough."

We found the white man still tied to the tree. As we approached he tried to yell through the gag, but all that came out was a hoarse croaking. Robert bent and pulled the gag loose and the man shouted, "Goddamit, let me loose! You goin' to pay for this, nigger!"

Robert touched the man's leg with his bare foot. The man jerked his leg, but the two legs were still tied together and it didn't move.

"You hog-tied him good," Robert said.

"They gonna come and burn out you goddam niggers!" the man shouted again. "They gonna torch the whole fucking bunch of you!"

"You don't have to shout so loud," Robert said. "I'se right here."

"What do we do now?" I asked.

"He goin' go to the bayou for a bit." He looked down at the man's legs. "You hobble him good. That's the way the slavers did to the old folks when they moves them from one plantation to another. They puts hobbles on them like you puts on a horse. How you learn to do that?"

"I remembered it from a book."

"Book learnin' can be a help," Robert said. "I can't read so it be no good to me, but I tells Esther she gots to get her childern to read some so's they don't get cheated at the store."

"I first saw the Lord God Bird in a book."

"Is that a fack?" Robert said. Listening to him, you would have thought that the bound white man wasn't at his feet. He looked down.

"We goin' to untie you now," he said, "only don't make no mistake. We kin kill you quick as a flash so don't do nothin' stupid. Although that may be a hard task for you." He turned and grinned at me.

I bent and untied the man's wrists behind the tree, put my hands under his armpits and lifted him to his feet.

"We goin' for a ride in my pirogue," Robert said.

"Where you taking me, nigger?"

"We goin' to feed you and give you somethin' to drink and we goin' to take good care of you."

We walked the man to the bayou, the man taking tiny steps because of the rope hobble. I tried to help steady him, but he shook off my hand.

"You going to pay for this," he kept saying.

The three of us got into the pirogue and Robert poled us into the dimness of the early morning. The man was silent now, hunched over, his bound hands behind him, his chest resting on his knees. Robert's two sacks were in the bow of the pirogue, and the one tied to the stick occasionally moved. Robert took us to the same shack he had taken Robin and me to months before.

We climbed into the shack, boosting the white man up the ladder and, when we were inside, Robert took one of the sacks and opened it, spilling the contents onto the floor. There was a fruit jar filled with a clear liquid, some Johnnycakes, a few pigs knuckles wrapped in a piece of cloth, and a pork chop, crusty and brown.

"Here," Robert said, setting the food in front of the man. "We goin' to untie your hands so's you can eat. This here's some white lightnin' what my cousin makes, and you kin wash your vittles down with it if you is a drinkin' man. If you ain't, then we take it ourselfs."

I untied the man's hands and he massaged his wrists, then unscrewed the lid of the jar and took a swig. He let out an explosive breath, said "Damn!' and took another mouthful. We watched him eat and when he was finished, he wiped his mouth with the back of his hand and picked up the jar again.

"Why you doing this?" he said

"Cause you needs to eat." Robert said.

"What you going to do with me?"

"Leave you here a bit. You go on, finish up that corn. My cousin make it good."

"Then what you going to do with me?"

"Maybe you come to your sense. You wants to live, and you don't want no trouble. Maybe that's the way it play out."

The man was silent, then took another gulp from the fruit jar.

"It be a long night," Robert said. "Now we all gets some sleep. You finish that corn 'fore we tie your hands again."

The man drank the last of the pint, then threw the jar at Robert, who dodged it. The jar smashed against the wall.

"You going to pay for this, nigger," he said. His speech was beginning to slur.

"I's a poor man," Robert said. "If I gots to pay, it won't be much." He nodded to me. "Git his arms behind him, Jake,"

I grabbed for the arms and the man struggled, but I managed to get them behind his back, pressing his body to the floor with my knees. Robert tied his hands with a short length of rope and then we rolled the man against the wall. We waited. Eventually the man fell asleep and Robert said, "Time we end this mess."

He took the other sack, lifted it by the rope and untied the knot. He took the sack over to the man, held the top of the sack open and suddenly, with a quick swoop, enveloped the man's head. He cinched the neck of the sack tight around the man's neck. There was a writhing inside the sack and the man came alive, his voice muffled by the sack and he thrashed, arms and legs banging against the floor and wall.

"What's in the sack?" I yelled.

"Cottonmouths. Three of them. They's not happy right now." He held the sack tight around the man's throat. "This take some time," he said.

I could not breathe.

"Why this?" I said.

`"He can't go back to town. He go there, folks come and burn us out, they find you and your woman. They's no way we can let him go. But if we kill him some other way, they goin' to find out and it be just the same. Man like this who come into the woods lookin' for you, he ain't goin' to tell nobody where he goin'. So his people won't look for him for a day or two. I go to town, tell the Sheriff I find a white man in the bayou. Man what take my pirogue and some of my corn liquor and he go off. When I go lookin' for him, I find him here, and it look like he git drunk and git bit by snakes."

The man still thrashed his legs against the floor, rolling his body back and forth and I could hear him cursing.

"We git you and your lady off from here. She go first, then you go. We gots a day or so. By then he be all swole up, nobody hardly know who he be."

The man continued to struggle.

"Snakes all done," Robert said. "Now they just tryin' to get away from him. This take some time now. But the poison go to his brain real quick and he goin' to be quiet real soon."

"Jesus," I said, under my breath.

"Jesus gots nothin' to do with this," Robert said. "Jesus gots nothin' to do with your dead baby, neither. Jesus done left us alone in the bayou, told us to fix things ourselfs. Jesus tell Judas, go ahead, take them pieces of silver. You needs them. They gonna kill me anyway. Jesus know how the world work. The Lord tell Moses, take that serpent by the tail and he done that and it turn into a stick and he led his people into the promised land. Serpents done take care of that white mans what messed with your chile."

It was light now, the morning sun lighting up patches of the bayou, streaming through the trees. The dawn chorus of birds was almost deafening, and the man was still. Robert took away the sack, closing the mouth of it. He went to the doorway of the shack and tipped the sack into the opening, letting it loose. The snakes cascaded out, falling into the water, swimming immediately, their brown bodies almost invisible, heads above the surface, undulating cords of rope that went off into the bayou.

"Adders," Robert said. "Moses' people call them adders. You know about Ponce de Leon?"

"The Spaniard?"

"That's the one. He come to Florida and then he come all the way to the Mississippi, and when he git here, he be wasted, hardly able to walk. His mens have to carry him."

"How do you know this?"

"My grandma's people, the Choctaws, they knows about him. White mens with hard skin that shines in the sun. That be their armor coats. The Choctaws help those poor souls and then poor ol' Ponce, he get bit by a cottonmouth. He swole up and die. He lookin' to be a young buck forever, but he not count on the adder what can swim. My people say if you can handle the adder, you be saved. Some of them say that."

"You believe that?" I asked.

"You gots to have strong hoodoo to touch the adder."

He looked at the motionless body of the white man.

"That's where I got those adders. I keeps them for a white man what pays for them. He use them in his church. Look like the Lord provide for us. Now we gots to go back to Esther and your woman. We leave him here."

Robert poled the pirogue silently through the bayou, and I lay back, looking up at the cypress and tupelo trees, imagining Robin high in one of them, the black cloak of feathers covering her body, clinging to the trunk; and I could see the Ivory Bill swooping toward her, its wings outstretched, pulling up as it approached the tree and then the screen went blank. I remembered when I was in school in Arlington Heights, when Mr. Weiner had shown a movie about volcanoes and the projector jammed. Something happened and the film stopped and suddenly the image on the screen had a brown hole in the center of it. Mr.

Weiner frantically pulled at something, swearing under his breath,

and the hole grew in size, became a white hot light as the film

began to burn, the brown edges creeping out until there was a

peculiar smell in the room and there was nothing on the screen

but the white light of the projector bulb.

It was like that, looking up into the trees, the pirogue

passing from shadow into sunlight and suddenly there was the

bright hot light of the sun and the Ivory Bill was gone, and so was

Robin.

24.

When we got back to the house the sun was low over the trees and Esther had supper ready. Robin sat up in the bed but Esther wouldn't let her do more than that, bringing her a bowl with broth in it and bits of green floating on top.

"This here's collard greens and chicken broth and you gots to take some to keep up your strength," she said.

Robin sipped at the broth.

"They's something else we gots to do before the sun goes off," Robert said when we had finished eating.

Esther shook her head but Robert continued. "We gots to bury the chile."

I wasn't prepared for this. I don't think Robin was either.

"It not something we wants to do, but we gots to do it," he said.

Robert did everything. Esther sat next to Robin and talked quietly with her. I couldn't hear what they were saying. I felt as if I were watching from some great distance. The children were quiet, something not usual for them. Robert disappeared with the basin that had the cloth over it and when he came back in, Esther helped Robin to her feet. I took her other side and we went out into the field in front of the house.

"This here field never gonna git plowed," Robert said. "It too wet here, too close to the bayou, so's it be a good place." He had dug a pit and next to it lay the skin of the Ivory Bill, wrapped so that it looked as if it had, once again, a body.

"I'se wrapped the chile in the Lord God Bird," he said. "That way the chile has wings. It won't have to walk in the next life."

We watched while Robert laid the Ivory Bill skin in the pit and began to methodically shovel the dirt back over it. No one said anything. The children held hands.

When Robert was finished he walked over the dirt, pressing it down with his bare feet and he held his hands, palms up, and he began to speak and I thought at first it was a prayer but I didn't recognize it.

"Our Lord," he began, "who lives in this place 'longside these dark waters, you watches over us childern." And then I realized it was the Twenty-third Psalm, something I had learned in Sunday school in Arlington Heights when I was not more than ten years old. But it was changed, and his dark voice intoned the words while he stood on the raw earth covering our stillborn child. I could hear Robin crying and Robert's voice became harsh and he said, "Ou con kouri, ou pa con kotchee," and then he fell to his knees and there were words I didn't understand, not English, something else, and I felt Robin's hand clutching mine and Robert rose and said, "Now I gots to finish things off. You two gonna go to Ezra's and stay there while I does what has to be done."

"What did you pray for, Robert?" I asked.

"I pray for the chile's soul."

"What was the other thing you said?"

"What other thing?"

"The words that weren't in English?"

"That be from my grandma. She know it from old folks what come from Haiti, mix with the Choctaw."

"What's it mean?"

"*Ou con kouri, ou pa con kotcheee.* You know how to run but you don't know how to hide. That for the white mans what cause the death of this special chile. Now you and your woman gots to go to Ezra's house 'fore it get dark."

Esther protested that Robin couldn't walk as far as Ezra's, but Robert insisted.

"I gots to go to town, find the Sheriff, tell him about the white man what got bit by congos. He come by here, I don't want no chance he look in the house and find them."

Esther said that Robin shouldn't walk, but Robert said, "No, we gots no choice. Jake carry her if she can't walk."

So Robin and I made our way though the woods in the failing light. We went slowly and by the time we had come in sight of Ezra's shack, I was carrying her, holding her over my shoulder, feeling her body press against mine, and when we came into the clearing Ezra was waiting, warned by one of Esther's children who had been sent ahead. The dogs gathered around him, but they remained silent. He helped me carry Robin into the house.

Robin lay on the corn shuck mattress and was quiet and then she said, "I feel empty, Jake. You know how you told me a snake sheds its skin?"

"Yes," I said.

"I feel that way. I've shed a skin, only there's nothing left, just emptiness."

"It will pass," I said.

"You say that, but you don't know it."

She looked past me and her eyes were green, like a creature that lived in the bayou, and they were flat and when I tried to look at her she looked off, first to the left, then the right, as if making eye contact with me would somehow force her to confront something, but she didn't know what it was that she needed to confront, and neither did I. There was nothing I could do, that much I knew.

Robin slept. Ezra's wife said nothing this time, hovered around Robin, and when she woke there was a broth for her and then we slept, all of us, Ezra and his wife, Naomi, and the children in that one room, and in the morning one of Esther's children showed up. We were to stay where we were until Robert sent for us, stay out of sight,

"I don't know why Robert so fire up to save your white

skins," Ezra said. "But Robert got his reasons so we keeps you."
His wife said nothing.

That evening another of Esther's children came and said
that Robert would come to us in the morning.

When it got dark Ezra and I sat out in front of the house
while the children played.

"Your wife doesn't want us here," I said.

"She a smart woman," he said. "She know if the Sheriff
come and find you here, it go hard on us. She don't want no truck
with you."

"We won't stay," I said.

"My wife be afraid for me and for our childern but she
know what kind of dogs be out there and she ain't going to throw
you and your woman to them. They not like my dogs. Them
other dogs eats their own kin."

Eventually Ezra and the children went inside but I stayed,
leaning against the wall of the house, watching the darkness of the
woods opposite, imagining that somewhere, deep among the trees,
was another ivory-billed woodpecker waiting inside the hollow
cavity left by a rotted limb, its cartoon head alert for the sound of

the wings of a bird like itself.

Robin was not my wife, but we had lived together for three-quarters of a year, and those who knew us assumed that we were husband and wife. Although I suspected that it didn't matter to any of them whether or not we had gone through a ceremony. Her name was that of a bird, but it was a small songbird, round-bodied, red-breasted, a short sharp bill that tipped from one side to the other when it looked at you, quizzically, cocking its head, making sharp darts at the ground to pick up insects. Robin was not like that. She was more like the Ivory Bill that she had imitated, slender, angular, a rare thing so imbued with magic that people exclaimed Lord God when they saw it. But it hadn't been seen for years until we had seen it sliding through the trees toward Robin as she clung to the trunk of a cypress high above the oily water of the swamp. I could recreate the wings of Robin's shoulder blades in my head as I looked at the black line of the woods, could feel my fingers trace the delicate bones of her ribs, her nose, her forehead, but Robin lay inside the house, asleep, emptied out. I thought of the cicada husks clinging to trees, transparent shells left when the insect unfolded its wings and took flight. I thought of Robin, high in the cypress, the black feathered cloak covering her, clinging to the trunk like a huge mythical bird, and the long slow sweep of the other bird that came toward her, lifted, and then crumpled, tumbling over and over; and I thought of Robin, too, falling, and I went into the house and felt my way to the bed and touched her hair, made sure that she was breathing, and I lay next to her, careful not to touch her, careful not to wake her. She turned restlessly and I held my breath and then her breathing was even again and I lay in the dark, trying to shut out the image of the Lord God Bird skin wrapped around the dead infant. The special chile, Robert said.

In the morning Robert was there. He told me the Sheriff and a deputy had come with him to the bayou and they had taken the dead man from the shack.

"He all swole up, blue and green like spoilt meat, and the Sheriff say he know who he be but only 'cause somebody say he gone to the bayou and don't come home. The Sheriff say it a dam shame the snakes done bit him but you a dam fool if you goes into the bayou all likkered up.

"He thank me for tellin' him and he ask again if I see any

white man and woman but I say no, this the only white mans what come through. So he's gone."

"What happens to us?" I said.

"We takes a chance. You goes north. But not at the same time."

"What's that mean?"

"Your woman go first. I gots a white man in Marion who comes to the bayou, I takes him huntin' for possum. He got a taste for that. I knows him for a long time and if I ask him to put this white woman on a bus goin' north, he do it. He think he puttin' one over on the Sheriff, somethin' I got cookin'. The special chile gonna go from here today. Ezra's woman take her to Marion. You goes tomorrra. But you don't go to the white man."

"Where do I go?"

"Ezra take you to the edge of the parish. Where the Sharkey road cross the dummy line. Then you finds a freight train goin' north. Hitch a ride."

"I don't like the idea of Robin going by herself."

"Ain't no choice," Robert said. "You gots money for the bus?"

"I have money from the loggers. I could go on the bus, too."

"No. Bus go slow. Word get out the two of you on it, you don't get to Pine Bluff. They be takin' you off and bringin' you back. You hitch a ride on a freight, maybe you get to where they can't touch you."

When I told Robin what was going to happen, she protested. She didn't want to go north alone. She was afraid that I wouldn't be able to follow and she wouldn't see me again.

"You don't know how I feel, Jake," she said. "If I lose sight of you, I think I'll stop breathing."

"No. You won't stop breathing. And you'll go to Arlington Heights and go to the garage at my folks' house and I'll show up and everything will be OK."

"Everything won't be OK. It won't ever be OK again," she said. "Everything will be different."

Naomi gave her an old dress to wear and they rubbed soot from the stove on her skin to darken it and I gave her a fistful of money. I watched as the two of them went down the dirt track and as they grew smaller I wanted to run after Robin, stop her, but Robert sensed what I was thinking, and his gnarled hand took hold of my arm and then they were gone.

"Tomorra morning Ezra take you to the dummy line," Robert said. He handed me a small pink stone. "You keep this in your pocket. It be a charm what keep you from wanderin' off."

25.

Ezra left me at the edge of the parish and I set across

the field as he told me to until I came to the railroad tracks.

Follow the tracks, he had said. The fields were fallow now, corn

harvested, cotton ragged with a few tufts clinging here and there,

little wads of white stuck in the rocks between the ties. It was

nearly an hour after I left Ezra that I saw the sand hill cranes. The

size of children, with bodies the color of slate, slender necks and

heads, a bright red cap just above the sharp black beak, they were

motionless, erect, aware of my presence on the tracks. There must

have been fifty of them, alert, watching from across a field. Above

me a half dozen more banked, like airplanes, their wings spread,

legs down, the long necks like arrows and they came in among the

grazing birds, slowing, touching down gently, folding their wings

so that they magically disappeared into the smoothness of their bodies. They were shaped like soft grey figs, their delicate necks and heads still, and I stopped and waited but they remained as they were, like one of Audubon's paintings, blue brush strokes in a brown field.

And then I went on, walking awkwardly along the ties, until I came to the edge of a town and the sidings where, as Ezra had told me, freight cars were shunted. This was the line that ran north and south, he said, and I could find an empty car and ride farther north, but I should be careful that no one saw me.

It seemed too easy.

Darkness came and I waited. A train rattled through, but never slow enough so I could climb aboard and I couldn't tell which cars were empty and which ones were full so I stayed in an empty boxcar facing the tracks. Other trains came through, two headed south, one north, and then, as the sky began to turn gray, a long train came through, and slowed, finally coming to a stop. A brakeman with a lantern appeared and he waved it and the train reversed itself and a dozen freight cars came onto the empty rails in front of the car where I hid. He waved his lantern again and the train reversed and I could see empty cars passing me, but they were going south. Then there was a clanking as the train again came to a stop and the brakeman was gone. The cars began to move north, imperceptibly, and I dropped out of the car and ran across to the empty cars opposite and climbed into one. It had scraps of cardboard in it, and a few sticks of wood, and I crouched in a corner as the train picked up speed. I was headed north. That was all I knew.

I thought of the cranes in the field I had passed. It was Fall, so they were headed south. Perhaps Robin, too, had seen the cranes.

It took four days to reach Arlington Heights. Once I reached southern Illinois I took a bus, riding all night, getting off in Elgin, hitching a ride and arriving at my parents' house in mid-afternoon. I went immediately to the garage, but when I looked inside, it was no longer my room. There were the lawn mower and garden tools, cartons, and the kitchen icebox with its door turned to the wall. There was a space where, apparently, my father now parked his car, an oily patch blotching the concrete floor, and the garage smelled of oil and gasoline. My bed was still there but boxes were stacked on it. There was no sign of Robin.

I went to the back door and found my mother in the kitchen. Her surprise was complete. She stood for a moment, then embraced me, exclaiming, "Jake! You're here!" and stood back and looked at me, saying again and again, "You've changed!"

She made me sit at the kitchen table and when I asked if Robin had been there she said no, they hadn't seen her. and where was my car and had I found the bird I was looking for and was I hungry?

When I asked again if there had been any sign of Robin, she said perhaps Robin had gone to her parents' house, no, there hadn't been any sight of her. My father would be home from school soon, and we would all have dinner and I would tell them where I had been, what I had been doing. I went to Robin's house but no one was home and when I asked a neighbor she said she hadn't seen Robin for nearly a year. I don't think she recognized me. I felt empty, imagined Robin on a bus that was broken down on the side of a road, imagined the fat sheriff stepping on board the bus where she sat, alone, in the back. The figure of a woman came toward me, walking under the leafless maples that lined the street but I knew it wasn't Robin, and somehow I knew that things had gone terribly wrong.

My father, too, was surprised to see me. But supper was strained. I couldn't tell them what had happened, and I knew that I looked strange, my clothes ragged, my hair long and unkempt. And I could feel my father's gaze, as if he were examining me the way I had seen him examine a set of draughtsman's drawings, and I knew that he was weighing what he was looking at, turning me over and over in his head.

But there was no evidence that Robin had returned to Arlington Heights. Her parents hadn't seen her, and I waited three days, sleeping in the room with my brother, who now seemed a stranger and who said little to me. My father asked if I had returned for good, but I told him something had happened that had changed things, that I had to go back to Louisiana, that something had happened to Robin. He pressed me for details but I was vague, that my car had broken down, I had to go back to get it repaired, I had expected Robin to meet me but her plans must have changed.

It was cold in the mornings, frost on the vacant lot next door, and I spent the days waiting. Once I telephoned the Sheriff

in Arkansas, feeding quarters into a pay phone, telling him I was
a reporter for a newspaper in Little Rock, that there had been
rumors of a sighting of an Ivory Bill by a couple from the north, an
ornithologist and his wife. Did the Sheriff know where they were?

On the fourth day I told my father that I was leaving. If
Robin showed up, they were to make sure she stayed, that I would
telephone him in a few days.

He asked if I had enough money for the trip. Yes, I told
him, I still had money left from my job with the loggers. He had
stopped asking me questions, only said that whatever it was that
had happened, if he could help, he would try, but I think he knew
that my separation from him and my mother and my brother was
now complete. And I was desperate to find Robin.

I went to a sporting goods store in Arlington Heights
and I bought a pistol, a small .38 that would easily fit in my coat
pocket. It was a cheap gun but I was not about to go back to
Louisiana unarmed.

My father drove me to Elgin to the bus station. I had new
boots and a jacket and I had cut my hair.

"I don't know what you need, Jake," he said as we waited

for the bus. "A boy left here and a man came back. I don't think I ever really knew you before. I have no idea who you are now." He put his hand on my shoulder. My father wasn't a toucher, and I could not remember him ever putting his arms around me, at least not since I was a tiny boy, and his hand resting on my shoulder felt strange.

And then the bus came and he shook hands with me and I went south again.

26.

The first bus took me to southern Illinois, crossing the Mississippi into St. Louis at night. The river glowed black as we crossed it, and the water lapped at the levee near the bus station. I had a long wait for the next bus that would take me into Arkansas and I watched while six black women in long white dresses and white turbans knelt along the stone and brick levee, chanting something to the water that flowed silently. I changed buses and went south again, following the same route Robin and I had driven, sliding down through Missouri into Arkansas, night becoming day and night again as we came to Pine Bluffs. The people in the bus changed color, more blacks now, their voices softer, and I could hear the familiar ring of Robert's voice in some of them.

We went by the turn-off to Crossett late in the morning

and when we reached the Louisiana line a few minutes later, I grew apprehensive, but when I stepped off the bus in Marion, no one paid any attention to me, and I set off toward the tracks and the fields beyond, retracing the steps I had taken only ten days before. Inside my trouser pocket I fingered the pink stone that Robert had given me.

At first Ezra didn't recognize me. His dogs set up a clamor and he stood in the doorway, watching me approach. When I called out, "Ezra, it's me, Jake," he yelled at the dogs to shut up and stepped down onto the dirt.

"What you doin' here?" he asked.

"I came back to find Robin. She never got north."

He called into the house and Naomi appeared in the doorway.

"Mister Jake say his woman never get to the north."

"I give her to that white man in Marion what Robert said would put her on the bus."

"But did you see her get on the bus?" I asked.

"I give her to the white man. He say he take care of things."

"Could you find that white man again?"

"You gots to talk to Robert 'bout that. I didn't take her to no house. We find him in a barn south of town."

I found Robert in the church on the other side of the woods, fixing a broken chair. Unlike Ezra, he didn't seem surprised to see me.

"Where's Robin?" I asked.

"She come back the day after you gone."

"What happened?"

"She say she can't go north, she gots to stay here and she want to know where you be. I tell her you go north to meet her, and she gots to get on the bus but she say no, she got somethin' to do here."

"What was that?"

"She don't say at first. Esther puts her to bed and we watches her and then she cuts her hair off, just leaves this little bitty top what looks like the Lord God Bird, only her hair is all black and she grease it up with fat so's it stick right up and she tell me she wants that coat of feathers."

"You gave it to her?"

"Wasn't no choice. She wrap herself in it."

He gathered up his tools and put them into the sack.

"She's at your house now?"

"No. She not there."

"Where is she?

"I don't know."

"What do you mean, you don't know?"

"Just that. Next day she gone. My pirogue gone, too."

"Gone where?"

"Like I say, I don't know. I get up and the pirogue be gone and she be gone."

"Why didn't you keep watch on her?"

"What you want me to do? Hog tie her to the bed?"

"You looked for her?"

" 'Course I did. Borried a boat and went lookin' but ain't no sign of her. Mebbe she went on to the other side to the Big Woods. I look there, too. Two days I find my pirogue but she not with it."

"Jesus, you just let her go off like that?"

"Sweet Jesus gots nothing to do with it, Jake."

Esther wasn't much help, either. She said Robin wasn't

herself, looked like she was faraway all the time, and then she was gone.

"We sorry, mister Jake, but she just slip out of here when we not lookin'."

I went to the house where we had stayed but there was no sign she had been there. I borrowed Robert's pirogue and went into the bayou and searched for the next two days, sleeping in the pirogue at night, working my way back to the Arkansas side. I came out into the fields and crossed to where our house had been but all that was left was a charred pile of timbers. My car was gone. I went back to the woods and followed my old blaze marks, sometimes stopping to make the Ivory Bill call or knock two blocks of wood together, imitating the knock of the Ivory Bill. There was no answer.

The third day I saw him.

27.

I heard the sound of the outboard motor long before I saw the boat. I poled the pirogue into some palmettos and waited for it to pass. But when it came into sight I recognized the man sitting in the boat, one hand on the arm of the motor, slowing as he approached, cutting the motor and letting the boat drift silently toward the base of the tree.

His tan shirt had half-moons of dark sweat under the arms and across his back. I watched while he floated, looking up into the tree, then across the water toward where I hid. I remained motionless, frozen, my breath coming in shallow exhalations through pursed lips.

It was the portly sheriff and he drifted for some moments, the boat turning in a slow circle while he looked up into the trees. He looked again at the palmetto thicket where I was hidden and pulled the motor to life, the noise shattering the silence of the bayou. He moved slowly off in the direction he had come, and I waited until the sound had faded before I came out. He was still looking for something and perhaps he was looking, as I was, for Robin. That he had come to the same tree where the bird had been shot told me he had been there before. He had probably been guided there by the man who had been with Billy when I had scrambled his brain. No one else would have known the exact tree.

When I told Robert I had seen the sheriff in the bayou at the tree where the bird had been shot, he said, "He lookin,' same as you."

"Is he looking for Robin or for me?"

"He lookin' for her, knows that if he find her, he find you."

"So he's still trying to track me down."

"They say he a stubborn man. Not like the Sheriff we got. He content to let things lay so long as they's no aggravation in Union Parish. But the Sheriff of Big Woods County, he the kind of dog what don't let go. You gots to hit that kind of dog with a stick, beat some sense into him 'fore he gets eat by a panther."

"You suggesting I beat some sense into that man?"

"No. I just tellin' you what is. You gots to be careful, pokin' 'round the woods."

I spent more time in the bayou and in the woods north of there but no one had seen anything of a woman or heard anything like the sound I described. Sometimes I whacked the two pieces of wood together like the sound of the Ivory Bill slamming at a tree trunk, but I never got any answer.

It was darker now. Fall had come on and there was cold rain.

Then I saw him again. I was sleeping at the old house, careful not to tramp down the weeds in front of it, never lighting a lamp. Crows rose on the trail leading to the house, rising in a raucous cloud, a sure sign that someone was coming. I thought it might be Robert, but I took my pistol and went to the outhouse, closing the door so that I could look out through the cracks. He came out of the woods into the clearing and waited, staring at the house.

I watched as he approached the shack carefully, sidling along the wall, peering in the window. He grew bolder, went to the door, opened it slowly and stood back. He disappeared inside and I slipped out of the outhouse, stood behind it with the door left open, my pistol in my hand. I eased the safety off. It seemed a long time before he reappeared. He stood in the doorway, surveying the clearing in front of the shack, looking back at the track where he had come, then at the outhouse. He stepped down onto the dirt and came toward me.

"I know you're somewhere, Hamrick," he called out. "Maybe you're hiding in the shitter. Maybe you're in the brush some place, but I can smell you. If I don't find you today, I find you tomorrow."

He came to the outhouse, looked in the open door to make sure I wasn't there, then turned toward the house.

"Maybe you're here, maybe you aren't. But I'll be back." He took a step forward and I stepped out behind him, clamping my arm around his neck, pulling his head back abruptly and, with the other hand, I pressed the .38 to the side of his head.

"You found me, sheriff. And if you move a muscle I'll spread your brains all over the ground."

I pressed the muzzle of the pistol harder against his temple. He stood still. I could feel the heat from his sweaty body, the softness of him pressing against me. His hat had come off and his hair was wet, thinning and slicked back.

"You won't shoot me," he said.

"I shot your boy in the woods, put a bullet in his brain."

"That was different. I don't think you're the kind of man who can pull a trigger on me, Mister Hamrick"

"Last time I saw you, you called me boy."

"The last time you saw me I offered to give your wife safe passage. Looks like you made a mistake."

"The last time I saw you was four days ago in the bayou, looking up at the tree where the Lord God Bird was shot by that peckerwood whose brain I scrambled. Somebody told you where it was. And you were looking for something."

"I was looking for you."

"And why would you look there? Somebody tell you they saw a woman in the bayou? A woman wearing a cloak made out of feathers?"

"There's all kinds of gossip running around. There's gossip that the Lord God Bird was seen and gossip among the niggers in Union Parish that there's a woman who's got the magic to call out to that bird and there's gossip that a white man lives among the blackies way back in the woods, but it's mostly gossip.

The stuff stories are made of. Except that you're right here."

"You're in Union Parish, Sheriff." I tightened my grip on his neck. "Looks like you're out of your home county. You aren't even in your own state."

His voice was not much more than a croak. "That don't bother me none. And it don't bother the Sheriff of Union Parish none, either. You're choking me, son."

I loosened my arm, but kept it pressed against his throat.

"What made you go into the woods to that tree? Did somebody tell you they saw the woman in the feather cloak?"

"I don't think she's anywhere near the woods. But gossip had it that you were back among the blackies and you were looking for her, so I went looking for you."

"Where did you hear that I was looking for her?"

"This place is full of secrets, but you're an outsider, and no matter what you think, you ain't no secret. You gonna shoot me, Hamrick?"

"I'm thinking about it."

"You ain't gonna shoot me."

"Maybe I'll find a sack full of snakes."

"Not that, either."

"Somebody said she was in the woods, maybe in that tree, or near it. Otherwise you wouldn't have gone there."

"Like I said, people talk. I heard talk that somebody saw the woman in the bird suit, but I couldn't tell if it was new talk or old talk from when Billy got shot."

"That's a lie!"

"You believe what you want, Hamrick. I ain't seen her and I ain't talked to nobody who has."

"So how do I find out who said they saw her?"

"You don't. Maybe nobody saw her. Maybe it's all just talk. Why don't you talk to those blackies you been so close to? They know more about what happens in the woods than anybody."

I loosened my arm, sliding it down to his chest, then stepped back.

He stood a moment, catching his breath before turning to face me.

"You ain't the skinny kid I seen before," he said.

"No. You're still the same fat sheriff."

"No need for that. You ain't going to shoot me, that much I'm sure of."

"Not unless you do something stupid."

"Not likely."

"I'm going to tie you up," I said. "I'm going to leave you in the house and when I get far enough from here, I'll tell someone where you are. They'll come for you and you'll go back to Crossett. I'm not worth the aggravation."

"You think I can just forget you put a bullet in Billy Galloway's brain?"

"You mistake me for somebody who cares what you remember, Sheriff. I don't give a shit what you remember. I can tell somebody you're tied up in that house or I can forget all about you. Nobody's going to come looking for you out here, and you know that."

He was silent. Then he spoke.

"You let me loose and I'll go back to where I came from and if you're gone when I look for you again, then you'll show some sense."

"No," I said. "We'll do it my way this time. You can walk

to that house or I can put a bullet in your knee and drag you."

He turned and began walking.

I trussed him up, hands behind his back, sitting against the wall, with his ankles bound together and a bowl of water on the floor beside him.

"What you gonna do now?" he asked.

"I'll go back the way I came, to Marion; and from there I'll send someone to cut you loose."

"That's all?"

"No. I'll ask some more people about my wife. People who move about in the woods. It may be a day or two before they come for you."

"It was a Lord God Bird what Billy shot, wasn't it?"

"Yes."

"I thought so. Everybody said there wasn't no more of them. They all died out when the loggers came. But you and your wife saw one. It came to her. Story has it she was dressed like one of them way up in that tree. Is that true?"

"Yes."

"You believe she could call the bird like the blackies say?"

"I don't know what they say."

"Some of them say she had some kind of charm that the bird could hear a long way off."

"I don't want to talk about her any more, sheriff."

"Suit yourself. You gonna leave me here, then?"

"That's right. Maybe you got some kind of charm to call somebody to find you."

28.

When I got to Robert's house there was a knot of people gathered. I found Esther who had a black shawl over her shoulders. Some women were in the house at the stove and there was food on plates on a plank in the center of the room. People stared at me, and there were faces I had never seen.

"Jake," Esther said. "Robert dead."

It took a moment for her words to register.

"How?" I said. "When?"

"Yesterday," she said. "He just give up. I find him sleepin' in the shade by the church only he don't wake up. He gone to Jesus."

"He was your father?"

"No. He like everbody to think he my daddy. But he my granddaddy."

"How old was he?"

"Old as Methuslah. He be a boy in the fields when they freed the slaves. Then he come back in the bayous and he live here ever since."

"So he was ninety years old?"

"Maybe more than that. He never know for sure when he was born. My mama run off when I was a chile. He and my grandma raise me. Then she die."

"I'm so sorry," I said. "He was a good man. He took us in. He cared for Robin and me when we were in trouble."

"Not you. The girl was what he said was special. He think she got some hoodoo and she call the Lord God Bird to her."

"What was hoodoo?"

"That be what Robert knows from his grandma. That be special charms what come from Africa. He mix it with the Lord's words. He say it make powerful charms."

"Not enough to keep Robin from harm."

Esther reached out to stroke my arm, as if to reassure me.

"Robert say she not of this earth. Robert say when he was a boy the woods was full of the Lord God Bird. That bird have a special magic. But they cuttin' the woods down and the bird gone

away. Nobody see one 'til your lady call out to it."

"I can't find her, Esther," I said. "I don't mean to add to

your troubles, but I can't find her and the Sheriff from Big Springs

found me. I've left him tied up in the house where we lived."

"You not goin' to find her," Esther said.

"How do you know that?"

"She talk 'bout another bird in the woods. She say that

the other bird would be the daddy bird and it be looking for the

lady bird what got shot. She dress up like the lady bird so she

might talk to that other bird."

"She told you this?"

"She told it to Robert."

"Why didn't you tell me this? Why didn't Robert tell me?"

She turned away from me to embrace a woman who had

come in the door and I stood, waiting. A blackness had descended

in the room and I had trouble breathing, as if my chest had

suddenly collapsed against my spine. When she turned back to me

I repeated the question.

"Robert say you got to spend some time lookin' for her

yourself. Maybe you see the Lord God Bird, too. I tell him he should tell you what he knows, but he a stubborn man. He say it be good for you to go in the bayou where she was."

"Did he expect me to find her?"

"No. He knows you won't find her."

"How did he know that?"

"He find her hisself when he find his pirogue. She fall from that tree."

I was suddenly cold.

"She was dead?"

"He say creatures had carry part of her off. The feathers was still there. He say he take care of her and when you come back he tell me to keep quiet, let you work it out for yourself."

She touched my arm again and said, "I gots to tend to these folk. We bury Robert this morning in the churchyard. They all come to pay their respecks."

I found Ezra among the people gathered outside the house and told him that there was a white sheriff tied up in the house we had lived in.

"What you expeck me to do?" he asked.

"You can let somebody know, get word to the Sheriff of Union Parish. He's got water. He'll be all right for a day or two."

Ezra said he would do that, but I could tell that he was nervous and wanted me gone. Robert was no longer there and I was a danger to them all, a magnet that would draw white men, upsetting the delicate balance of their lives.

Something moved in the dirt at my feet and I bent to look and it was a wasp. It was dragging a beetle twice as large as it was, pulling it along. The insect had been paralyzed by the wasp's sting and its legs moved sporadically but the wasp was determined, sometimes buzzing its wings, towing the carcass a jerk at a time. It came to some rocks and pulled the insect under the edge of a rock, pushing at it, tucking it out of sight before backing off and flying away.

I did not know if I were the wasp or the stunned beetle. One moment I had been watching Robin high in a tree, and the next moment something happened and she was gone. I tried to imagine her by herself, climbing the cypress, and I knew that things had gone wrong, that she was like the half-paralyzed beetle, climbing only because it was somehow familiar, as if she could once again bring back the bird and the house where we made love

and the long slow nights and then I was the wasp, busily tucking

her body under a rock, stowing it away where it was safe. I felt

empty. I was the skin the snake had shed. I remembered Robin

saying she had felt like the empty snake skin and now I felt that

way, too.

I stumbled off through the woods toward Marion but

I didn't go north. I ended up in New Orleans and then went

east. They said there were Ivory Bills in the swamps of northern

Florida and I spent two years there. I guided some biologists from

a university the second year, but we never found any sign of the

Ivory Bill.

Sometimes, when I was out among the northern Florida

rivers I thought about Robin. An egret flashed white in the

sun, low across the green water and another one slowed, wings

outstretched, stopping gently on the muddy edge.

And in my head was a Louisiana egret, standing on a rock,

fixing its golden eye on us, its sharp beak as yellow as a school

pencil, and then there was a swallow and the soft coo of a pigeon

and the quickness of breath and the rising of a thousand egrets, their wings filling the air, and she shuddered and the birds were gone, the echo of their wings still in the empty air.

The cloud of birds returned, egrets again, so many of them settling over the water, turning it into a pulsing white surface, the current slowly moving them downstream, piling some of them against rocks where they flapped their wings and moved to float again and in the rapids they rose and half-flew and settled again, pooling in the quiet water. She rose and fell, only to rise again, over and over and over until the birds emptied into the sea.

A woodpecker in the forest beyond the river drummed on a tree, and a meadowlark somewhere beyond the cattle trilled and it was silent, the heat rising from the brown grasses, and she was filled with lassitude and wanted only to sleep or to lie in the shade until dusk came. Overhead a single crow, black against the hazy blue, rowed silently toward the wood.

I heard the sound of falling water inside my head and I pursed my lips and there was softness and muscle. I imagined cracked crab and chilled wine and the shadows lengthened on the river. A bird called from the wood, a clear bell-like voice as if it were speaking to us. She slept, her arm under her head and I watched the almost imperceptible rise and fall of her rib cage and I picked the hair off her cheek and tucked it back. All of this was in my head with the falling water.

29.

I went back to Arlington Heights several years later and found that my father had died and that my mother no longer lived in the house on South Mitchell Street. My brother had graduated from college and was working in Chicago. The lilacs were still there.

I have not been back to Arlington Heights since then. Sometimes I think of Robin standing in the empty room of the tiny house we rented from the farmer, naked, her arms lifted.

"Imagine I'm a bird," she says. "What kind of a bird do you want me to be?"

"Right now you look like an egret," I say to her. Her skin is white, almost porcelain, and her neck seems longer and as I look at her, I imagine an egret, wings outstretched, rising to leave the water in the ditch by the roadside, lifting its wings gracefully, catching the air.

"What does the egret sound like?" she asks.

"Not pretty. It's a croak. As if you startled a big frog."

She lets out a hoarse belching sound and lowers her arms, lifting them again.

"Fuck me," she says. "Now."

No one ever saw another Lord God Bird.

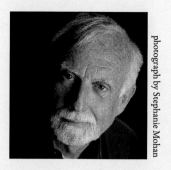

Russell Hill has published poetry, essays, short stories and novels. His novel, *Robbie's Wife* (Hardcase Crime), was a finalist for the 2008 Edgar Allan Poe prize from the Mystery Writers of America. The recipient of a Fulbright Award, he spent a year in England as an English teacher. and taught high school students for more than 50 years. An avid fly fisherman, he has written for outdoor magazines, and is the author of *The Search for Sheepheaven Trout*, a book about a two-year quest for a nearly-extinct trout. Other novels include *The Edge of the Earth* and *Lucy Boomer* (Ballantine Books). Married, with three children, he has lived most of his life in California.

Books from PLEASURE BOAT STUDIO: A Literary Press

(Note: Caravel Books is a new mystery imprint of Pleasure Boat Studio: A Literary Press. Caravel Books is the imprint for mysteries only. Aequitas Books is another imprint which includes non-fiction with philosophical and sociological themes. Empty Bowl Press is a Division of Pleasure Boat Studio.)

Island of the Naked Women · Inger Frimansson, trans. fm. Swedish by Laura Wideburg · $18 · a caravel mystery

Crossing the Water: The Hawaii-Alaska Trilogies · Irving Warner · fiction · $16

Among Friends · Mary Lou Sanelli · $15 · an aequitas book

Unnecessary Talking: The Montesano Stories · Mike O'Connor · $16

God Is a Tree, and Other Middle-Age Prayers ·Esther Cohen · poems · $10

Home & Away: The Old Town Poems · Kevin Miller · $15

Old Tale Road · Andrew Schelling · $15 · an empty bowl book

Listening to the Rhino · Dr. Janet Dallett · $16 · an aequitas book

The Shadow in the Water · Inger Frimansson, trans. fm. Swedish by Laura Wideburg · $18 · a caravel mystery

The Woman Who Wrote "King Lear," And Other Stories · Louis Phillips · $16

Working the Woods, Working the Sea · Eds. Finn Wilcox and Jerry Gorsline · $22 · an empty bowl book

Weinstock Among the Dying · Michael Blumenthal · fiction · $18

The War Journal of Lila Ann Smith · Irving Warner · historical fiction · $18

Dream of the Dragon Pool: A Daoist Quest · Albert A. Dalia · fantasy · $18

Good Night, My Darling · Inger Frimansson, trans. fm. Swedish by Laura Wideburg · $16 ·a caravel mystery

Falling Awake: An American Woman Gets a Grip on the Whole Changing World — One Essay at a Time · Mary Lou Sanelli · $15 · an aequitas book

Way Out There: Lyrical Essays · Michael Daley · $16 · an aequitas book

The Case of Emily V. · Keith Oatley · $18 · a caravel mystery

Monique · Luisa Coehlo, trans. fm. Portuguese by Maria do Carmo de Vasconcelos and Dolores DeLuise · fiction · $14

The Blossoms Are Ghosts at the Wedding · Tom Jay · essays & poems ·$15 · an empty bowl book

Against Romance · Michael Blumenthal · poetry · $14

Speak to the Mountain: The Tommie Waites Story · Dr. Bessie Blake ·
278 pages · biography · $18 / $26 · an aequitas book
Artrage · Everett Aison ·fiction · $15
Days We Would Rather Know · Michael Blumenthal · poetry · $14
Puget Sound: 15 Stories · C. C. Long · fiction · $14
Homicide My Own · Anne Argula · fiction (mystery) · $16
Craving Water · Mary Lou Sanelli · poetry · $15
When the Tiger Weeps · Mike O'Connor · poetry and prose ·15
Wagner, Descending: The Wrath of the Salmon Queen · Irving Warner
·fiction · $16
Concentricity · Sheila E. Murphy · poetry · $13.95
Schilling, from a study in lost time · Terrell Guillory · fiction · $17
Rumours: A Memoir of a British POW in WWII · Chas Mayhead ·
nonfiction · $16
The Immigrant's Table · Mary Lou Sanelli · poetry and recipes · $14
The Enduring Vision of Norman Mailer · Dr. Barry H. Leeds ·
criticism · $18
Women in the Garden · Mary Lou Sanelli · poetry · $14
Pronoun Music · Richard Cohen · short stories · $16
If You Were With Me Everything Would Be All Right · Ken Harvey
·short stories · $16
The 8th Day of the Week · Al Kessler · fiction · $16
Another Life, and Other Stories · Edwin Weihe short stories · $16
Saying the Necessary · Edward Harkness · poetry · $14
Nature Lovers · Charles Potts · poetry · $10
In Memory of Hawks, & Other Stories from Alaska · Irving Warner ·
fiction · $15
The Politics of My Heart · William Slaughter · poetry · $13
The Rape Poems · Frances Driscoll · poetry · $13
When History Enters the House: Essays from Central Europe ·
Michael Blumenthal · nonfiction · $15
Setting Out: The Education of Lili · Tung Nien · trans. fm Chinese by Mike
O'Connor · fiction · $15

OUR CHAPBOOK SERIES:

No. 1: ***The Handful of Seeds: Three and a Half Essays*** · Andrew
Schelling · $7 · nonfiction
No. 2: ***Original Sin*** · Michael Daley · $8 · poetry
No. 3: ***Too Small to Hold You*** · Kate Reavey · $8 · poetry

No. 4: ***The Light on Our Faces: A Therapy Dialogue*** · Lee Miriam
Whitman Raymond · $8 · poetry
No. 5: ***Eye*** · William Bridges · $8 · poetry
No. 6: ***Selected New Poems of Rainer Maria Rilke*** · trans. fm German
by Alice Derry · $10 · poetry
No. 7: ***Through High Still Air: A Season at Sourdough Mountain*** ·
Tim McNulty · $9 · poetry and prose
No. 8: ***Sight Progress*** · Zhang Er, trans. fm Chinese by Rachel Levitsky ·
$9 · prosepoems
No. 9: ***The Perfect Hour*** · Blas Falconer · $9 · poetry
No. 10: ***Fervor*** · Zaedryn Meade · $10 · poetry

FROM OTHER PUBLISHERS (In Limited Editions):

Desire · Jody Aliesan · $14 · poetry (an empty bowl book)
Deams of the Hand · Susan Goldwitz · $14 · poetry (an empty bowl book)
Lineage · Mary Lou Sanelli · $14 · poetry (an empty bowl book)
The Basin: Poems from a Chinese Province · Mike O'Connor · $10 / $20
· poetry (paper/ hardbound) (an empty bowl book)
The Straits · Michael Daley · $10 · poetry (an empty bowl book)
In Our Hearts and Minds: The Northwest and Central America · Ed.
Michael Daley · $12 · poetry and prose (an empty bowl book)
The Rainshadow · Mike O'Connor · $16 · poetry (an empty bowl book)
Untold Stories · William Slaughter · $10 / $20 · poetry (paper / hardbound) (an
empty bowl book)
In Blue Mountain Dusk · Tim McNulty · $12.95 · poetry (a Broken Moon
book)
China Basin · Clemens Starck · $13.95 · poetry (a Story Line Press book)
Journeyman's Wages · Clemens Starck · $10.95 · poetry (a Story Line Press
book)

Orders: Pleasure Boat Studio books are available by order from your bookstore,
directly from PBS, or through the following:
SPD (Small Press Distribution) Tel. 8008697553, Fax 5105240852
Partners/West Tel. 4252278486, Fax 4252042448
Baker & Taylor 8007751100, Fax 8007757480
Ingram Tel 6157935000, Fax 6152875429
Amazon.com or Barnesandnoble.com

Pleasure Boat Studio: A Literary Press
201 West 89th Street
New York, NY 10024
Tel / Fax: 8888105308
www.pleasureboatstudio.com / pleasboat@nyc.rr.com

HOW WE GOT OUR NAME

...from *Pleasure Boat Studio,* an essay written by Ouyang Xiu, Song Dynasty poet, essayist, and scholar, on the twelfth day of the twelfth month in the renwu year (January 25, 1043):

"I have heard of men of antiquity who fled from the world to distant rivers and lakes and refused to their dying day to return. They must have found some source of pleasure there. If one is not anxious for profit, even at the risk of danger, or is not convicted of a crime and forced to embark; rather, if one has a favorable breeze and gentle seas and is able to rest comfortably on a pillow and mat, sailing several hundred miles in a single day, then is boat travel not enjoyable? Of course, I have no time for such diversions. But since 'pleasure boat' is the designation of boats used for such pastimes, I have now adopted it as the name of my studio. Is there anything wrong with that?"

Translated by Ronald Egan

home studies, on the other hand, together with studies of "separation effects," have enabled us to investigate a group of babies and young children who had known mothering and human partnerships at one or another period of early development and who suffered loss of the mother and often repeated separations from a succession of substitute mothers. In one set of studies, then, the groups of babies had in common the experience of no human partnerships; in the other, the babies had suffered ruptures of human ties in early development.

Within these two large groups the data from all studies confirm each other in these essential facts: children who have been deprived of mothering, and who have formed no personal human bonds during the first two years of life, show permanent impairment of the capacity to make human attachments in later childhood, even when substitute families are provided for them. The degree of impairment is roughly equivalent to the degree of deprivation. Thus, if one constructs a rating scale, with the institution studied by Spitz[6] at the lowest end of the scale and the institution studied by Provence and Lipton[7] at the other end of the scale, measurable differences can be discerned between the two groups of babies in their respective capacities to respond to human stimulation. But even in the "better" institution of the Provence and Lipton study, there is gross retardation in all areas of development when compared with a control group, and permanent effects in the kind and quality of human attachments demonstrated by these children in foster homes in later childhood. In the Spitz studies, the degree of deprivation in a hygienic and totally impersonal environment was so extreme that the babies deteriorated to the mental level of imbeciles at the end of the second year and showed no response to the appearance of a human figure. The motion picture made of these mute, solemn children, lying stuporous in their cribs, is one of the little-known horror films of our time.

men without potency and women without sexual desire, under any of the conditions that normally favor sexual response. These men and women who have never experienced human bonds have a diffuse and impoverished sexuality. When it takes the form of a violent sexual act it is not the sexual component that gives terrible urgency to the act, but the force of aggression; the two drives are fused in the act. When we consider the ways in which, in early childhood, the love bond normally serves the redirection of aggression from the love object, we obtain a clue: the absence of human bonds can promote a morbid alliance between sexual and aggressive drives and a mode of discharge in which a destructive form of aggression becomes the condition under which the sexual drive becomes manifest.

From these descriptions we can see that the diseases of non-attachment give rise to a broad range of disordered personalities. But if I have emphasized the potential for crime and violence in this group, I do not wish to distort the picture. A large number of these men and women distinguish themselves in no other way than their attitude of indifference to life and an absence of human connections.

The hollow man can inform us considerably about the problem we are pursuing, the relations between the formation of human love bonds and the regulation of the aggressive drive. In those instances where we have been able to obtain histories of such patients, it appears that there were never any significant human ties, as far back as memory or earlier records could inform us. Often the early childhood histories told a dreary story of lost and broken connections. A child would be farmed out to relatives, or foster parents, or institutions: the blurred outlines of one family faded into those of another, as the child, already anonymous, shifted beds and families in monotonous succession. The change of address would be factually noted in an agency record. Or it might be a child who had been reared in his own family, a family of "no connections," unwanted, neglected, and sometimes brutally treated. In either case, by the time these children entered school, the teachers, attendance officers, or school social workers would be reporting for the record such problems as "impulsive, uncontrolled behavior," "easily frustrated," "can't get close to him," "doesn't seem to care about anything." Today we see many of these children in Head Start programs. These are the three- and four-year-olds who seem unaware of other people or things, silent, unsmiling, poor ghosts of children who wander through a brightly painted nursery as if it were a cemetery. Count it a victory if, after six months of work with such a child, you can get him to smile in greeting or learn your name.

Once extensive study was begun on the problems of unattached children, some of the missing links in etiology appeared. We now know that if we fail in our work with these children, if we cannot bring them into a human relationship, their future is predictable. They become, of course, the permanently unattached men and women of the next generation. But beyond this we have made an extraordinary and sobering discovery. An unattached child, even at the age of three or four, cannot easily attach himself even when he is provided with the most favorable conditions for the formation of a human bond. The most expert clinical workers and foster parents can testify that to win such a child, to make him care, to become important to him, to be needed by him, and finally to be loved by him, is the work of months and years. Yet all of this, including the achievement of a binding love for a partner, normally takes place, without psychiatric consultation, in ordinary homes and with ordinary babies, during the first year of life.

This brings us to another part of the story, and to further links with the biological studies of Lorenz. Research into the problems of attachment and non-attachment has begun to move further and further back into early childhood, and fi-

nally to the period of infancy. Here too it is pathology th has led the way and informed us more fully of the norm course of attachment behavior in children.

Clinical Studies: Lost and Broken Attachments in Infancy

Since World War II, a very large number of studies h appeared which deal with the absence or rupture of hu ties in infancy. There is strong evidence to indicate tha ther of these two conditions can produce certain dis bances in the later functioning of the child and can imp varying degrees the capacity of the child to bind hims human partners later in childhood. A number of these s ies were carried out in infant institutions. Others follo children who had spent their infancy and early years succession of foster homes. In each of the studies that I refer to here, the constitutional adequacy of the baby at was established by objective tests. When control g were employed, as they were in some of the studies, was careful matching of the original family backgr These investigations have been conducted by some most distinguished men and women working in chil choanalysis, child psychiatry, and pediatrics—among Anna Freud, Dorothy Burlingham, René Spitz, John B William Goldfarb, Sally Provence, and Rose Lipton.

The institutional studies have enabled us to follow velopment of babies who were reared without any po ity of establishing a human partnership. Typically, e the best institutions, a baby is cared for by a corps of and aides, and three such corps, working in shifts, h sponsibility for large groups of babies in a ward.[5] The

As we group the findings on all the follow-up studies it becomes clear that the *age* at which the child suffered deprivation of human ties is closely correlated to certain effects in later personality and the capacity to sustain human ties. For example, in some of the studies, children had suffered maternal deprivation or rupture of human connections at various stages in early childhood. As we sort out the data we see a convergence of signs showing that the period of greatest vulnerability with respect to later development is in the period under two years of life. When, for any reason, a child has spent the whole or a large part of his infancy in an environment that could not provide him with human partners or the conditions for sustained human attachments, the later development of this child demonstrates measurable effects in three areas. First, children thus deprived show varying degrees of impairment in the capacity to attach themselves to substitute parents or, in fact, to any persons. They seem to form their relationships on the basis of need and satisfaction of need (a characteristic of the infant's earliest relationship to the nurturing person). One "need-satisfying person" can substitute for another, quite independently of his personal qualities. Second, there is impairment of intellectual functions during the first eighteen months of life which remains consistent in follow-up testing of these children. Specifically, it is conceptual thinking that remains depressed even when favorable environments are provided for such children in the second and third years of life. Language itself, which was grossly retarded in all the infant studies of these children, improves to some extent under more favorable environmental conditions but remains nevertheless an area of retardation. And third, disorders of impulse control, particularly in the area of aggression, are reported in all follow-up studies of these children.

The significance of these findings goes far beyond the special case of infants reared in institutions or in a succession of

53

foster homes. The institutional studies tell us how a baby de-
velops in an environment that cannot provide a mother, or,
in fact, any human partners. But there are many thousands of
babies reared in pathological homes, who have, in effect, no
mother and no significant human attachments during the
first two years of life. A mother who is severely depressed, or
psychotic, or an addict, is also, for all practical purposes, a
mother who is absent from her baby. A baby who is stored
like a package with neighbors and relatives while his mother
works may come to know as many indifferent caretakers as a
baby in the lowest-grade institution and, at the age of one or
two years, can resemble in all significant ways the emotionally deprived babies of such an institution.

Biological and Social Foundations of the Human Bond

The information available to us from all of these studies in-
dicates that the period of human infancy is the critical period
for the establishment of human bonds. From the evidence, it
appears that a child who fails to make the vital human connections in infancy will have varying degrees of difficulty in
making them in later childhood. In all of this there is an extraordinary correspondence with the findings of ethologists
regarding the critical period for attachment in animals.

If I now proceed to construct some parallels, I should also
make some cautious discriminations between attachment
behavior in human infancy and that in animals. The phe-
nomenon of "imprinting," for example, which Lorenz describes, has no true equivalent in human infancy. When
Lorenz hand-rears a gosling, he elicits an attachment from
the baby goose by producing the call notes of the mother

54

goose. In effect he produces the code signal that releases an instinctual response. The unlocking of the instinctual code guarantees that the instinct will attach itself to *this* object, the producer of the signal. The registration of certain key characteristics of the object gives its own guarantees that this object and no other can elicit the specific instinctual response. From this point on, the baby gosling accepts Dr. Lorenz as its "mother"; the attachment of the baby animal to Lorenz is selective and permanent. The conditions favoring release of instinctual behavior are governed by a kind of biological timetable. In the case of attachment behavior, there is a critical period in the infancy of the animal that favors imprinting. Following this period the instinct wanes and the possibility of forming a new and permanent attachment ends.

It is not difficult to find analogies to this process in the attachment behavior of the human infant, but the process of forming human bonds is infinitely more complex. The development of attachment behavior in human infancy follows a biological pattern, but we have no true equivalents for "imprinting" because the function of memory in the first eighteen months of a human baby's life is far removed from the simple registrations of stimuli that take place in the baby animal. Yet even the marvelous and uniquely human achievements of cognitive development are dependent upon adequacy in instinctual gratification, for we can demonstrate through a large body of research that where need satisfaction is not adequate there will be impairment in memory and consequently in all the complex functions of human intelligence.

Similarly, there is no single moment in time in which the human infant—unlike the animal baby—makes his attachment to his mother. There is no single act or signal which elicits the permanent bond between infant and mother. Instead, we have an extended period in infancy for the development of attachment behavior and a sequential develop-

N.B.

ment that leads to the establishment of human bonds. By the time a baby is eight or nine months old he demonstrates his attachment by producing all of the characteristics that we identify as human love. He shows preference for his mother and wants repeated demonstrations of her love; he can only be comforted by his mother, he initiates games of affection with her, and he shows anxiety, distress, and even grief if a prolonged separation from her takes place.

I do not wish to give the impression that this process is so complex or hazardous that only extraordinary parents can produce a baby with strong human bonds. It is achieved regularly by ordinary parents with ordinary babies without benefit of psychiatric consultation. It requires no outstanding measures beyond satisfaction of a baby's biological and social needs in the early period of infancy through feeding, play, comfort in distress, and the provision of nutriments for sensory and motor experience—all of which are simply "givens" in a normal home. But above all it requires that there be human partners who become for the baby the embodiment of need satisfaction, social interaction, comfort, and well-being. All of this, too, is normally given in ordinary families, without any reflection on the part of the parents that they are initiating a baby into the human fraternity.

Finally, where the attachment of a baby animal to its mother is guaranteed by interlocking messages and responses on an instinctual basis, we have no such instinctual code to guarantee the attachment of a human infant to his mother. This means, of course, that there are an infinite number of normal variations in patterns of mothering and great diversity in the mode of communication between baby and mother. Any of a vast number of variations in the pattern can be accommodated in the human baby's development and still ensure that a human bond will be achieved. The minimum guarantee for the evolution of the human bond is prolonged intimacy with a nurturing person, a condition that was once biologically insured through breast feeding. In the case of the bottle-fed baby, the insurance must be provided by the mother herself, who "builds in" the conditions for intimacy and continuity of the mothering experience. As bottle feeding has become common among all social groups in our society, continuity of the nurturing experience becomes more and more dependent upon the personality of the mother and environmental conditions that favor, or fail to favor, intimacy between the baby and his mother.

The bond which is ensured in a moment of time between a baby animal and its mother is, in the case of the human baby, the product of a complex sequential development, a process that evolves during the first eighteen months of life. The instinctual patterns are elicited through the human environment, but they do not take the form of instinctual release phenomena in terms of a code and its unlocking. What we see in the evolution of the human bond is a language between partners, a "dialogue," as Spitz puts it, in which messages from the infant are interpreted by his mother and messages from the mother are taken as signals by the baby. This early dialogue of "need" and "an answer to need," becomes a highly differentiated signal system in the early months of life; it is, properly speaking, the matrix of human language and of the human bond itself.

The dialogue begins with the cry that brings a human partner. Long before the human baby experiences the connections between his cry and the appearance of a human face, and long before he can use the cry as a signal, he must have had the experience in which the cry is "answered." Need and the expressive vocalization of need set up the dialogue between the baby and his human partners. Normally, too, there is a range of expressive signs in a baby's behavior which his mother interprets through her intimacy with him: the empty mouthing—"He's hungry"; fretful sounds—"He's cranky, he's ready for his nap"; a complaining sound—"He wants company"; arms extended—"He wants to be picked up." Sometimes the mother's interpretation may not be the correct one, but she has acted upon the baby's signal in some way, and this is the crucial point. The baby learns that his signals bring his mother and bring satisfaction in a specific or general way.

The institutional baby has no partner who is tuned in to his signals. As Provence and Lipton demonstrate in their institutional study, since there is no one to read the baby's signs there is finally no motive for producing signals. The expressive vocalizations drop out or appear undifferentiated in these babies. And long after they have been moved to homes with foster families, speech development remains impoverished.

The animal baby makes a selective response to his mother in the early hours of life, and distinguishes his mother from other members of the species. The human baby discovers the uniqueness of his mother in a succession of stages throughout the first year. How do we know this? Among other ways, through the study of the smiling response of the human infant. Our tribal greeting sign, the smile, undergoes a marvelous course of differentiation in the first year. Since the smile connotes "recognition," among other things, we may study differential smiling as one of the signs in the evolution of attachment behavior. In this way Peter Wolff of Harvard has found that the human baby in the third and fourth weeks of life will smile selectively in response to his mother's voice.[8] Wolff can demonstrate experimentally that no other voice and no other sounds in the same frequency range will elicit the baby's smile. Wolff's finding should end the controversy over the "gas smile," and mothers who always disagreed with pediatricians on this score are thus vindicated in their wisdom.

At about eight weeks of age, the baby smiles in response

to the human face. As René Spitz has demonstrated, the smile is elicited by the configuration of the upper half of the human face.[9] A mask, representing eyes and forehead, will also elicit the baby's smile at this age. The baby of this age does not yet make a *visual* discrimination among his mother's face, other familiar faces, and strange faces. But between the age of six weeks and eight months the smile of the baby grows more and more selective, and at about eight months of age the baby demonstrates through his smile a clear discrimination of the mother's face from the faces of other familiar persons or the face of a stranger. Presented with a strange face at the close of the first year, the baby will typically become solemn, quizzical, or unfriendly, and may even set up a howl. This means that a form of recognition memory for familiar faces has emerged in the infant. But in order that recognition memory appear, there must be thousands of repetitions in the presentation of certain faces, to produce the indelible tracing of *this* face with *these* characteristics, which can be later discriminated from all other faces with the general characteristic of the human face. This does not mean that a mother or other family members need to be constantly in the baby's perceptual field. It does not mean that, if someone else occasionally takes over the care of the baby, his memory capacity will be impaired. But it does mean that there must be one or more persons who remain central and stable in the early experience of the baby so that the conditions for early memory function be present. And it means, too, that such a central person must be associated with pleasure and need gratification because memory itself becomes selective through the emotional import of experience. By the time a baby is eight to twelve months old, the mother is discriminated from all other persons, and the baby shows his need for her and his attachment to her by distress when she leaves him and by grief reactions when absence is prolonged beyond his tolerance. At this stage, when the mother has become the indispensable human partner, we can speak of love, and under all normal circumstances this love becomes a permanent bond, one that will embrace not only the mother but other human partners and, in a certain sense, the whole human fraternity.

The baby who is deprived of human partners can also be measured by his smile, or by the absence of a smile. If the human deprivation is extreme, no smile appears at any stage of infancy. In the institution studied by Provence and Lipton the babies smiled at the appearance of a human face, and while the smile was not joyful or rapturous, it was a smile. But whereas at a certain age babies normally discriminate among human faces by producing a *selective* smile, the institutional babies smiled indifferently at all comers. There was nothing in the last months of the first year or even in the second year to indicate that these babies discriminated among the various faces that presented themselves, nothing to indicate that one person was valued above other persons. There was no reaction to the disappearance or loss of any one person in this environment. In short, there was no attachment to any one person. And in this study, as in others, it was seen that even when families were found for these children in the second or third year of life there was a marked incapacity to bind themselves to any one person.

These were the same babies who showed a consistent type of mental retardation in follow-up studies. In the areas of abstract thinking and generalization these children and, in fact, institutional babies in all studies, demonstrated marked impairment in later childhood. In ways that we are only beginning to understand, this disability in thinking is related to impoverishment in the structures that underlie memory in the first year of life. The diffusion and lack of focus in the early sense-experience of these infants, and the absence of significant human figures which normally register as the first mental traces, produce an unstable substratum for later and more complex mental acts.

③

The third generalization to be drawn from all these studies has to do with "impulse control," and specifically the control of aggression. From all reports, including those on the model institution directed and studied by Anna Freud and Dorothy Burlingham [10] and the "good" institution investigated by Provence and Lipton, it emerges that such children show marked impulsivity, intolerance of frustration, and rages and tantrums far beyond the age in childhood where one would normally expect such behavior. Over thirty years ago Anna Freud drew the lesson from her institutional study that the problems of aggression in these children were due to the absence of intimate and stable love ties. Under the most favorable circumstances, the group care provided by the institution usually cannot produce durable love bonds in an infant. Everything we have learned since this sobering study by Anna Freud has confirmed her findings twice over.

And this brings us back full circle to Lorenz's study of aggression and the bond. The progressive modification of the aggressive drive takes place under the aegis of the love drives. Where there are no human bonds there is no motive for redirection, for the regulation and control of aggressive urges. The parallel with animal studies is exact.

A Summary of the Evidence

If we read our evidence correctly, the formation of the love bond takes place during human infancy. The later capacity of the ego to regulate the aggressive drive is very largely dependent upon the quality and the durability of these bonds. The absence of human bonds in infancy or the rupture of human bonds in early life can have permanent effects upon the later capacity for human attachments and for the regulation of aggression.

It would be a mistake, of course, to blame all human ills on failure in early nurture. There are other conditions in the course of human development which can affect the capacity to love and the regulation of drives. Yet the implications of maternal deprivation studies are far-reaching and, if properly interpreted, carry their own prescription for the prevention of the diseases of non-attachment. As I see it, the full significance of the research on the diseases of non-attachment may be this: we have isolated a territory in which these diseases originate. These bondless men, women, and children constitute one of the largest aberrant populations in the world today, contributing far beyond their numbers to social disease and disorder. These are the people who are unable to fulfill the most ordinary human obligations in work, in friendship, in marriage, and in child-rearing. The condition of non-attachment leaves a void in that area of personality where conscience should be. Where there are no human attachments there can be no conscience. As a consequence, the hollow men and women contribute very largely to the criminal population. It is this group, too, that produces a particular kind of criminal, whose crimes, whether they be petty or atrocious, are always characterized by indifference. The potential for violence and destructive acts is far greater among these bondless men and women; the absence of human bonds leaves a free "unbound" aggression to pursue its erratic course.

The cure for such diseases is not simple. All of us in clinical work can testify to that. But to a very large extent the diseases of non-attachment can be eradicated at the source, by ensuring stable human partnerships for every baby. If we take the evidence seriously we must look upon a baby deprived of human partners as a baby in deadly peril. This is a baby who is being robbed of his humanity.

CHAPTER III

"Divide the Living Child"

> And the king said, Bring me a sword.
> And they brought a sword before the
> king. And the king said, Divide the
> living child in two, and give half to
> the one, and half to the other.
>
> I Kings 3:23

A CHILD is claimed by two mothers. The wisdom of the court is sought by two contestants. In this century, which a blind prophet once called "The Century of the Child," the ancient tale of Solomon renews itself in the modern court. The rights of child ownership prevail. The child himself remains a mute contestant. Few voices are raised to claim his human rights.

We are all made witness to the horror through the video screen, the news story, the picture magazine. And we are all made judges. "How would I choose? Who is worthy to make the awesome judgement?"

Solomon's sword has become a metaphor. But for the child the metaphor is exact. In the psychological sense, a child can be "cut in two" when the law decrees that his love for the two people who are mother and father to him must be severed, and that he must be given to strangers whom the law decrees to be his parents.

Those of us who are specialists in child development are making a strong claim upon the modern court. We are asking for nothing less than "the moral rights of infants and children," the right to know love through enduring human partnerships. This means that any violation of that right through custody decisions becomes a matter of gravest concern to us. It must also become a concern shared by every citizen, by all of us who care about children.

The Moral Burden

In fairness to the modern judge, his moral burden is a larger one than that of Solomon. For the ancients, the claims of blood and blood ties were compelling: in the mystical sense, blood ties united human partners, and were the essence of the human bond. In our time, we have come to know that a child's love for his parents is not instinctive, is not a heritable trait like the color of hair and eyes; it is very largely a love that is born of love. The child loves because he is loved, and the beloved partners may be his natural parents or his foster parents or his adoptive parents. Nor do "instinct" or "blood ties" guarantee that a natural mother or natural father will love their child and therefore be loved in return. If our laws do not reflect these modern truths we must look for other reasons.

Certainly there cannot be an enlightened judge today who does not share these beliefs regarding the nature of a child's love. But there are other traditions with ancient roots which may govern decisions regarding the welfare of children. For today, as in archaic times, the child is regarded as the property of his natural parents. "Who *owns* the child?" may be the principle that determines many custody decisions. The "fitness of the parent" can be a consideration when such "fitness" is questioned in extreme cases. "The best interests of the child" is generally regarded as the cardinal principle, but court decisions regarding it more commonly reflect the prior claim of natural parents under circumstances in which the "fitness" of the natural parent is undisputed.

While straining under the weight of archaic law, the enlightened judge of today has another moral burden thrust upon him. The new burden derives from the findings of contemporary psychology which have illuminated the origins of human bonds. As we have seen in earlier chapters of this book, the love bonds between a child and his parents are formed during the early months and years of life. Any circumstances which break these bonds or prevent their formation may damage the psychological development of the child and may permanently impair the capacity to love and to form enduring human partnerships in later life. The judge who must make the crucial decisions for binding and unbinding these ties for children has the crushing moral burden of this knowledge as he makes decisions each day which govern the future of children.

In our courts today there are a few enlightened judges who have brought this new knowledge of the nature of human bonds into their decisions. This knowledge, I am sure, does not help them sleep well at night. For if we understand fully the meaning of loss of love to a young child, the burden on the conscience of the court is a terrible one.

In the story that follows, I have examined a large number of custody cases which have been brought to my attention. I am not a lawyer, of course. My only task is to examine the human implications of these custody decisions for the child and his family.

Baby Lenore

The case of "Baby Lenore" [1] was widely publicized in 1971. Baby Lenore had been surrendered for adoption by her natural mother soon after birth. In the story that follows we should keep in mind that the legal procedures for adoption were strictly followed.

Baby Lenore was placed with the DeMartino family in June 1970 at the age of five weeks. The adoptive family had been thoroughly investigated and their qualifications as parents were exceptionally high. When Lenore was four months old the natural mother commenced a *habeas corpus* action to reclaim her child from the agency. The litigation that followed involved a contest between the adoption agency, which claimed that the mother was bound by her contract, and the natural mother, who claimed that she had a right to her child. The natural mother prevailed and in May 1971, when Lenore was one year old, the New York Court of Appeals affirmed the decision to return the child to her natural mother.

The events of the next year are well known. The DeMartinos took up residence in Florida just before the Court of Appeals decision was handed down and, with Baby Lenore still in their care, carried on the fight with the State of New York, which now judged them to be in contempt.

In the trial proceedings, counsel for the DeMartinos argued that the sole issue for the Florida court was "the best interests of the child." Two distinguished psychiatrists, Dr. Stella Chess and Dr. Andrew Watson, testified as to the possible trauma which removal might precipitate in the thirteen-month-old child. On the basis of medical testimony the court decided that the baby should remain with the DeMartino family.

From the evidence reported I concur with the decision that

66

"the best interests of the child" in the case of Baby Lenore were served by her remaining in her adoptive home. If I now speak on behalf of the "best interests" of Baby Lenore, from the psychological point of view, I do not want to put aside the personal anguish of the natural mother or that of the DeMartinos during this nightmare in the courts. For the natural mother, the original decision to give up her baby for adoption must have been a torment. Yet once the decision has been made, the child's interests must, I believe, be paramount. For the adoptive parents, who loved their baby, the terror that the child would be taken from them can be fairly equated with that of parents whose child is in danger of death or abduction.

If I say, then, that the child's interests are paramount, it is not without feeling for the natural mother. But the psychological grounds for the decision of the Miami court represent the best that we know about child development today.

Baby Lenore, like every baby who has known parental love, had begun to form her permanent attachments to her adoptive parents in the early months of life. The DeMartinos *were* her parents. At six months of life, or earlier, a baby clearly discriminates between the faces and voices of parents and those of strangers. Even his smile and his vocalizations become "special," preferential for these two people who are the center of his universe. Between six months and one year of age this love is already so binding that even temporary separation, for a day or two, will create distress, refusal to eat, difficulties in sleeping and mood changes in which sadness and apathy become recognizable signs of grief. When the parents come back, the baby behaves in ways that we all can recognize as "when the beloved returns." There is relief, comfort, clinging, and gradually a return to his old self.

In brief, if we try to describe the reactions of a baby who

67

loses his parents and his world, we can only find analogies with our adult experience of loss through death. The analogy is fair. Since a baby has no way of imagining the return of a "lost" beloved person, he experiences this loss as total, even as we adults experience the death of a loved person. And when the "lost" mother is replaced, even by a devoted substitute or foster mother, the baby does not automatically transfer his love to the new mother. Love has its own laws, even in infancy. Once love is given it belongs to the loved partners.

What could have been expected if Baby Lenore had been returned to her natural mother as the New York Courts had ordered? No instinct exists which would have caused the year-old child to recognize the woman who bore her. The natural mother would, with terrible irony, be the foster-mother, and the baby who had lost her beloved parents—the adoptive but actual parents—would find her natural mother a stranger. There would have followed a sequence of events which I and others have seen in clinical work: a long period of distress for the baby, a turning away from the stranger who was her natural mother, hopeless crying, and finally resignation. If the stranger, who is her natural mother, is patient and loving, some measure of the baby's capacity to love will return and be given to the new mother. But the cost to the child in suffering is incalculable and the effects of this traumatic loss may endure for all the years to come.

But how do we know this? Can a baby under one year "remember" this traumatic separation from his original partners? No, he will probably not remember these events as a series of pictures which can be recalled. What is remembered, or preserved, is anxiety, a primitive kind of terror, which returns in waves in later life. Loss and danger of loss of love become recurrent themes or life patterns. What is preserved may be profound moodiness or depression in later life, the somatic memory of the first tragic loss, which returns

68

from the unremembered past even, ironically, at moments of pleasure or success. What is preserved is the violation of trust, of the ordered world of infancy in which love, protection, and continuity of experience are invested in people. The arbitrary fate that broke the first human bonds may damage or shatter that trust, so that when love is given again it may not be freely returned. And finally, what is preserved is likely to be a wound to the embryonic personality in the first year which may have profound effects upon later development. In the early years, personality is essentially "interpersonality," the self evolving in relation to human partners, the binding of that self to those partners through love and reciprocal love. When the bond is broken, the very structure of personality is endangered, and the mending of personality will be an arduous task for the new partners.

The risks are very great. Whenever we disrupt the love bonds of infants and children, we take an action which has grave implications for the future of the child. When the New York Court of Appeals awarded Baby Lenore to her natural mother, the decision was reached out of simple ignorance of a large body of scientific knowledge that now informs us of the meaning of human bonds in the early years. I am also sure that Miss Scarpetta, the natural mother, could not have known that her baby's best interests now lay in the preservation of the ties to her adoptive parents. However terrible the choice may be, the good mother who understands this can only decide in favor of her baby's future.

In the largest number of custody cases which I have examined, the court's decisions have been based upon the proprietary rights of the natural parents without regard for the nature of the child's real attachments. There are cases in which children have been reared by grandparents or other relatives, or by foster parents, who are "mother" and "father" to the child in all ways, while the natural parents are strangers or at best comparatively insignificant figures in the child's life. Upon petition by the natural parents the court may award custody to them (if no evidence of gross unfitness is presented) and the child whose love resides with grand-parents or foster parents is "cut in two." He may never be made whole again.

It is not only in the courts that the rights of infants are violated. In hundreds of child-welfare agencies throughout the country, babies and young children live in foster homes or institutions for extended periods, because the natural parent or parents are unable to bring themselves to the deci-sion of formal surrender. During the waiting periods, the baby in a foster home has made his human attachments to the foster parents. When the decision is made in favor of sur-render by the natural parents, the baby becomes available for adoption. He may be six months old, a year, or two years, or older, when he is wrenched from the foster parents whom he loves, and placed with adoptive parents who are strangers to him. In a number of cases known to me, the foster parents have applied to become the adoptive parents of the child they have grown to love and have been denied by the social agency because agency policy does not permit foster parents to apply for adoption of a child in their care. Such agency policies are buried in antiquity, and I cannot tell you how they came to be. Neither can I tell you why they persist. But in the light of everything that is known about babies and human attachments, thousands of children throughout our country are removed from foster homes where they have known secure love and are delivered like small packages to adoptive parents who are strangers to them. Even the most loving and devoted adoptive parents will suffer many trials before the baby transfers his love and trust to them.

"Fitness of the Parent"

In still another group of cases, the issue of parental "fitness" is paramount in the court's decision to award custody. What constitutes "fitness" of a parent? I would consider, as you would, that physical and emotional brutality toward a child, neglect or abandonment of a child, severe mental pathology in the parent (certain forms of psychosis, drug addiction, criminal behavior), would under all normal circumstances raise questions regarding the "fitness" of a parent. But my practical experience as a consultant to social agencies and my reading of custody cases shows a pattern that is as eccentric as that which governs the earlier group of cases I have described.

The proprietary rights of the parent have prevailed in courts under circumstances in which children have been beaten, tortured, and sexually assaulted by a parent. There are cases recorded throughout the country in which parents who are criminal psychopaths and child murderers have regained custody of their children after a few months of "treatment" in a mental hospital. The same blind justice has declared parents "unfit" when judged on the basis of I.Q. alone, or on something which a court judged "a bohemian style of life," or marriage to a person of another race.

In two cases which I have reviewed, parental rights were terminated on the basis of a "low I.Q." in one or both parents. In the A. case (Iowa, 1972)[2], no clinical evidence of retardation was produced at any of the hearings. If there was other evidence of parental incapacity, this was not included in the brief court opinion. Is there scientific evidence that a parent's capacity to love and care for a child is related to intelligence? I know of none. If the judgment of incapacity is made, it must be made on the basis of other evidence, in fact, the evidence that normally applies in the judgment of "fitness" of a parent. If consideration is given to the child's "best interests," then the questions to be asked are still the essential ones: Are there strong affectional ties between child and parent? Are the parents employing their capacities (however limited) to provide the reasonable minimal guarantees to a child—that he be loved, valued, protected, educated? A parent with "a low I.Q." may be able to provide the essential nutriments for child development. If he or she cannot provide "an intellectually stimulating environment" it is only fair to say that there are other parents at the other end of the spectrum who can provide the nutriments for intelligence and yet be unable to provide love and protection.

The "moral fitness" of a parent in a number of cases reviewed by me became an issue in custody cases. In the absence of absolute standards of "moral fitness" each judge is free to judge "fitness" according to his own views. Thus, in New York in 1972,[3] a family court judge transferred custody of a seven-year-old girl from her divorced mother to her father on these moral grounds: the mother was known to be "cohabitating" [sic] with a man described by the court as "the paramour." The judge also cited "the character of the neighborhood" in which the mother was living. The Lower East Side, said the judge, was not "a safe place for a small female child to play." The father, who had remarried, was living in a suburban garden apartment. No other evidence of superior "fitness" of the father was introduced beyond legal marriage and a garden apartment.

Both the mother and father were professional middle-class people. The practice of "cohabiting" without marriage is not, of course, restricted to any class, but I have observed that among the poor it is rarely a factor which governs custody decisions. I have also observed that the issue of community environment, which presumably affects all children, is rarely introduced into decisions regarding child welfare when the family is poor. If the moral principles enunciated by this judge were given general application in custody and child-welfare cases, a large part of the child population of New York City would become wards of the court.

The relevant questions for the child in this case were not examined in the summary that was available to me. What was the nature of the child's attachment to her mother? To her father? What were the demonstrated capacities of the mother to rear her child? What qualified professional opinions did the judge have available to him in making his decision?

In Alabama, in 1972,[4] welfare authorities brought child custody proceedings against a young white woman, twice divorced, who gave birth to a child fathered by a black man. The state tried to take away this baby and her four other white children on the grounds that the mother was unfit. No evidence of moral unfitness of the mother was introduced beyond the implied "unfitness" of a woman who had borne a child to a black man. The juvenile court ruled that the state could take none of the children.

Consider the alternatives. Had the court removed these five children from their mother's custody, the children would, of course, have been placed in foster homes or institutions. The baby, child of a black father and white mother, would have been among the "difficult to place" babies, in this community as in others, and his tragic story could be predicted from that moment on.

Here the court's wisdom prevailed; but in many other instances known to me a righteous judge, committed to his private moral beliefs, has removed children from their homes, from the only human attachments they have known, and set them on a course which is marked like a refugee trail. The family is split up. The children are placed with licensed foster parents whose good intentions, devotion, and humanity are rewarded by that court with the sum of $80 or $90 a month in many communities. The children, if they have had strong attachments to their own parents, are not grateful to their foster parents. Within a year or less, it is entirely possible that circumstances within the foster home might require that the children be placed in another home. It is not unusual in foster-home agencies that children placed at the age of five will know six or seven foster homes before they have reached the age of 12.[5] These are the children who learn at an early age that they are unwanted, unworthy, shabby cast-offs who come to rest briefly in still another place, until they cease to please or to give satisfaction, and then move on again. In one way or another, these cheated children avenge themselves upon society in later years.

The same blind justice that declares a white mother with a black baby "morally unfit," a mother with a low I.Q. "unfit," or a father with a garden apartment more fit than a mother with a Lower East Side apartment is at work in another group of custody cases, where the manifest unfitness and brutality of parents does not move the court to take custody of a child in danger.

The capricious motives which have led some courts to remove children from parents to whom they had strong attachments are matched, in these instances, by an irrational justice which is blind to gross neglect and brutality on the part of parents and sustains the rights of these parents to own the children whom they have abused and will continue to abuse.

There *are* times when children *must* be removed from their own homes. There are children whose lives are endangered by criminally psychotic parents, children who have been beaten, tortured, starved, sexually assaulted by parents who are, themselves, beyond cure for their terrible mental diseases. There are parents who do not even experience feelings of guilt for their sadism, or guilt for the killing of a child. This is not to say that all abusive parents are beyond cure; a very large number of them can be helped. But among abu-

74

sive parents there are a considerable number whom no known psychiatric treatment will endow with the capacity for love or simple human caring, or moderate the rage to kill which breaks through like a savage storm that is beyond their control.

In every community in this country there are documented cases in which a judge has sustained the parental prerogative, ownership of the child, when the evidence of torture, brutal assault of a child, or incest was not only presented to the court but uncontested. Peter and Judith Decourcy have collected a number of these documents in their book, *A Silent Tragedy.* [6] The documents read like a medieval horror story, made all the more terrible by the court decision: ". . . returned to parental custody." "Parents admonished to be exceedingly careful to prevent further injury to these children."

These, then, are the children whose very survival and human potential is in great danger if they remain with their parents. Foster home placement will provide protection and, under the best circumstances, a chance to know love and to be loved. To remain in their own homes is to be destroyed emotionally—and in many cases it is literally a sentence of death.

Who Are the Decision Makers?

The decision to maintain or dissolve a child's relationship with parents or substitute parents to whom he has attachments, or the decision to dissolve or maintain a child's relationship with parents who are endangering the life of a child, are made by a juvenile court judge on the basis of evidence presented to him. He may be assisted in making his decisions by the testimony of social workers, psychologists, psychiatrists. These decisions affect a child's destiny as surely as a pronouncement from the gods did in ancient justice.

We are all unworthy, being less than gods. Those of us with professional training in child development know how unworthy. When we are brought to make decisions we may call upon our best knowledge and we will surely tremble in awe before the task. But decisions regarding custody are finally in the hands of a juvenile court judge, with the assistance of a supporting staff. What qualifies the judge to make these decisions which affect the destinies of children and their families?

Throughout the country, the holder of this office needs no qualifications beyond his legal training. On the judicial ladder, this office is lowest in prestige, least likely to attract a man or woman of superior qualifications and career interests in children and families. The man who must play god need not be informed about the psychological needs of children and their families and is free to exercise his private beliefs and prejudices regarding the best interests of the child without tormenting doubts.

In the majority of our courts, the supporting staff of social workers and psychologists have neither the specialized professional training nor the vocational commitment to children which qualifies them as advisors to the court. In many of the records I have examined, the professional staff dispenses shabby counsel to the court, in which psychological ignorance and confusion are cloaked in pretentious scientific language. Yet they, too, are the decision makers for tens of thousands of children and their families.

Who shall speak for the child in the courtroom? In 1973, Goldstein, Freud, and Solnit published a book in which this question is examined. In *Beyond the Best Interests of the Child*,[7] the authors address themselves to some of the same problems we have considered here. The child's best interests are paramount, these authors assert throughout. The child must have personal representation by counsel in the court. Counsel for the child "must independently interpret and formulate his client's interests, including the need for a speedy and final determination."

What all of us are seeking is an enlightened court which affirms the priority of a child's needs and his affectional ties over all other considerations. A humane court endowed with psychological wisdom may invoke the principle "in the best interests of the child" and give it a precise twentieth century meaning—that protection and preservation of a child's love for his human partners is a paramount value in establishing "the best interests of the child."

CHAPTER IV

Child Care Industries Incorporated

WANTED: MATURE WOMAN. CHILD
CARE. CHILDREN TWO AND
FIVE. EMPLOYED MOTHER.
LIGHT HOUSEKEEPING. LIVE
IN. MUST LOVE CHILDREN.
MORE FOR HOME THAN
WAGES. CALL AFTER 5:00
P.M.

KENNEY 220-7482

ALAS for the Kenneys as they wait for the phone to ring. This devoted nanny will not be found. I believe she was last employed by David and Agnes Copperfield, London, circa 1850, having been the childhood nurse of Mr. Copperfield since the untimely death of his father. For a modest wage this cheerful, red-cheeked woman performed all household duties, consoled and advised the widow, and mothered the orphaned child. This good woman literally burst with maternity. Her hearty embraces, recalled by Copperfield the younger, caused the buttons of her bodice to fly off in all directions.

Child Care Industries Incorporated

Name: Clara Peggotty; b. 1780 (?); Yarmouth, Exc. ref. . .
D. Copperfield, C. Dickens, London.
Current employment status: Unknown.

The plight of the Kenneys is shared by approximately 14
million working mothers in search of substitute mother care
in 1974. Of these there are 5 million who have 6.5 million
children under the age of six. The Kenneys, with their two
preschool children, belong to this second, rapidly growing
group of families who must find child care in a society that
has been depleted of "substitute mothers." Licensed day-
care centers and family day-care homes cannot cope with the
demand. The estimated number of day-care "slots" is
1,000,000 [1]. In any case, the question must be raised whether
these institutions are actually providing "substitute mother
care" for babies and preschool children.

To accommodate the millions of children of employed
mothers, an industry has grown up which includes sitters-
by-the-hour, sitters-by-the-week, "mother's helpers," "day
care in my home," and public and private day-care centers. In
the last category some enterprising merchants of child care
have set up chains which, like Colonel Sanders and Howard
Johnson, claim to dispense uniform service and hospitality at
reasonable cost. The industry includes hourly service centers
for any domestic emergency. Recently I heard of a place
called "Kiddie Park," which I thought, naturally, was a play-
ground for small children. This turned out to be literally "a
parking place for kids," i.e., you drive up to park the kiddie
and for a fee of 50 cents an hour your baby or toddler can
have the services of a smiling lady and the society of eight or
ten disgruntled and scrappy customers in training pants.
We also have "drop-in centers" for babies and young chil-
dred which operate on the same principle, the principle
of the cash and carry laundry or the deposit box at the
bank.

For queasy parents who leave a tearful child in the care of

anonymous sitters and care-givers, the industry has a slogan: "THE MINUTE YOU LEFT HE STOPPED CRYING."

As an industry, Child Care Industries Incorporated is in a unique position. Its services and personnel can range from "good" to "deplorable," and the consumer in the age range one month to six years will not write letters to the management regarding the quality of service. (Nor is he in a position to withdraw his patronage.) Since his parents are not really the direct consumers of the services rendered, they are rarely in a position to judge the quality. In other trades this is known as a seller's market. The question for us is, "How fare the children?"

As the consumer's advocate I propose to examine the services of Child Care Industries Incorporated from the point of view of both the direct consumer (the child in care and his needs) and the indirect consumers (his parents and their needs).

The Child in Care

We start with the child. But we cannot speak of "the child" or "the working mother" or "the care-giver." The needs of children are different for each developmental stage, and caregiving or substitute mother care must be judged in relation to the reasonable or optimal requirements for nurture at each of these developmental stages.

If we can generalize at all, we can say that all children at all ages need stability, continuity, and predictability in their human partnerships for the fullest realization of their potentials for love, for trust, for learning and self-worth. The human family, which has been unjustly castigated in recent years, is a durable and rugged institution which was invented for this purpose and while fallible at times, it normally provides the conditions for the fulfillment of these needs. When substitute mother care is considered for a child of any age, the questions which need to be asked are: (1) What are the needs of my child at *this* stage of development? (2) Who can serve as a mother substitute for my child, given these needs?

Infants and Toddlers

For infants and children under the age of three, the developmental needs make special requirements upon the mother and unique requirements for substitute mother care. These are the years in which the foundations for love and for learning are being laid down. Under all favorable circumstances the baby's primary attachments emerge through the mother's and father's care-giving. As in all partnerships of love, the baby's love flourishes through continuity and stability of these experiences with his partners.

The baby's love, like love at all ages, is more or less exclusive. The baby is not more likely to switch partners and bestow his love upon a stranger—even a beguiling one—than any other member of the human family who values his partner in love. By the time the baby is six months old, love and valuation of his mother take on poignant meaning; even minor separations from her can be distressing. And if extraordinary circumstances such as hospitalization or a prolonged journey take his mother away for several days, even the six-month-old baby will show signs of grief and bereavement, more poignantly felt because at six months the baby does not yet have the elementary concept that a person or object that disappears must be "some place."

Between the ages of six months and three years, children who are strongly attached to their parents will show distress and even panic when they are separated from their parents and left with strangers. Parents who understand these reactions as a sign of love take special pains to see that a sitter employed for the parents' night out, or the mother's afternoon away, will be a person known to the child and trusted by them and their child. Most babies and young children can tolerate these brief, everyday separations if substitute care is carefully worked out and if the child, with even minimum language comprehension, can be told that mommy and daddy are going bye-bye, that Susan (the known sitter) will take care of him, and that mommy and daddy will be back soon. In these ways separation from them need not disturb the child's trust of his parents.

As the direct consumer's advocate I must make a blanket indictment of Kiddie Park, the Drop-in Center, Baby Sitters Unlimited, and all such services of Child Care Industries Incorporated, which provide anonymous sitters for small children. During the years when a child must learn trust and valuation of himself and others, these industries teach values for survival. A child cannot feel valued when he is left in the care of a succession of anonymous sitters. And in the population of under-fives which I know well there are large numbers of toddlers and small children who show excessive anxieties around separation and loss which can be attributed in some measure to experiences in which separation has brought a succession of strangers into the child's life.

In the case of the mother seeking employment, who has a baby or toddler, all these developmental considerations take on larger dimensions. Typically, the mother will be gone for ten hours each day, five days a week. Since babies and toddlers make extraordinary demands upon their own mothers, the requirements for a "substitute mother," in the true sense of the word, are also extraordinary. A mother who is in tune with her child, sensitive to his signs and signals, his unique patterns of personality and his idiosyncrasies, will want no less in a substitute mother. If her own pleasure in her child and her own valuation of his love is large, she will want a mother substitute who finds pleasure in babies and small children and who values a child's love. Such a person would also feel that care of a child is a personal commitment and that if she has earned the affection of a small child she would not capriciously change jobs or desert the child and the family to whom she has bonds of affection.

At this point I can feel my readers rise up in bitter protest: where do you find such a "mother substitute?" And in truth, such mother substitutes are in short supply. But remember, I am the consumer's advocate in this essay. And if we are asking the questions, "What are the needs of the child?" and "What are the needs of the family seeking child care?" and "What constitutes 'substitute mother care'?"—these are not the same questions as "What does the market offer?"

If a mother is considering a group day-care program for her baby or toddler, the same questions need to be asked. If group care in a home or a day-care center is considered, the criteria for "substitute mother" do not change.

Is there, in fact, in the home or nursery under consideration "substitute mother care?" Is the program designed in such a way that one person on the staff is the primary and consistent care-giver for each baby? And is this care-giver the "primary person" for one or two babies, or seven or eight babies, under the age of three? Considering the unique needs of the baby and toddler, can one person provide substitute mother care for numbers of small children even if she is highly qualified? And, assuming there is a primary care-giver for each child under the age of three, is this person one who has the personal qualifications of "substitute mother" which we have identified?

Again, I can feel the reproaches of good and conscientious mothers who have sought day care which meets their own high standards. With great fortune some mothers have found an extraordinary home day-care program in which a devoted woman provides substitute mother care. With luck and perseverance some mothers have found an extraordinary day-care center in which the principles of child care are derived from the psychological needs of babies and small children, programs in which exceptionally qualified teachers or aides provide mother substitute care, highly individualized for each child, consistent and mindful of the needs of the small child for continuity in relationships.

I myself know of only a handful of day-care centers in this country which operate on these principles. I do not know of any state licensing laws which include these principles among their standards. Thus, it is possible under existing state laws to prescribe a ratio of adults to children (one adult to four children) in the age range birth to three years and not require that each group of four children should have one primary person who stands in as "mother substitute." It is entirely possible (and usual) that each baby has four to six rotating staff members who care for him, in which case, of course, no one person stands for "mother substitute."

Preschool—Three to Six Years

Around the age of three, but sometimes later, most children can tolerate separation from the mother for a half day, morning or afternoon, without distress when a good and stable substitute care plan is provided. In developmental terms, the child at the age of three can transfer some part of the trusting relationship with his parents to a care-giver or a teacher who knows how to earn the trust of children. Advances in cognition also help him in tolerating separation; he knows that a mother who is absent will return, that a mother not-present is "some place," while earlier, in the period under three, this concept was either not available to him, or easily lost under tension.

In the years three to six, a half-day group care program

based on good educational principles can facilitate the child's development. In a small group social learning can be advanced. In a good preschool program under the leadership of qualified teachers, a child's potential for learning can be enhanced through introduction to stories, to music, to drawing and painting, and exploration of the natural world.

The capacity for peer relationships and friendships at this age has advanced far beyond the two-year level. But the natural tendency of this age is to seek one or two partners in play. A good preschool program is responsive to this tendency and flexibility promotes the conditions under which sub-groups in the larger group can be formed (and reformed). A classroom situation in which twelve or twenty preschool children are put through a daily regimented schedule of "group activities," or a program in which twelve or twenty children mill around a large room without any social structure, are equally inimical to the developmental needs of small children.

The adult care-giver or teacher remains central to the child's well-being during these years (and long after). (The recommended adult-child ratio for preschool [3- to 5-year-olds] is one to seven or eight children. Far better, some of us think, is a one-to-four ratio in which one primary care-giver or teacher is available to four children as "mother substitute" or "special teacher" even though the child will have ties to other teachers.) In a good group program for preschool children one can see the centrality of the adult, as children in the course of a single hour move from peer group play to the adult, "touching base," returning to an activity or to a private pursuit. In an ideal group-care program an adult is available for conversation, for reading a story, for comforting a distressed child, for enhancing a talent or an interest, and responding to this child's personality and his individual needs. (This is also what a good parent does for his child at home.)

Under the favorable conditions described above, most children can profit from a half day in group care. But there is a consensus among good preschool educators that the benefits of a good preschool program diminish or are even cancelled when the school day is prolonged to six hours or beyond. Most children begin to show the strain of prolonged separation from mother and home after a few hours.

When preschool education is the family's only objective in bringing a child to a preschool program, the half day at nursery school is best adapted to the child's own needs. But when the primary consideration is *substitute care for a working mother employed full time,* the 9- to 10-hour-a-day group program can strain the child's tolerance to its limits.

Under the most favorable circumstances, in "ideal" day-care programs known to me, directors and teachers have been unanimous in their reports. When preschool children are separated from their mothers for 9 to 10 hours there is a point of diminishing returns in the nursery day, and finally a point where no educational benefits accrue to the child. By afternoon, after nap time, restlessness, tearfulness, whininess, or lassitude become epidemic in the group of 3- to 6-year-olds. Even the most expert teachers have difficulty in sustaining the program and restoring harmony. What we see is longing for mother and home. The nice teacher, the "best friends," the lovely toys can no longer substitute.

Once again, as I write this, I can feel the reproaches of mothers who for personal or financial reasons must work full-time. As the "consumer's advocate" I am not unmindful of the needs of women who are employed or are seeking employment. But we are addressing ourselves to questions of children's developmental needs and capacities and are examining issues of substitute mother care and education for preschool children. From these points of view it appears to me and others in the field of early child development that an 8- to 10-hour-day group care program for 3- to 6-year-olds does not serve the educational needs of small children, and the professional staff even under the most favorable circumstances find that they do not serve as "mother substitutes" or "teachers" beyond the half-day tolerance of most preschool children.

Are we asking too much? Has anyone proved that the 9- to 10-hour nursery day, under *optimal* circumstances is harmful to the child? As far as I know, no one has "proven" this. And certainly we would expect that in the ideal nursery I am using for reference, good teachers will exert themselves to see that no child is harmed. In the case of a child who was showing ill effects they would carefully examine the psychological needs of the child with his parents, which might lead to better solutions or alternatives in care.

But here we are speaking of "ideal" nurseries, providing child care for working mothers.[2] They are rare. The majority, by far, of the preschool full-day nurseries that are known to me do not have expert teachers or professional staffs attuned to the individual needs of each child and his family; the programs themselves are not educational programs; they offer, at best, "custodial care." For mothers who are seeking "mother substitute" care and an educational program, these nurseries fail on every count. We do not need to "prove" that such programs can be damaging to many children. When a child spends 11 to 12 hours of his waking day in the care of indifferent custodians, no parent and no educator can say that the child's development is being promoted or enhanced, and common sense tells us that children are harmed by indifference.

The mother who must work for personal or financial reasons has poor options for her preschool children. If she is looking for substitute mother care in a home or a school she will learn that such care will be hard to find "at any price." If we, as consumer's advocates, will not settle for "anything but the best" for children, we are faced with the sobering fact that in our country we will need over 2,000,000 devoted and dedicated "substitute mothers" with professional qualifications to serve the needs of 6,500,000 children under the age of six whose mothers are employed.

For the poor and the socially disadvantaged families, who are a majority in this particular population, a mother's options are usually so limited that "substitute mother care" and "education" are not even among her choices. Children already disadvantaged by poverty, poor nutrition, health problems, domestic stress and confusion, and the risks of high-delinquency neighborhoods, spend their days "at a neighbor's," or several neighbors or relatives in the course of a week, or in a "center" which more likely than not is a storage place for babies and preschool children which, licensed or unlicensed, may offer nothing more than a hot lunch and distracted and overburdened, untrained care-givers.

The School-Age Child

Normally, the school age child at the age of six or older can manage the full day school session and separations from home with a fair degree of independence. He also demonstrates in his after-school activities some degree of independence in moving outside the orbit of the home. Most parents will agree that supervision and availability of parents or parent substitutes in the after-school hours remain a vital need for the child.

Most mothers who work full time or part time find that the task of combining work and child care becomes easier in the school years. If a good and stable after-school child-care plan is made, the school age child seems able to manage well in most cases. He may, in fact, take considerable pride in his mother's work and can share responsibilities in the home to ease the after-work domestic chores.

The standards for a mother substitute during the after-school hours remain as we have described them for the early years. Someone who can, in fact, "stand in" for the mother between the hours of 3:30 and 6:00, someone who shares the family's standards of devotion to children and responsibility for children. And here, it appears, the task of finding a mother substitute for the after-school hours is not as formidable as in the infancy and preschool years. This is a two-and-a-half-hour work day for another woman. The number of women available for child care on a part-time basis is considerably larger than the number available for full-time child care. In this labor pool are women whose children are grown and who are interested in part-time work, college students who may find part-time child care a satisfying way of supplementing income, women in the neighborhood who are mothers and can accommodate part-time child care in their own homes, and so on.

It seems, then, that if a mother is in a position to choose whether or not to work, if financial and professional needs are not pressing, her options for substitute mother care are better in the school years than in the preschool years.

It is the problem of child care in the infant and preschool period that presents the largest obstacles for most mothers who are considering employment or are already employed.

Three Fictional Families

As the consumer's advocate I will invent three fictional families for illustration of the problems which an employed mother faces in seeking child care that meets the high standards I have proposed. The fictional families are composite portraits of many young families I have known in my work. I have endowed the parents with good capacities for love and nurturance of children. Their children are at different developmental stages, infancy, preschool, school age. The family options in two families are limited by income. One family, by contrast, has a high income. All three families are served by the enterprise which I have called Child Care Industries Incorporated. The child care people and care facilities are fictional but are drawn from my visits to various homes and centers throughout the country.*

The Neustadts

This fictional family is composed of Peg, John, and their six-month-old son, Anthony. John is employed in a food store, earning a net income after taxes and other deductions of $7,000. Peg, who had worked as a clerk-typist before Anthony was born, earned $5,000 after taxes. Peg has taken a leave of absence from her job. Without her earnings the Neustadts are just not making it and are already several hundred dollars in debt. Peg makes plans to return to work.

The Neustadts place an ad in the local newspaper. "Mature woman wanted for child care; warm, reliable, must love children." What they had in mind, I suppose, was a 20th-century Peggotty. A single applicant appears, a Mrs. Rosemary Grimm. She is, in fact, a tough old girl, an unsentimental grandmother who states her terms of employment in flat English. She last earned $100 per week at the Masons, and she will not work for less. She produces a long list of references, for the past five years, and two letters from former employers in which she is commended chiefly for her "reliability." It is she who conducts the interview. She is a non-stop talker who notices the baby only once in this hour. With a sharp glance at Anthony (dressed this July day only in a diaper and a cotton vest), she recalls the infant son of a previous employer who nearly died of pneumonia.

* I have chosen the device of "the composite portrait" to protect the identities of real families and day-care programs known to me.

The rattled Neustadts bring the interview to a close. "Not for us!" they say to each other later. And John makes a quick calculation. At $5,000 per year for child care, even with tax deductions for the working mother, the family would net about $1,000 through Peg's employment.

The Neustadts wait for the other applicants to appear. But nobody comes.

So the Neustadts enter the world of the sitter and the mother's helper.

A friend recalled a darling college girl, named Betsy, who needed daytime employment and had late afternoon and evening classes. Betsy loved babies. Her rate was $1.00 per hour.

Three months later, when Anthony was nine months old, Betsy found a job as counter girl at an ice-cream parlor for $1.50 per hour. Her girlfriend, Penny, who loved babies, came to the Neustadts and left when Anthony was eleven months old. Penny was followed by Deedee, and Deedee was followed by Olivia. Olivia was followed by Joanna who was, herself, the mother of two preschool children who were cared for by a neighbor. When Joanna left (she developed migraine headaches) Anthony was eighteen months old.

Anthony began to cry out in his sleep when he was ten months old. By fourteen months he wakened several times at night screaming "Mama," and clung to his Mama in terror when she picked him up. Peg was alarmed and spoke to friends about this. Cindy, the neighborhood expert on child rearing practices, said it was teething. Peg was doubtful. So am I.

Since I have invented this family anyway I will invent a nightmare for Anthony which caused him to waken in terror. In Anthony's nightmare he is lost in a department store and he can't find Mama. There is a revolving door which goes round and round and Betsy and Penny and Deedee and Olivia and Joanna and lots of strange ladies keep spinning around, and somebody reaches out and picks up Anthony, and he is sucked into the revolving door and goes round and round. He screams "Mama," and he wakes up and finds Mama beside his bed. He clings to Mama to make sure she won't get lost again.

The Neustadts made another try. A friend recommended the services of Mrs. Nancy Gordon, a young mother herself, who said that she was never happier than when she had a houseful of children. She provided day-care in her home for eight children and she could always accommodate one more. Her fee was $16 per week. Peg went to visit.

Nancy turned out to be a pleasant, vivacious, unflappable young woman. Her basement recreation room housed eight children, four of whom were under two years of age. Two babies were in bouncing seats, suspended from the ceiling. They bounced steadily with glazed eyes. One six-month-old baby was curled up with a bottle propped beside him. A fifteen-month-old baby, clutching pacifier and diaper, roused herself from stupor when Peg came near and cried "Mama!" in an exultant voice. Nancy was amused. "Aw, c'mon, Missy," she said, "that's not your mama." And she gave her a friendly pat. "She says that to everyone who comes in the door," Nancy explained. Three children (ages probably two to three) were sitting transfixed before a television set, oblivious to the world. One child, a boy of four, was riding a trike and appeared to be very much at home. This child turned out to be Nancy's own son.

Question: Is Nancy providing substitute mother care for these babies and young children? Well, not unless the mothers of these babies follow the practice of leaving them unattended for hours with propped bottles, pacifiers, and bouncing seats. Not unless their toddlers spend the day before a TV screen.

But is Nancy an uncaring woman? Is she cruel? Not at all, it appears. If these children seem dispirited and joyless it is not because their caretaker is malevolent or grossly neglectful.

She simply doesn't have a sense of what babies and young children need. She is not personally attached to any of these children. She is the custodian of a baby bank, dispensing necessary services such as diapering, a meal and a snack, kleenex for the tears, rescue from assault by peers, safe storage for the ten hours when mother is at work.

In the end Anthony did not go to Nancy's basement day-care program.

Peg's friend, Karen, thought that the Neustadts should look for a good day-care center with people who could give babies the kind of love they need and would ordinarily get at home. The Neustadts now entered the world of the Day-Care Center.

They learned that there were two kinds of day-care centers. One was called "non-profit" (subsidized by public funds) and the other "proprietary" (i.e., privately owned and operated for profit). The Village Nursery (non-profit) charged a fee of $14.00 per week for each child. The director had a teacher's certificate, and the education of her assistants ranged from high school to two years of college. It was rated "good" by local authorities. The Neutstadts learned that they were not eligible for The Village Nursery. Their combined net income far exceeded the ceiling for eligibility for a subsidized center.

The Merry Mites Day Care Nursery (proprietary) charged a fee of $18.50 per week (average for proprietary centers in the Neustadts' community). John Neustadt began to do some calculations in his head. If the subsidized day-care center charges $14.00 per week and the proprietary day-care center charges $18.50, how does the proprietor make his profit?

I went to the library for the Neustadts (I find myself growing increasingly attached to this family) and pulled together some figures. I found that Mary Keyserling (former director of the Women's Bureau, U.S. Department of Labor) had directed a study for the National Council of Jewish Women

EVERY CHILD'S BIRTHRIGHT

in 1971.[3] At that time the estimated cost of "quality day-care" was $40.00 per week per child. This means that the non-profit "good" day-care center, such as The Village Nursery was subsidized for the difference between its $14.00 per week fee and actual costs of $40.00 per week. Without subsidy, the Merry Mites Day-Care Center was charging $18.50 per week and was making a profit, or it could not stay in business. And how were they managing to make a profit?

We will accompany the Neustadts to the Merry Mites Day-Care Center. Merry Mites is located in an elderly house in a low-rent residential neighborhood. There is a small back yard which is fenced off for a play space.

There are thirty children under the age of six at Merry Mites. In the birth-to-three-year range there are ten babies and toddlers. In the three-through-five-year range there are twenty children.

The director of Merry Mites is Mrs. James Craven. She is not a teacher, she is a business woman. There is one teacher on the staff of Merry Mites, Jenny Gruber. She has had no training in early childhood education. She earns $6,000 per year, which is considerably under the pay scale for teachers in the local school system, but in the surplus teacher market of 1975 she is not doing badly. Jenny is in charge of the three-through-five-year olds. There is one full-time aide on the staff. Her name is Barbara Martin. She has had 2 years of high school and earns $4,160 per year. She is in charge of the infant and toddler group. This gives Merry Mites a staff ratio of one adult per fifteen children. The national median is somewhere between 1:10 and 1:19. The recommended federal day-care staff-child ratios are: infants 1:3, toddlers 1:4, preschoolers 1:7–1:10.

We visit the infant and toddler nursery with the Neustadts. There are two fair sized rooms, one equipped with cots for napping. The play room is equipped with a television set, some mangy stuffed toys, a few battered plastic trucks, a doll

94

carriage, and masonite "doll-corner" furniture, which has not resisted the revenge of a number of Merry Mites. For the babies there are the ubiquitous bouncing swings, each with a mesmerized occupant, and two playpens in which babies in an alert state can engage in brutal socialization of one another. Four of the six toddlers are stretched out before the television set, eyes blank. Two of the toddlers are in battle over the one fire truck (ladders and one wheel missing) and their screams rise above the shrill cries from the TV screen. A mutiny among three prisoners in the playpen group sends Barbara flying in both directions with a shrill command to the firemen to cease and desist—which they do not—and a sharp reproof to the oldest mutineer, Blue Shirt (one year), for causing the mutiny (which he did not). In the clamor Blue Shirt is removed from the playpen and carried off wailing to the cot room, leaving two mutineers still in good form for another round.

There are better moments. When two of the TV watchers desert the screen, they seek out Barbara and climb into her lap. She embraces them both and speaks gently to them. This brings the two firemen and one more TV member over to Barbara's knees. They clamor to be held too. "I ain't got enough lap for everyone," Barbara says kindly. One fireman comes over to the strangers with a beguiling smile and snuggles against Peg's knees. The second fireman, his face blank, moves across the room where he finds his tattered blanket and a pacifier and curls up on the floor.

Who is to blame for this dreary nursery, with its joyless babies? Is it Barbara, who governs this baby bank with a mixture of rough justice and tenderness? I think not. For who could do a better job of playing mother to ten babies for eight to ten hours per day? It is conceivable that even an All Star day-care team composed of Dr. Spock and the American Mother of the Year could not provide substitute mother care for ten babies under these circumstances.

Later we visit the Merry Mites preschool nursery. Jenny Gruber, we remember, is the teacher in charge. The preschool division is housed in the basement recreation room of this old house. Twenty children between the ages of three and six are milling around as we enter. The equipment and toys are battered and ill-chosen by educational standards. A scratchy record player is booming with a rock record. The sound of unearthly laughter is coming from a TV, where a cartoon animal chase is performed before the glazed eyes of five children. There are two trikes with two solemn boys pedalling around the room. Six children are grouped around a table with Jenny, all with crayons and coloring books. The shabby "doll corner" is occupied by three small girls who at this moment are engaged in a shrill fight for possession of one ill-used doll carriage. "It's Joy's turn, girls," says Jenny in a mechanical voice from the table. No one is listening, and the fight continues until Joy wrestles the empty carriage from her competitors and sets out victoriously, wheeling it across the room.

One small fellow attracts our attention. He is the only member of the group who is engaged in what teachers call "creative play." He is at work in a corner of the room with a set of large cardboard construction blocks. He is quite alone, oblivious to the clamor around him. He is methodically building two walls to enclose the corner. There are just enough blocks to bring the height of the walls to the height of a small boy. He leaves an opening at the southeast corner. He crawls in. Over the wall we see him sitting cross-legged on the floor. He has a smile on his face, and it is the first smile we have seen in this joyless throng of children. It strikes me that this lad who has carved out an island of privacy for himself, through his own creative efforts, has exhibited a capacity for adaptation under extreme stress which will insure his survival.

But not for long. Joy and her doll carriage have found him. She pushes her doll carriage through the door of the block house and announces herself. "Stay out!" the hermit screams. There is a tussle in the block house and the walls collapse. The hermit, still cross-legged on the floor, has a monumental tantrum. He is carried from the wreckage, screaming and kicking in Jenny's arms. "You just have to learn to share," Jenny broadcasts above the din. She exiles him.

It is ten o'clock in the morning and Jenny's face looks pinched and hard. Shall we fault her for this mockery of preschool education? I would not. Nothing in her formal teacher education has prepared her for the education of preschool children. Nothing has been added to her education since she took this job. Moreover, even a well-trained preschool teacher could not bring a respectable educational program to this group of twenty assorted kids, ages three to six. One fully trained teacher for four to six children is considered a desirable ratio for a preschool education program.

What Merry Mites is offering the infants and preschool children in the two programs we have visited is "custodial care." Moreover, since Merry Mites has one licensed teacher, good sanitation and adequate lunches, its rating on Keyserling's scale would be "fair," meaning "largely custodial . . . meeting basic physical needs." About 36 percent of the proprietary centers in the Keyserling study were rated "fair." About 50 percent were rated "poor," among them some which were found to be actually injurious. Only 1 percent of the proprietary centers visited were rated "superior"; 14 percent were rated "good."

Merry Mites "custodial care" for infants and preschoolers begins to look high-grade when we compare it with some of the proprietary centers rated "poor" in Keyserling's study. One excerpt from the report on a day-care center:

> "Very poor basement, dark room. All ages together. Rigid control and discipline. Babies are kept next door in double decker cardboard cribs in a small room with a gas heater. . . ."

97

Another report, another center:

> "At the time of the survey visit to the center there were two children aged 10 and 12 in charge. This center should be closed. Absolutely filthy. Toilets not flushed, and smelly. Broken equipment and doors. Broken windows on lower level. . . . Broken chairs and tables. No indoor play equipment. One paper towel used to wipe the faces and hands of children. Kitchen very, very dirty."[4]

Then will the Neustadts have to settle for "custodial care," grade "fair," for Anthony? But the Neustadts, we remember, were not seeking "custodial care." They had set out to find "substitute mother care" for Anthony. If the Neustadts were eligible for a subsidized day-care center, would Anthony get "quality day-care?" In the Keyserling study of non-profit day-care centers, only 37 percent were rated "good" or "superior," 50 percent were rated "fair," and 11 percent were rated "poor." This was a better score than the proprietary centers earned in the same study, but no guarantee of "quality."

And if the Neustadts found one of the non-profit centers rated "superior" (9 percent), and if Anthony, competing for its space, could be enrolled, would Anthony get "substitute mother care?" The rating does not guarantee "substitute mother care."

The options for the Neustadts are not good.

The Andersons

If the Neustadts were a more affluent family, would they fare better in their search for "substitute mother care?" Probably not. The employed mother in a metropolitan community who earns $20,000 or more per year, and who can pay the going rate of $5,000 to $7,500 per year, will find herself in grim competition with her sisters for the vanishing nursemaid. No Peggottys. Not even a latter-day Mary Poppins will appear, although the legend persists. If one is found, lured with TV and private bath, a handsome wage and all fringe benefits, her maternal qualities may not be larger than those of the Neustadts' Mrs. Grimm. But faithful to the legend and the script, this latter-day Mary Poppins will soon rise on her umbrella and leave the nursery vacant once again. The small children of many affluent professional or business women may come to know a procession of indifferent caretakers who come and go. They are interchangeable parts of the child-care industry.

The Andersons are an affluent young couple in their late twenties. Christy, their daughter, is twenty months old. Helen Anderson is a social worker and her husband, Carl, is a lawyer. Helen's salary is $15,000 per year, Carl's income is approximately $25,000. The Andersons live in a suburb of New York City.

When Helen made plans to return to work, Christy was six months old. Helen and Carl had carefully considered plans for Christy's care. They wanted, of course, a nursemaid who was mature, dedicated to children, knowledgeable about babies—a person who would be, properly speaking, "a mother substitute" during the hours when Helen was at work. They were prepared to pay the highest salary without reservations. Helen's own income was not essential to maintain a good standard of living. She chose to work because she loved her work.

The Andersons then set out to find a worthy and capable woman who met their own high standards for "a mother substitute." They registered with employment agencies, placed ads in the newspapers, asked for the help of their friends. The first surprise was the discovery that "at any price," even $7,500 per year, the number of applicants for this special job was pitifully few. Two applicants turned up during the first week of interviewing. Both were women who had unstable employment records and were singularly lacking in the personal qualities that the Andersons were seeking. The trickle of applicants continued for some weeks. . . . A tired grandmother who had reared her own four children and six grandchildren, whose only employment references were in restaurant work. . . . A frayed member of a religious cult whose sentences rambled. . . . A lady who smelled of gin. . . . A cheery girl from a Caribbean Island who spoke little English. . . . an illiterate woman who wrote her name in a labored childlike scrawl. . . .

"At any price" these were all women who had no choice but domestic work. They represented the rock bottom of the woman's labor market, unskilled, uneducated, and without hope in a competitive market.

There were others. Women who were themselves mothers, with their children in the care of grandmothers, aunts, neighbors, desperately seeking work because they were the only source of support for their families. And Helen, who understood these things very well, considered the irony which brought these women to become substitute mothers to the children of other women.

Yet, it was just such a woman, Gladys Harrison, who finally met the high personal qualifications of the Andersons. Gladys was thirty, the mother of three children ranging in age from four to seven. Her two younger children were cared for in a neighborhood day-care center. The oldest boy went to a neighbor after school. Gladys was a personable and intelligent woman. She was charmed by the Andersons' baby and showed beautiful tact in making friends with Christy. She liked the Andersons, and they liked her.

Helen went back to work after Gladys had been with the family for a month of trial employment. There was no question that Christy missed her mother during the day, but there was no question either that Gladys was an adequate "mother substitute." Gladys was always reliably on time early in the morning; she was greeted warmly by Christy, and Christy showed only a few days of transient distress when Helen returned to work. It was a good and a comfortable arrangement.

When Christy was twelve months old, Gladys left the Andersons. Her youngest boy was sick; her oldest boy was having trouble in school; her children needed her at home. She was very sad to leave Christy and the Andersons.

Helen stayed home from work during the next two weeks and began the melancholy interviews again. The second round was not better than the first. And, in fact, one old timer was sent back by central casting for a repeat interview. It was the tired grandmother. In the second interview Mrs. Johnson, the grandmother, seemed to gain in personal qualities and energy. She had the virtue of having no young children at home and her restaurant credentials praised her reliability. After a trial of a week the Andersons decided that Mrs. Johnson had her merits. Her maternal capacities were not as large as those of Gladys. She was competent with Christy, and kind, but the years of rearing too many children and grandchildren had left her without zest for babies. Christy cried now when Helen left. Well, Christy was older, too, and separation from her mother was harder. When Helen called home during the day the sounds of the TV drowned out all conversation and Helen realized uneasily that during Christy's waking and sleeping hours Mrs. Johnson spent a very large amount of time watching soap operas. So did Christy. Christy was whiny and clinging now. Was it the age? Or missing her mother? Certainly as soon as Helen and Carl arrived home from work Christy began a whiny complaint and required a lot of holding and comforting.

When Christy was fourteen months old Mrs. Johnson failed to show up one morning. She called to say that her ulcer was bothering her and the doctor thought she ought to stay home and rest for a while. She wasn't sure when she'd be well enough to come back.

After she left the telephone, Helen wept. There was anguish for Christy and for herself. Anguish, too, for the lot of women like herself whose early careers did not depend upon their personal gifts or even the state of their own professional market, but on the services provided by Child Care Industries Incorporated.

Mrs. Johnson was followed by Martha Williams in the succession of nannies for Christy. And Christy is now twenty months old. Mrs. Williams has four children of her own. She is a decent, kindly woman, in her thirties, overburdened by the strains of raising her own family without a husband. When one of her own children is ill, Mrs. Williams must stay home. When Mrs. Williams stays home, one of the Andersons must stay home from work. Most frequently it is Helen herself. It is an uneasy plan. Mrs. Williams is wondering whether it might not be better for her to go on welfare until her children are a little older. The Andersons are bracing themselves for another change.

From all this we can see that the options in child care for the affluent Andersons are not really much better than those of the Neustadts. However, since Helen's income is not a critical issue in the Anderson family, Helen has more alternatives open to her.

If her own professional needs seem imperative to her she can examine the options within her community for a stable child-care plan. If her own high standards of child care can be met by a day-care center she may consider that a first rate day-care center with a trained professional staff might provide more stability and continuity of care than the procession of nannies who have entered Christy's life. She may find, however, that "at any price" such a day-care center does not exist in her community. What Helen would ask for in substitute mother care is found in a handful of model nurseries throughout the country, which provide highly trained personnel for their children and adhere to a philosophy of child care which values intimate human connections be-tween a baby and parents, a baby and substitute parents.

It is not cost alone which keeps such model nurseries from proliferating. To operate such model nurseries we would need approximately 2,000,000 professionally trained teachers and aides to serve as mother-substitutes for children under the age of six whose mothers are employed. Substitute mothers with these qualifications are in short supply.

And Helen has other options. If a stable child-care plan at home or at a nursery cannot be worked out, Helen can assess her baby's needs and her own professional needs and make rational choices. She may choose to work part-time for the next two years, which would give her better options in child care since there are more women available for child care on a part-time basis than full time. (Helen is also working in a profession which is accommodating to part-time employ-ment both for women and for men.) Or Helen may choose to stay home until Christy is three and can be enrolled in nur-sery school while Helen works part-time. (Good half-day preschool programs for the three-to-five-year olds are gener-ally more available and, as we have seen, the preschool child can not only manage separations from his mother for a half day but can profit from his experiences in a good nursery school.)

In summary: The affluent family is not better served than the marginal family by Child Care Industries Incorporated. But the mother whose income is not critical for maintaining the family has the freedom of making rational choices on behalf of herself and her children.

The Martins: "Who Takes Care of the Caretaker's Children?"

Barbara Martin, whom we met as the aide in charge of the infant nursery at Merry Mites, has her own story. She lives in the Looking Glass World of Day Care in which hundreds of thousands of mothers on welfare take care of the children of hundreds of thousands of working mothers and other mothers on welfare, while hundreds of thousands of women take care of the children of the mothers who are taking care of the children of mothers on welfare and other mothers.[5]

(If this sentence causes dizziness, I recommend that it be read slowly as you turn. With each full rotation, fix your eyes on a distant point. I myself use the dome of Capitol Hill.)

Barbara is the mother of three children, Margaret, ten; Charles, seven; May Ellen, four. Barbara's husband deserted the family four years ago. The family is black. In 1971, Barbara and the three children received an AFDC allowance of $370.00 per month. This covered rent, utilities, clothing, and food for four.*

In 1972 public outrage at welfare costs reached a high pitch. It was an election year and our Christian spirit (banish poverty) wrestled with old devils (the welfare cheater, the squanderer of public funds, the shiftless breadwinner, the AFDC mother who procreates in order to increase her welfare check). It was also the year in which a group of the nation's statesmen conspired to raise the price of the children's milk in order to re-elect the president who employed our public funds to improve the quality of his life. It was not a good year for Christians or for the Republic. Defense costs were rising; there were warnings of inflation. It became increasingly clear that the reason our economy was in danger and public morality at the lowest point in modern history was that Barbara Martin and her three children were draining our national resources and our public purse. One of the nation's highest priorities was to get the Martins off the welfare rolls. "Mandatory employment of welfare heads of family" and "Work Incentive Programs" were slogans of the day.

*This provides an annual AFDC income of $4,440 per year. The poverty line for a family of four in the Martin's community was $5,000 per year in 1972.

(Recall that 75 percent of AFDC heads of families are mothers.)

Around the time that Barbara Martin and her three children were found to be the cause of our national decline, Barbara was a full-time mother. And doing a decent job of it. Like most welfare mothers I have known, she cared about her kids and they cared about her. She was a no-nonsense sort of person and she kept a sharp eye on her kids as they dodged the neighborhood toughs and the junkies on the street.

Early in 1973 Barbara was placed in a Work Incentive Program with the acronym WIN.[6] She was to receive job training and a chance to improve the quality of her life. The children were placed in a day-care center, subsidized by federal funds.

Since Barbara, like most WIN mothers, had less than a high-school education there weren't too many career choices open to her. She could be trained for restaurant kitchen work (average pay $2.00 per hour) or she could be trained as a child-care aide (average pay $2.00 per hour). Barbara liked children and thought the working hours might be better for a mother in child care than in kitchen work.

In her job training Barbara had a course in child development in which an instructor stressed the importance of the one-to-one relationship in working with small children. And Barbara graduated, and she got a job at Merry Mites, where she alone supervised ten babies between the ages of three months and three years, and she earned $2.00 per hour.

In 1975 May Ellen, four, spent eleven hours a day in a subsidized day-care center. Margaret, ten and Charles, seven, spent the after-school hours in a subsidized day-care center. The taxpayer's subsidy for the day-care of the three Martin children amounted to $346.00 per month. May Ellen's day-care center was rated "fair," "largely custodial," but it included one hour a day of "cognitive enrichment." The after-school day-care center attended by Margaret and Charles was rated "fair" and, with twenty children supervised by one harassed aide, we must assume that the children provided their own cognitive enrichment.

When Barbara picked up May Ellen at 6:00, she found her four-year-old very cranky because she hadn't seen her mother since 7:00 in the morning. After a full day with ten cranky babies and toddlers, Barbara found that her own kids got on her nerves, and she hated to admit it. Meals were pick-up because Barbara didn't have time to shop regularly, and her apartment refrigerator didn't hold more than two days' food.

And the Martins were still on welfare! They received supplementary AFDC assistance of $303.80 per month to bring them to the level of the lower-budget Federal Standards.

To explain this we have to go through the Looking Glass.

The Looking Glass Economy

It is only natural that when I pass through the Looking Glass I find myself on a platform wearing my unpressed academic gown, and that a class materializes before my eyes. I recognize Alice, the White Queen, and the Red Queen. The blackboard behind me is covered with figures and calculations all carefully set down in mirror writing, including the label " ⊤ƎϽᗡႮᗺ ".

"Then how does it happen," asks Alice, "that if Barbara Martin is working, the Martins are still on welfare?" There is a pointer waiting for me, and I begin an explication of the figures on the board.

"In Column I, you will see that if Barbara Martin was not employed she would receive in 1975 a monthly AFDC allowance of $426.40 for her three children and herself. This would cover rent, utilities, food, household necessities, and clothing for four people.

"In Column II, Barbara has graduated from the WIN (Work Incentive) program and has a net income of $317.60 per month after F.I.C.A. and taxes are deducted. This is $108.80 less per month than the family support from AFDC and would not provide a Work Incentive. If Barbara had to assume the costs of day-care for her three children, which comes to $347 per month, and her own costs of employment, estmated at $40 per month, the family income would be wiped out.

"Clearly, then, Barbara and her family will need income supplementation from AFDC and a work incentive. Therefore, AFDC must cover (a) the deficit in family income, (b) Barbara's costs of employment, and (c) costs of child care for the employed mother. But these are costs which would not occur if Barbara were not working. Therefore the AFDC provides an additional incentive which is called 'Income Disregard.' This is a form of 'not counting,' and this figure is arrived at by a method of calculation that I will not present to you until you enroll in my Advanced Seminar.

"Now, in computing the AFDC supplementary cash income, the Martins will get the difference between Barbara's net earnings and her former AFDC allowance, *plus* a fraction which constitutes her Work Incentive. The total AFDC cash supplement will be $303.80 per month, but the net gain for Barbara and her children over the former AFDC allowance will be $247.60 per month."

"Then," says Alice, "isn't Something Good Accomplished? I mean like if Barbara Martin is partly self-sufficient and AFDC only has to supplement her income by $303.80, well, isn't that a Saving of $122.60 for the taxpayer?"

"So it would appear, Alice. But scholars who have gone through the Looking Glass and returned have a curious tale to tell. Remember that Barbara Martin's costs of day-care for her three children must be subsidized by the government. If we now add the costs of day-care ($346.60) per month and the cash supplement from AFDC, which is $303.80, we obtain the figure of $650.40, which means that the Federal Government (i.e., the taxpayer) is spending $224.00 *more* per month on the Martin family with Barbara employed than it did when Barbara was unemployed and supporting her family on an AFDC grant.*"

"Still," says Alice staunchly, "isn't the Quality of Life improving for the Martins? If the Martins' *net* income is increased by $247.00 per month, isn't that something?"

Alice will surely get an "A" in my course for her nimble mental arithmetic, but I must point out that if the net gain in Barbara's income improves her living standards, we could improve the quality of her life and that of her children by simply adding $100 plus to her cash AFDC allowance while Barbara stays home with her children. The taxpayer, in our computation, would still come out ahead, the children would have their mother's care, and the Martins would be above the poverty line.

"Treachery!" cries the Red Queen, "That would be a Guaranteed Income and that is illegal, unconstitutional, and contrary to the Looking Glass way of life." This is greeted by applause.

---

*From *The Detroit News*, Tuesday, October 24th, 1972, p. 3A "Few Good Posts for ADC Mothers: Job Plan's Net Loss Is 3.2 Million," by Don Ball.

"The jobs do not pay enough for the ADC recipient to earn her way off welfare and do not provide promotional opportunity so that she can eventually achieve a salary which would make her independent of ADC. Instead, her ADC is continued as she works, with the government paying her employment expenses and child care costs.

Michigan ADC payments were reduced an estimated $1.2 million in the 1970–71 fiscal year because of earnings by ADC recipients who found jobs through WIN programs. But for the same period, the federal government paid $4.6 million more than if the ADC recipients had stayed at home. In other words, the taxpayers were out an overall $3.2 million as a result of the WIN program in Michigan during the 1970–71 fiscal year."

The class is getting out of hand. "Ladies and Gentlemen," I say, above the din, *"this is a class in Child Development. Our primary concern is the child and his family and the effects of the Looking Glass Economy upon the developing child."*

Alice, who sees an "A" in her future, raises her hand. "Enrichment," she says. "May Ellen is getting one hour a day of Cognitive Enrichment in her nursery school. That's a plus. For development, I mean."

"That may be true," I say, "but if May Ellen can profit from one hour a day of Cognitive Enrichment (and who can't in these melancholy times), does she need ten more hours a day to consolidate this learning? And when does the plus become a minus for the four-year-old girl who still needs her mother?"

"Are you against Cognitive Enrichment?" It's the White Queen. (I place an "∃" in my book for her.) "I am *for* Cognitive Enrichment," I say. "I am also in favor of Emotional Enrichment. They go together. In fact, it has been proved that they *must* go together. I most respectfully urge Your Majesty to consult the text which has been provided for this course.

"Your Ministry of Child Development has discovered, after spending millions of dollars on research, that mental and emotional development cannot be separated. You cannot add 'cognitive enrichment' like a vitamin supplement to a child's daily needs. The child who thrives is the child who has *both* the nutriments for love and the nutriments for learning. If we can all agree that Barbara Martin is at least an adequate mother, then she is the most certain source of those emotional supplies for her child. No one has yet claimed that May Ellen's nursery school director and her four aides will give as much love, or more love, or better love than May Ellen's mother.

"So, if we are only considering May Ellen and her developmental needs, she could profit from a half-day in nursery school (most children do) with a good educational program,

109

and the balance of the day with her mother. This would cost the taxpayer about half the present costs of the eleven-hour-day nursery care and May Ellen would get what she deserves—the best of both worlds.

"May Ellen spends eleven hours each day in a subsidized nursery only because your Ministry of the Budget has persuaded the taxpayer that he is saving money while he is actually losing money. Your Ministry of Child Development has spent millions of dollars to discover that maternal love is one of the great national resources which can still be provided without cost to the taxpayer, and without immediate danger of depletion. And Your Majesty herself has claimed on ceremonial occasions that Our Children Are Our Greatest National Resource."

Alice's hand is raised again. "You haven't said a word yet about some preschool children who might get more from being in a day-care center all day then being at home."

"Well, then, I should," I agree. "Because there are some small children who suffer such emotional impoverishment and instability in their homes that a first rate day-care staff might compensate in some measure for the deficits at home. And then there are small children like Anthony Neustadt. His parents are perfectly adequate, but as long as his mother *must* work, a first rate day-care nursery would be preferable to the revolving-door sitters who appeared in his life in a one-year period. But we've examined the Neustadts' options. And there are no good solutions."

Alice's hand is waving. Urgently. A groan arises from the class.

"What I don't understand," she says, "is what a mother is supposed to *do*. You haven't given any answers at all in this class."

"That," I say, "is because I don't have the answers. I only have the questions.

"That means: If a mother of an infant or preschool child

can freely choose to work or not to work, she can ask herself the questions. If she chooses to work full time for personal reasons, or career reasons, she can examine her options in terms of her child's needs and her own needs and make her decision on the basis of the best information available to her and the real choices she has in substitute care.

"If she *must* work for financial reasons, her options for substitute care are poor and there are almost no good solutions open to her—at least so far—which serve the needs of her child.

"I am worried about millions of children who are being served by Child Care Industries Incorporated. I worry about babies and small children who are delivered like packages to neighbors, to strangers, to storage houses like Merry Mites. In the years when a baby and his parents make their first enduring human partnerships, when love, trust, joy, and self-valuation emerge through the nurturing love of human partners, millions of small children in our land may be learning values for survival in our baby banks. They may learn the rude justice of the communal playpen. They may learn that the world outside of the home is an indifferent world, or even a hostile world. Or they may learn that all adults are interchangeable, that love is capricious, that human attachment is a perilous investment, and that love should be hoarded for the self in the service of survival."

A sound like the surf at high-tide is rising in the room. Is the Looking Glass World dissolving? No, it is only the sound of shuffling feet and the gathering of papers and books. I recognize it instantly. The class hour has come to an end.

CHAPTER V

Priorities for Children

IN THIS CENTURY we have come into knowledge about childhood and the constitution of personality that can be fairly placed among the greatest scientific discoveries in history. But the children themselves are not yet the beneficiaries of our science. Our juvenile laws are chained to archaic principles, and the social policies which govern the welfare of children are shaped by the needs of the moment, or the budgetary crisis of the year. They are blind to the psychological needs of the child and his family.

In this chapter, I propose to examine certain aspects of child welfare law and social policy in relation to the central question of this book, the nurturing of human bonds.

The Scientific Legacy

It is now over seventy years since Freud discovered that the most severe and crippling emotional disorders of adult life have their genesis in early childhood. During the past thirty years our studies have led us deeper and deeper into the unknown territories of childhood, into infancy and early childhood and the origins of personality. We now know that those qualities that we call "human"—the capacity for enduring love and the exercise of conscience—are not given in human biology; they are the achievement of the earliest human partnership, that between a child and his parents.

And we now know that a child who is deprived of human partners in the early years of life, or who has known shifting or unstable partnerships in the formative period of personality, may suffer permanent impairment in his capacity to love, to learn, to judge, and to abide by the laws of the human community. This child, in effect, has been deprived of his humanity.

How we learned this has been described in Chapter II. It was a discovery that emerged from the wreckage of World War II. The lost children, the abandoned children, the children of Hitler's camps, and the babies without mothers brought about an impassioned inquiry on the part of scientists into the meaning of war to children. What emerged from this inquiry was that even the life-threatening dangers of war were not as destructive to the minds and emotions of children as separation from their mothers and fathers. For many of these children the damage to personality was permanent, even though some of them were later reunited with their parents.

At the war's end, the scientific inquiry moved ahead. It is not only in times of war that children are deprived of mothering and family nurture. There are circumstances today in which tens of thousands of children in our country are deprived of a mother or a mother substitute. Small children in institutions, children in foster homes, children in storage while their mothers work, and children in their own homes with unstable partnerships form a vast population of sufferers.

As scientists from a number of disciplines examined the

113

effects of maternal deprivation on the developing personality, a consensus of findings emerged. We learned that the developing ego of the young child is inextricably interwoven with the maintenance of the early love bonds and that deprivation of these bonds, or a rupture of bonds already formed, can have permanent effects upon the later capacities of the child to love and to learn. We also learned, from the clinical side of the inquiry, that the most severe and intractable emotional diseases of childhood are the diseases of non-attachment and of broken attachments. A commitment to love is normally given in the early years of life, the gift of ordinary parents, without benefit of psychiatric consultation. But a child who at school age has not yet received this gift may require the whole of our colossal apparatus of psychiatric clinics and remedial education to help him to love and to learn.

These are the extreme cases, yet the number of such children is growing year by year. There are also less virulent but ominous forms of the same disease that are afflicting tens of thousands of other children in our country.

The children of poverty know lost and broken human connections to a frightening degree. There is the father who is not now present or who has never been. There is the mother who works at an ill-paid job and whose babies and young children are delivered like small packages to the doorsteps of neighbors, relatives, day-care centers—"anyone handy"—as it happens in the desperate child-care plans of the poor.

And finally, over the months and years there is no one in this ghostly procession who is mother or stands in the place of mother and no one to bestow identity upon a child. When Head Start began, its teachers were astonished to discover that there were children aged four or five who did not know their own names.

All of this tells us that during the thirty years in which our scientific world made revolutionary discoveries regarding the nature and origin of human bonds and the origins of the diseases of non-attachment, the children themselves have not been the beneficiaries of these discoveries. We have identified a group of malignant diseases of personality, disturbances of the primary human attachments. These diseases are preventable at the source. In a rational world, an army of mental health workers and citizens would gather together to ensure the human bonds of children, to guarantee their human rights.

The mending of children's lives is a very large part of the work of my profession. It would be folly to say that *all* childhood disturbances of personality can be prevented, but a large number that I have seen could have been prevented; and in nearly every case these have been caused by disturbances in the primary human relationships during the early months and years of life.

We have traditionally considered child psychotherapy as a form of prevention. And so it is. If we are successful in treating the childhood form of the neurosis, we may prevent the crippling neuroses of later life. But prevention must be seen in social terms as well. For every child who has been cured of enuresis, bogey men, and youthful pilfering, there are thousands of children waiting, already endangered or damaged because our social institutions and our social policies have robbed them of some measure of their humanity. In the most terrible irony, the mental health professions have been witnesses and sometimes even unwilling collaborators in the tragedy.

The Department of Soma and the Department of Psyche

The history of social work as a mental health profession has cruel paradoxes and many lessons for us.

In the 1920's social workers were among the first to see the implications of Freud's theory of the infantile neurosis for the prevention of adult mental disturbances. In collaboration with psychiatry and psychology they set up child guidance clinics for the identification and treatment of the emotional disturbances of childhood.

The child guidance movement had barely entered its first decade when the disaster of the Great Depression occurred. Poverty, hunger, the emasculation of jobless fathers, desertion of families by broken men, and the placement of children in foster homes were the problems that flooded social agencies and clinics. Social work was also responsible for the development and administration of new programs of public assistance. It was during the period 1935–1939 that a strange bureaucratic marriage was initiated.

The child was divided in accordance with the ancient dichotomy of soma and psyche. The soma of the child was given to the public assistance agencies to be fed and sheltered, and the psyche was given to the child guidance clinic. In the Department of Soma, social workers collaborated with legislators to bring forth the first federal public assistance programs for dependent children (Aid to Dependent Children). This was a remarkable achievement in itself for it guaranteed the subsistence needs of hundreds of thousands of children. But in order to feed the child, they compromised with intransigent legislators and wrote into the enabling laws certain eligibility requirements which have had their effects upon the psyche of the child for over thirty years. The model ADC child would have no father, an absent father, or a disabled father. In all cases, the family that qualified for ADC received higher relief allowances than a family might receive from local welfare sources. This meant, of course, that the family which had an absent father was rewarded by the system and the system of rewards was so effective over three decades that it helped to institutionalize the family without a father among the poor.

The lesson can be summarized in briefest terms: at the same period in the history of social work that brought forth new programs for child mental health, the profession launched and administered public assistance programs which eroded family structure. On one side of the street we had the Department of Soma, issuing mental health problems along with its relief check. On the other side of the street we had the Department of Psyche rapidly expanding its waiting list. In the classic image of Penelope, we wove our cloth by day and unraveled it by night.

The ghost of Penelope haunts the child guidance movement. History records that during the second, third, and fourth decades of our crusade for child mental health there were three wars. For half of those years tens of thousands of children in our country were reared in the family chaos bred by war, and the result was the steady erosion of family bonds, which is the only certain and predictable outcome of war. If the era of child mental health has not brought large rewards to the children, we must reflect that mental health cannot be sustained by clinics alone.

The irony is underscored. These thirty years of intermittent war are the thirty years which gave us the research on the origins of love and the origins of human bonds.

As custodians of this scientific treasure the mental health professions have somehow failed to share the wealth among the social institutions that serve children. Our juvenile

117

courts, as we saw in Chapter III, are privileged to make decisions regarding custody and social treatment for tens of thousands of children. The mental health principles upon which they base their decisions were laid down in the Old Testament. In 1976 the child can remain the property of his natural parents even though they may be strangers to him.

Many thousands of babies and young children spend the early years of their lives in a succession of foster homes and institutions while decisions regarding surrender and custody drag through the courts. The court is empowered to act in the best interests of the child. Since the best interests of the child are incontestably served through sustaining stable human partnerships for the child, the power to act decisively to protect the child and his future surely resides within the law.

These unwanted children who have never known stability or continuity in human partnerships fill the waiting lists of our child guidance clinics and psychiatric hospitals. In truth, they are not wanted there either, for no one has yet invented a treatment that fills the vacancy in personality which occurs when no human partners have entered.

The archaic principle of ownership prevails strangely in another group of custody cases. There are children whose lives as well as psyches are endangered if they remain in their homes with their criminally psychotic parents. But today, even as it was fifty years ago, the court is loath to take protective custody of children who are the property of deranged parents. These children, too, are brought to the doors of the child guidance clinics. But we have not yet found a cure for children whose nightmares are real.

And finally since no one has yet banished Penelope from the social policies that affect children, we have come full circle on poverty too. Since 1936 we have rewarded the families that had an absent father. Since 1967 we have inaugurated relief policies which reward the welfare mother who works and penalizes the mother who doesn't work. Since our government has also closed the door on bills for the development of "quality" day-care facilities, we are now creating an expanded population of little wanderers who are already arriving at the doors of mental health agencies.

We have become partners in a surrealist charade in which society assaults the developing ego of the child and charges the child guidance clinic with the responsibility for repairing it.

On Poverty, the Family, and Human Bonds

If the ghost of Penelope has haunted these pages, it is only fair to ask how she got into this story.

At the Child Development Project, University of Michigan, we provide psychiatric services for families with babies and very young children. Most of our patients are the children of poverty. Across the street from us is the County Department of Social Services which administers the AFDC* program and licenses day-care facilities. In children's services in our county, we belong to the Department of Psyche; they belong to the Department of Soma. We are supported by a grant from the National Institute of Mental Health, U.S. Department of Health, Education and Welfare; they too are supported by the U.S. Department of Health, Education and Welfare and the State of Michigan. To the best of my knowledge, the highest policy makers in Washington in the Department of Soma have rarely met the highest policy makers in the Department of Psyche.

---

* In 1950 the ADC program was modified to include payment to the mothers of these families and was renamed Aid to Families of Dependent Children (AFDC).

119

In fact, as we have seen, the taxpayer supports two divisions in HEW: one to impair the development of children and another to repair it. Or, if you prefer, one to weave and one to unravel. It is worth mentioning that the larger part of the budget goes into weaving and the smaller into unraveling. However, the taxpayer doesn't know this, and periodically he cries, "A pox on *both* your houses! Where are the benefits from the fortune that is drained from my purse?"

The Federal Department of Soma has a clear mandate. It is required to minister to the bodily needs of AFDC children, to provide food, shelter, clothing, and health care. It is not required by law to minister to the psychic needs of children. That's not their department.

Since one cannot reproach a bureaucracy for exercising its mandate, I will only ask, for the moment, whether the Department of Soma can actually fulfill its obligations under the law.

Can the nutritional needs of a child be met on an AFDC allowance? In my own area, Washtenaw County, Michigan, and in New York City, two high-cost communities which provide high levels of AFDC support, the maximum food allowance is the same: $1.38 per day per person for a family of four. This figure includes food stamp values. Since food costs are 7 percent higher in New York City than in Washtenaw County, the New York City AFDC food allowance is less than our own.

It is conceivable that a nutritionist with expert knowledge of low-cost food exchange values and expertness in marketing could provide nutritional adequacy for a child on this budget; most of us could not. There are many regions in our country which provide much lower levels of support for AFDC children. This means that malnutrition is virtually guaranteed for large numbers of AFDC children.

Poor nutrition *in utero* and during the early years of childhood can create irreversible effects upon all bodily systems.

It is directly related to birth defects, serious health problems, and impaired learning. The Department of Soma finds itself in the extraordinary position of inventing new health problems with each relief check.

The free health care available to welfare families is generally of the poorest quality in nearly every community I know. Medicaid (which by 1976 had become the subject of public scandal for widespread fraud within the medical professions and for abuses which have cruelly affected the welfare recipients) has not delivered quality health care on the scale which is necessary to prevent and treat the alarming incidence of illness and death among children of poverty and the debilitating effects upon health of poor nutrition and environmental hazards which affect every child who lives in poverty. Infant mortality rates in the United States are now higher than those of sixteen other countries. Non-white children in our country rank 31st compared to the mortality rates of other countries.[1]

As for the shelter of the body which is furnished by the welfare department, it will virtually guarantee that a child will be reared in a slum dwelling and that he will learn survival tactics in a jungle while he is still a toddler.

However, the subject of this volume is human attachments, so, with a strong warning to myself to keep to the subject, I will now try to examine those policies of public assistance which affect the development of human bonds in the early years of life.

The Invisible Father

We have already seen in my brief historical summary that welfare policies have favored the development of female-headed, one-parent families. And while there are many factors that have contributed to this trend in all sectors of our society, there is probably no other condition in our society outside of public assistance (and imprisonment) in which the absence of a father is a requirement and not a choice. This means, of course, that the child in poverty, already disadvantaged by meager sustenance, is deprived of a father or a father substitute—if his mother complies strictly with the rules of eligibility.

Since few young mothers will elect celibacy in exchange for AFDC eligibility, an AFDC household may include a male visitor who serves as father surrogate (or may, in fact, be the "absent" father), and his presence or his connection with the family must be a well-kept family secret. Since harboring a male in an AFDC family is nearly as dangerous as sheltering a fugitive from justice, the male visitor or the surrogate father is, for the children, the center of a shady family conspiracy.

For those who share the old-fashioned view that fathers are central persons in a child's development, a sneak-in and sneak-out father or surrogate father does not provide an elevating model for the children. Also, since his status in the family is uncertain and he may have no real privileges in child rearing, both the attachment between him and the children and the beneficial uses of that attachment in the rearing and discipline of the children may be lost in the family. Further, if one holds to the old-fashioned view that patterns of parenting are transmitted to children through the parental model, we can argue that this model becomes a strong factor in the repetition of one-parent families through generations.

It is the mother, then, who is the central person of a typical AFDC family. In 1975 over 75 percent of AFDC heads of families were women. Since the total number of AFDC recipients is eleven million, and since eight million of these are children[2], approximately six million children on welfare belong to families in which the mother is the head.

The "Welfare Mother"

The phrase "welfare mother" now enters our story and requires a brief digression. Since everything that follows will conjure up pictures in our heads, it is important to sort out the pictures. My pictures, which derive from a large experience with "welfare mothers," are not the same as my neighbor's, or that of many public spokesmen, or even of the debaters in Congress. In the public image "the welfare mother" is believed to be profligate with public funds, canny in getting the most out of the system. In heated congressional debate she has been accused more than once of "breeding children out of wedlock in order to extort money from the taxpayer." It is thought by many that she is incapable of rearing children.

In my own large experience with "welfare mothers" it is the rare woman who fits any one of these stereotypes. In Washtenaw County, which is really a large metropolitan community, and in our program, which serves a large number of county families in poverty, we have a fair cross-section of welfare families, black and white. Their babies and young children are in trouble, or they wouldn't be seeing us, and in this respect we should note that so are a large number of middle class families with babies and young children and that's why they are seeing us.

What we see among the "welfare mothers" are large numbers of women who are willing, and able, to make extraordinary personal sacrifices for their children, who show devotion and love for their children that cruelly test the quality of maternal love. We see in them hopes and daydreams for their babies and young children which distinguish them in no way from economically advantaged parents. And we do not even understand where the hopes and the daydreams come from.

When we visit them in their bleak and horrible apartments, see them wrestle with the blind bureaucracy that issues the relief check (not always on time), witness a meal that leaves every child hungry and ill-nourished, sit with them for hours in clinics where they and their children are ill-served and degraded, we can only ask ourselves how they have found resources within themselves to meet each day.

A few of these mothers (actually very few—we should note for later reference in this story) are themselves the children of welfare. When we listen to their life stories in which childhood poverty, absent parents, street tyranny, and school failure have brought them full circle to the conditions which are now re-created for their children, we cannot imagine how the human spirit can survive such assaults and yet generate dreams for the children.

Nor are they as a group "hopeless cases." A very large number of our "welfare mothers" have used our help for themselves and their babies. The babies are thriving; their mothers have found new pleasures in their children, a heightened self-regard, and hope for themselves. The majority will not be on welfare long; some are already moving toward employment as the children reach the age of nursery school and grade school. In this respect, we should not take full credit as a psychiatric unit. Welfare, for the majority of AFDC welfare families, is a way station, usually during the period when the children are small and the mother has poor alternatives in employment and for child care. I will expand upon this point later.

1967: "Mandatory Employment for Welfare Heads of Families"

The original intention of the AFDC program, when it was inaugurated in 1936 as ADC, was to provide basic support for the children and to encourage mothers to stay home with their children instead of seeking employment to support their families. In 1967 this policy underwent a total reversal. As welfare rolls and welfare costs rose to new heights, there was a great push in Congress to get "welfare heads of families" into jobs, and job training and the work incentive program, WIN, was inaugurated in the Johnson administration. The 1967 Social Security Amendments established programs to encourage welfare mothers to become self-supporting. *Compulsory* work requirements and job training were written into the law, penalties for mothers who refused to participate were stated clearly (a reduction of the AFDC payment). And the law made no exception for the mothers of small children.

The reasons for this shift in policy are highly complex. I will try to sort out some of the components in economic, social, and psychological motives.

MOTHERS IN THE LABOR MARKET

First, it is important to remember that the stay-at-home mother who was being supported by public policy in 1936 was no longer a symbol of public virtue. In the Sixties hundreds of thousands of women with children were entering the job market each year. There were voices emerging which claimed work as a right for all women. These voices were mainly those of career women. If the national trend was moving strongly toward employment of mothers, why exempt the welfare mother?

In fact a substantial number of AFDC mothers *were* in the labor force, part time or full time, even in 1967, and because of low earnings needed AFDC supplementation to support their families. They were, of course, counted as AFDC recipients.

The *compulsory* work requirement was addressed to a large number of AFDC women who were believed to be slothful and indifferent toward work and self-support. In the inflamed public imagination there were plenty of jobs "out

125

there" for women who were willing to work. And this may even have been true. However, in the heat of debate neither we nor our congressmen were able to grasp the budget arithmetic which turned real income through employment into a surrealist nightmare for the woman in poverty and for the Government Accounting Office (GAO) and its computers as well.

For illustration we can employ a hypothetical AFDC mother and her three children in Los Angeles in the late Sixties.[3] She was receiving $200 per month in support from AFDC. She had a 10th-grade education, no skills. If pride or a mandatory work requirement had brought her to the necessity for employment, she might have found work in a low-paying service job at $2.00 per hour. Would she then have had the dignity of self-sufficiency? Her gross income per month for a forty-hour week would have been $346. Payroll deductions, work related expenses, and the costs of child care (the last computed at the lowest levels) would have consumed $242 of her gross earnings. This would have left $104 for the family as real income to be spread over rent and utilities, food, clothing, and incidentals for four persons. The mother would then have had these alternatives: she could have fed the children and not paid the rent and utilities, or she could have paid the rent and not fed the children, or she could have paid the rent, partly fed the children, and left them to shift for themselves without substitute care while she worked.

If she were to remain on AFDC, the real income of the family would be $200 per month and her children would remain in her personal care.

If the AFDC mother chose the debasing alternative of welfare, we do not have to impute sloth, cunning, and apathy to her motives. It is just as likely that she was a woman who cared about her children and had the basic intelligence required of all of us to manage 5th-grade arithmetic.

In Congress, however, this lady was not praised because there were just too many of her, and we had even larger budget headaches. While motives for choosing welfare over low-paid work could easily be derived from the budget arithmetic of a family in poverty (and all this information was available to our legislators and to the taxpayer) it was a difficult idea to hold onto. There is nothing that stirs our passions like a page of figures which reveal an unpalatable truth. Our congressional debates record that the woman who did her arithmetic and came up with the same answers as the GAO computers was, nevertheless, transformed into a harpy who preyed upon the taxpayer. (I have chosen my language carefully. The language employed in congressional debate was coarser.)

THE RISE IN AFDC ROLLS AND COSTS

The other part of the story which led to reversal of AFDC policy can be stated in straightforward terms. Over a decade there was a tremendous rise in the number of families on AFDC, and the public costs of welfare were escalating at a frightening rate. The taxpayer was rebelling, and his representatives in government were speaking for him. The phrases "hard core welfare clients" and "welfare as a way of life" entered public oratory and drowned out the sober reports of economic analysts which made the issues more complex and more perplexing. Since "hard core welfare" inflames the imagination and economic studies do not, it is probably a good idea to take up the "hard core" issue first.

There is, I am sure, a category of welfare clients who represent the third generation of their families on welfare. What their numbers are and whether the incidence of such families on welfare was or is increasing is a mystery which has not been illuminated by any of the sources I have consulted. My impression in reading the work of respected scholars in the field is that whatever the numbers of "hard core" families,

127

they appear *not* to be the cause of the tremendous rise in relief rolls during the past decade.[4]

However, since the whole issue of "hard core welfare" pervades the climate of opinion and muddies our vision of the real problems of poverty, it is worth reporting these facts which bear upon entering and exiting from the welfare system. Sar Levitan, writing in 1971 says, "Steady growth of the (AFDC) rolls masks a tremendous turnover. . . ." "Most families join and leave the AFDC rolls quickly. In recent years approximately one quarter of the cases left within six months; 30 percent left within a year; half closed within two years; and three-fifths within three years."[5]

How to account, then, for the steady rise in welfare rolls? I think there is a fair consensus among social scientists that the rise in relief rolls reflected in large measure social and economic changes and conditions which were affecting the population at large. Thus the increase in the number of families on AFDC reflected the steep rise in the number of female-headed families over the course of a decade, a trend that was seen in all sectors of our society. This increase, in turn, was related to a sharp rise in divorce and desertion rates and the rise in illegitimate births, which increased every year from 1960 to 1968. (The highest increase in illegitimacy was in white births.) To these factors we need to add the rise in the number of women of childbearing age in the general population who had been themselves the babies of the post World War II baby boom.[6] Then, since all women who head families are disadvantaged in the labor market and limited in choice by the needs of dependent children, women with young children and limited education have the poorest options in work, in wages, and in the availability of jobs.[7]

Our wage structure itself failed to provide adequate earnings to sustain a very large number of families in which the head of the family was employed full time. Nearly one out of seven persons employed in 1970 earned less than $2.00 per hour, according to Levitan.[8] If the wage earner was employed full time and supported a family, he could scarcely sustain it above the poverty level. If the wage earner and family head was a woman with young dependent children, the costs of child care would reduce her real income to starvation levels.

We are back, then, to the budget arithmetic which we worked out for the hypothetical Los Angeles mother with three children. The truth was that the rise in the number of AFDC cases reflected economic and social changes which were beyond our grasp in 1970, and are still not fully grasped in 1977.

It would be unnecessary, then, to impute motives of avarice or sloth as reasons for the swelling AFDC caseloads. AFDC actually became the only alternative for large numbers of women with small children.

And a sad and shameful alternative for most of them. Surveys during this period confirmed that the majority of women on AFDC would prefer work to welfare if there were real choices in work and child-care plans. The largest number of AFDC recipients considered welfare shameful and gave heartfelt testimony that the American work ethic was right, that one *should* be self-supporting and not dependent on others.[9] And a substantial number of AFDC mothers (more black than white) were in the labor force, part time or full time, and were still "not making it" without AFDC supplementation.[10]

HOW IS POLICY MADE?

All of this information was available to the policy makers of the Sixties, but policies are not immediately responsive to the knowledge available to us at critical points in the decision-making process. Issues of public welfare stir profound feelings in all of us. Anger, disillusionment, weariness, helplessness, and an urge to take action seize the taxpayer and his elected representatives, and the facts cannot be assimilated. Not right away.

A strong push for action came not alone from the rise in welfare recipients and costs, but public agitation in which "the welfare bum" and "the profligate woman" were marked as the real villains, and these labels drowned out the sober realities of the charts, the tables, and the testimony of experts that the issues were larger and more formidable and lay within the fabric of our economic system and changes in the American family. Wisdom would have dictated postponement of action until it could be guided by solid facts and sound principles. Instead, if I have fairly read the debates of this era, the "hard core welfare family" took on mythic proportions, welfare and hardcore became synonymous, and in anger and desperation we put together a hodgepodge of reforms to save us from the mythical beast who was devouring our house and threatening to set up permanent residence within it.

It was in this climate that we invented our own Creature and named it WIN. As one of the last legacies of The Great Society, the WIN program has proven to be a costly disaster and, like so many legacies of its kind, after nearly a decade of tinkering and patching, it cannot be made to work and cannot even be junked. In the budget arithmetic which I worked out for the Martin family (Chapter IV) you will recall that direct welfare payments were reduced by the costs of child care during job training and employment brought the total costs of the program to a figure that far exceeded the original AFDC payment while the mother remained at home with her children.

On the face of it, it is hard to argue with the idea that welfare families should become self-supporting, that work incentives should be provided to halt the proliferating numbers of families which are being supported through public assistance. If there is no work incentive, it is argued, these families will continue to be sustained at public expense, and larger and larger numbers of families will become dependent upon welfare aid. Already, it has been pointed out, in many states the AFDC payments to families exceed the income of the working poor. And this is true, even though the AFDC support is under the poverty line in every state.

Like any rational person, I too believe that families should have incentives to become self-supporting. But there are six million children in the AFDC families with female heads who require substitute mother care if their mothers are employed, and the services which are provided by Child Care Industries Incorporated do not provide substitute mother care. In fact, as we have seen in Chapter IV, they are, typically, child storage houses, staffed by care-givers who are mostly indifferent and often outrageously neglectful.

Children at all ages are endangered by indifferent care-givers. But children under the age of six are endangered during the most critical period of development. One of the 1967 Social Security Amendments made no exceptions in its compulsory work requirements for the mothers of small children. It is very likely, of course, that there was no intention of enforcing this compulsory work requirement; it was a threat, a legislative temper tantrum, and a wholly dishonest gesture of appeasement to irate congressmen and taxpayers. In practice, in the years that followed, the penalties were not broadly exercised, and discretion in enforcing the work requirement was left to the states. Most states, like my own, do not *require* mothers with children under six to seek job training or employment. But the ambiguities in the law leave much room for "encouragement" and even pressure upon the AFDC mother to seek employment or job training if "suitable child-care arrangements" are available. Since in our state the Department of Social Services is responsible for

131

both the administration of AFDC and the licensing of day-care homes and centers, an extraordinary number of homes and centers have been licensed and judged "suitable." The majority of those I have known would be rated by me as "poor" or even worse.

Then, since the dollar incentives offered to an AFDC mother who works will bring a modest benefit to a family living in extreme poverty (see the budget arithmetic in Chapter IV), there are real incentives to the AFDC mother with small children to seek employment. This combination of "encouragement," subtle threats, and dollar incentives has resulted in a rise in the numbers of AFDC mothers with young children who are employed or in job training throughout the country, and if I can judge the temper of the taxpayer and our legislators, this number may increase each year.

The Department of Soma, then, has complied with the voter's demands that "welfare heads of families" be pushed toward employment and self-support. It has provided incentives and encouragement to mothers to seek employment and it has provided the costs of day care for the children. It has carried out both the voter's mandate and the laws which govern welfare.

And Then the Children

But the children are not faring well. And that is our department. In the Department of Psyche we are seeing babies and very small children who are not complying with the law. In spite of everything their government is doing for them—jobs for their mothers, day care for themselves, Medicaid and food stamps—they are not cooperating.

We are seeing an alarming number of babies from AFDC families and other families in poverty who are showing signs of emotional starvation. We see many solemn babies who rarely smile or vocalize. We see some babies who are already developmentally retarded, yet our refined testing may show mental capabilities beyond those reflected in the standard test score. We see babies who do not recognize their mothers at an age where normal babies show recognition and preference for their mothers. A number of these babies are in severe and even life-threatening states of malnutrition.

These are signs and symptoms which are commonly associated with "maternal deprivation." In classic form these signs were first identified in the 18th and 19th centuries in institutionalized infants who were deprived of mothers and mother substitutes.

It would be easy, then, to leap to the generalization that the mothers of these babies in poverty were all guilty of gross neglect, but only in exceptional cases was this found to be so. In our work at the Child Development Project we withhold judgment until all aspects of the baby's life have been examined by us. Our staff is composed of pediatric specialists in medicine, psychiatry, psychology, and social work. Through careful study of these families we made the discovery that many of our most severely endangered babies were children in poverty whose mothers were employed, and who were cared for through the desperate child care plans of the poor. These included the baby storage home provided by "somebody" in the neighborhood (and sometimes a different "somebody" several times a week) or a baby bank (it could be a child-care center subsidized by the government) in which a procession of indifferent care-givers of doubtful qualifications ministered to twenty babies for ten hours of a baby's day. For all practical purposes, these were motherless babies.

As illustration, I will cite the figures which emerge from one category of severely endangered babies, referred to us for failure-to-thrive (growth failure, no primary physiological causes, associated with severe emotional deprivation). These are babies whose survival is in danger both in the physiological and psychological senses. Among eleven babies referred to us with the diagnosis "failure-to-thrive," ten were in families with incomes below the poverty line. Six of the ten babies in poverty were AFDC recipients. In eight of the eleven cases the mother was not the primary caregiver; she was employed or in job training, and the baby was being cared for in homes or day-care centers, licensed and unlicensed, in each case unable to provide substitute mother care as judged by us. In some cases this was due to indifference and gross neglect in substitute mother care; in others it was the incapacity in a crowded day-care center to provide for the physical and emotional needs of infants and young children.

In this life-threatening disorder we can see that poverty has placed these babies in double jeopardy. First, it will virtually guarantee nutritional inadequacy. Second, in the event that the mother must work, poverty deprives the mother of decent options in substitute mother care and most frequently reduces her options to baby storage places. The result, in such extreme cases as "failure-to-thrive," is a baby who is suffering both a severe nutritional disorder and a severe psychological disorder.

I have used "failure-to-thrive" as a small model for study in this illustration. The majority of the infants in our program who show disorders of attachment have not reached the alarming state of growth failure. But in a very considerable number of cases in which we see disorders of attachment, poverty and the miserable choices imposed upon the poor have brought babies and young children into the care of indifferent and even abusive substitute care arrangements which can be beyond the control of the mother herself.

In speaking of poverty and its effects upon this subgroup of imperiled babies—or any others—there is no reason to distinguish between the poverty of AFDC (the so-called "dependent poor") and the poverty of the "working poor" who do not seek financial aid. The effects upon the children are not easily discriminated, although it must be said that the children of the working poor will be spared some measure of the degradation and humiliation of poverty which every "welfare child" will know as soon as identity and consciousness of self begin to emerge in his development. And it is a solemn thought, as we pursue certain issues of poverty in these pages, that there are as many families among the "working poor," living below the poverty line, as there are families in the class of the "dependent poor," who are also living below the poverty line.

If I now return to issues of "public policy" and their effects upon children, I am mindful of the fact that poverty can reflect public policy whether the policy is institutionalized, as in welfare, or sanctioned as a kind of personal privilege, in the case of the working poor. In either case, so far as children are concerned, the policy, whether implicit or explicit, is one of indifference to the nation's children.

I have chosen to pursue the issues of public *welfare* policy chiefly because an institutionalized policy provides the most economical route into issues, biases, beliefs, myths, rationalizations, and self-deceptions. It registers as law and written policy and recorded debate and cannot be denied or put out of mind as readily as the unwritten policies which govern our opinions. If we are interested in examining policies which affect the children of poverty, our public welfare policies become a useful guide into the interior.

Who Are the Policy Makers?

If the reader will agree with me that such AFDC policies can adversely affect the minds and bodies of children, that they can erode the vital human ties between small children and their families, then we must ask, "How did this nation, which loves its children, bring itself to this alarming state? Who are the policy makers who deprive children of emotional and physical sustenance? Who creates a Department of Soma, which assaults the child, and a Department of Psyche to heal him?"

Alas, in our Republic it is the whole lot of us: the taxpayer, the voter, our representatives in government, the bureaucrats, all reflecting, it would appear, a popularly held sentiment. A sentiment *against children?* Not really. How could it be? Since in all the public outrage against The Welfare Mess, nobody ever mentions the children at all.

In the Newspeak which we have all embraced, there is something called Welfare, which is devouring our public purse and cheating the taxpayer. Public outrage is directed toward a group of public enemies called "Welfare Heads of Families." The image which is conjured up is that of a shiftless male, a community bum who could work if he wanted to but prefers to spend the taxpayer's money on booze, or dope, and causes his children to go hungry. Since it is clearly this welfare bum who is starving his children, we, the taxpayers, are not responsible. With each bite the IRS takes from our paychecks, the image of this publicly-supported bum arises like Frankenstein's Monster, and cries for vengeance come to our lips. We write to our newspapers. We write to our congressmen. Get rid of the Welfare Cheaters!

Our congressman has been plagued by this Welfare Bum too, and so he forms committees or joins committees to subdue this monster who is draining our public purse. Periodically, in a cleansing rite which we perform before election, the welfare books are inspected, and it is found that there is bad cheating on welfare going on all over. Auditors report that 5 percent of welfare recipients are ineligible for payments. The careful reader will find that this figure does not represent the incidence of fraud, but an aggregate figure which includes clerical errors in payments or in establishing eligibility. Actual cases of fraud are small in number and the incidence of fraud has changed little over the decades.[11] However, "welfare fraud" is regularly cited in inflammatory prose in our newspapers, and is popularly accepted as a sign of the decline of morals in our Republic. It also has the beneficial and cleansing effect of taking our minds off other frauds.

Being as much a puritan as anybody, I don't like fraud in any form or any place. And I don't think "small frauds" are entitled to apologists any more than "large frauds." So if I now diverge for a moment into the subject of "comparative fraud" I am not concerned about relative proprieties, I only wish to pursue a psychological problem. I am interested in the Welfare Cheater as a durable villain.

The *New York Times* (18 Sept. 1976)[12] reports that a congressional investigation of Medicaid has revealed "widespread fraud and waste" which may amount to as much as 25 to 50 percent of the $15 billion annual expenditures in this program. An earlier story in *Newsweek* (9 Aug. 1976)[13] reported that of the combined Medicaid and Medicare funds amounting to $32 billion annually, "at least ten percent are pilfered annually" as the result of abuses and outright fraud by all segments of the medical profession."

In the year in which these stories were written, 1976, our congressional offices were riddled with scandals. The matrimonial fidelity and moral purpose of a number of statesmen were tested and found wanting by playmates on their office payrolls. These diversions were unknowingly subsidized by the American taxpayer, whose indignation knew no bounds when it was learned that these office bunnies could not type and kept irregular hours.

In this year, too, our national police force, the FBI, was found with a hand in the taxpayer's pocket. Our CIA has devoted a large chunk of the taxpayer's money to burglaries ("unauthorized burglaries," as the phrase goes) and has committed hundreds of millions of the taxpayer's money to the "destabilization" of the governments of foreign countries. With a few blueprints for murder.

When we consider the number and cultural diversity of this gang of rogues and crooks who have been feasting on the taxpayer's money, it is remarkable how durable as a national villain the Welfare Head of the Family has been. Scandals come and go, but on our public enemies list there is really no one else who consistently makes the headlines every day and who can stir our passions to such a frenzy.

Who is he?

I have gone in search of him. In the library stacks. Where else?

Levitan reports: "Although one welfare family in six includes a father, two-thirds of these men are incapacitated; only about five percent of AFDC families include an able-bodied father. More than seven families in ten include only the mother. One family in ten includes neither the father nor the mother, and the children live with a caretaker relative or in a foster home." [14]

The Welfare Bum is apparently hiding out in that 5 percent of AFDC families. However, since a good number of those men may be temporarily unemployed or may, in fact, be working full time or half time at hourly rates that cannot support a family without AFDC supplementation, we have to search further in these figures for the Welfare Bum who refuses to work in order to exploit the taxpayer. Does he represent one percent? Two percent? I cannot find further information. However, even at 2 percent the taxpayer should feel some relief. The incidence of able-bodied men on AFDC who are unwilling to support their families through work (or cannot find work) would not appear to be high enough to threaten the American work ethic.

This leaves us with the problem of identifying the Welfare Heads of Families for our rites of exorcism and, alas, the figures and the gender will not change.

Seventy-five percent of Welfare Heads of Families are women, mothers of dependent children. Since dependent children are by definition in need of a mother's care, these Welfare Heads of Families are not, strictly speaking, unemployed. The battle cry "mandatory employment for welfare heads of families" has a hollow ring when our public crusaders come charging down the hill to find the shiftless bum who is feasting upon the taxpayer's money and find a woman with three children. And they are not feasting.

Who, then, is stealing the taxpayer's money? Is it the children? Or their mother? Since we are a nation that loves its children we will not accuse them of stealing the taxpayer's money. And since "mother" is a word that evokes the wrong sentiments for tax cutting, we are left without a villian unless we can engage the welfare bum (male) to furnish his valuable services.

It is the children, of course, who are ultimately responsible. Once the children get into the picture they louse up policy decisions. If we keep them in the picture and label them as "welfare recipients" we can't reduce welfare expenditures. We might even have to increase them. And since the children are not spending the taxpayer's money on booze, there is no one to blame for our fiscal crisis and the deterioration of public morals. In order to preserve our economic policies, which call for "drastic cuts in public spending," we have to get the children out of the picture. This can be done through a massive act of repression: there are no children in Aid to Families of Dependent Children. And now, since someone clearly is stealing the taxpayer's money, we discover to our relief that it is the welfare head of family—and the male bum offers himself (with a lewd smirk) for ritual sacrifice.

When the male bum is not available (hired elsewhere; everyone needs him) a carefully selected female counterpart can be employed. In another version of this national soap opera the welfare head of family *is* a woman. The phrase "welfare mother" is deleted from the script because the word "mother" will introduce the wrong sentiments for "mandatory employment." There are still a lot of taxpayers and congressmen who don't like the idea of working *mothers*. But if it can be demonstrated that these female heads of welfare families are unworthy of the sacred name "mother," well then, by God, we and our congressional representatives will support "mandatory employment."

So it is necessary to prove that these women are unworthy. Well, then, a large number of them have conceived their children out of wedlock. They are sinners who should now do penance. (Senatuh, we could all do with a little penance.) And some of these women have continued to procreate while receiving public funds. That makes them *unrepentant* sinners, and they should pay. (Let's send the bill to the children.) And the reason that they procreate and continue to procreate is *in order to get public funds.* (Any unrepentant sinner could figure out an easier way of making a living.) And they let their children go running loose on the streets. (Not proven. But the rental allowance on AFDC does not get the kids a garden apartment.) Anyway, as the picture of a sinful and profligate woman emerges, a woman who neglects her children and profanes the word "mother," it is not difficult for the taxpayer and the congressman to chant in unison, "Get the cheaters off of welfare!" And "mandatory employment of AFDC heads of families" is a shoo-in.

Here, again, the children louse up the script. Somebody, perhaps a bureaucrat who is paid to keep these things in his head, will bring up the question of the children. "What children?" "Those Dependent Children that we are giving Aid To. If the woman goes to work, who will take care of those Dependent Children?" There is a pause for everyone to collect his thoughts. "Day Care!" someone remembers. He is greeted with a cheer. The children will all go to day-care centers. Nice clean day-care centers with a hot lunch, and teachers who will give them cultural enrichment and keep them off the streets. Then, says the bureaucrat, we will need day-care funds for six million AFDC children whose female heads of family are employed during the day. *That,* says the committee, is inflationary and we will vote against it. The committee adjourns with the recommendation that day care be provided for all children of welfare mothers who are employed and that no new money be appropriated for day-care centers.

The children can now be obliterated from consciousness and conscience. As the ill-served consumers of Child Care Industries Incorporated, they will not complain to their congressmen. They have no vote anyway. They are an invisible constituency in every congressional district.

Finally, it appears that the duplicity which has governed our public policies affecting the welfare of children is not the result of a master plan to defraud the children of basic human needs, but the result of mental trickery in the public conscience. By getting the children out of the picture we are free to pursue our tough-minded policies with respect to public aid and to cut the budget without a tear. With the children out of the picture we can vote for mandatory employment of "welfare heads of families," provide dollar incentives to the AFDC mother who works, and build a costly subsidy for day care. By keeping the direct costs of welfare allowances in a separate budget from the subsidies, we console the irate taxpayer. The net additional costs of this program to the taxpayer can be calculated in the hundreds of millions. The child-care programs provided for the children have been generally of the poorest quality, although the taxpayer has paid heavily for storage costs. The costs paid by the children who are in storage have not been calculated by anyone.

Alternative Poverty Proposals

The alternatives to The Welfare Mess have been various forms of income redistribution plans in which the welfare apparatus is dismantled and the poor are provided with a minimum base income which would be accountable through the mechanisms that already exist in IRS. In principle it is equitable. It gets rid of the public assistance caseworkers and functionaries who police the poor and degrade them, and it leaves the problem of who is cheating and who is not reporting income to the IRS, which bring the poor to the same status as taxpaying citizens that the rest of us enjoy.

However, the fate of Nixon's Family Assistance Plan is highly instructive to those who seek welfare reform and a plan to eradicate poverty in our country. The plan, sensibly enough, included income supplements for the "working poor" as well as the so-called "dependent poor," and evolved from the concept of a negative income tax. The base levels proposed in the various modifications of this proposal would not eradicate poverty, but were conceived as a first step toward a policy of income support and a redistribution of the tax burden. The arithmetic involved would bring us back into the Looking Glass Economy, and I have no heart to go through the looking glass again.[15]

The Nixon plan was introduced on October 3, 1969. The House approved the plan with some modifications in April 1970. The Senate Finance Committee balked on a number of issues. Liberals felt the level of payments was too low. Many conservatives were against the program from the start and called it "a guaranteed annual income." The arguments circled around the issues of "work incentives," and the Welfare Bum and the Profligate Woman came on stage for their ritual

142

performance.* The arithmetic of work incentives, worked and reworked in endless revisions, never closed the gap in the arguments. And, alas, no arithmetic could cover the gap between the proposals for income support and the prevailing level of support of 90 percent of welfare recipients.[16]

While salvage operations were begun by FAP supporters, another storm broke out—the Cambodian incursion—and FAP was abandoned.

New income redistribution plans are again in preparation as I write the final pages of this chapter. If a wizard appears who can close the gaps in the old plan, or devise a new one, it is safe to predict that the cry "inflationary" will create turmoil once again. And it may take another wizard to get the Welfare Bum and Profligate Woman off the stage in our national soap opera so as to leave a decent space for the children.

In 1974 there were 10.2 million children living in "official" poverty, the term for the federal "poverty line." For a nonfarm family of four, the threshold in that year was $5,038. A more accurate measure of poverty based upon Department of Labor minimum income standards would bring the figure to 17 million children who were living on less than the minimum required for basic needs. Of these there were about 5.5 million under the age of six.[17]

Budget Priorities and Priorities for Children

This has been a long discourse on poverty for a small book dealing with the child and his human bonds. If I have dwelt

---

* Would a negative income tax with graduated work incentives result in a reduced work effort or withdrawal from the labor force? In a recent field ex-

at length on social welfare policies and their effects upon human attachments, it is because I firmly believe that the children of poverty are the single largest group in our nation which is robbed of its human potential in infancy and the early years.

The children of poverty suffer lost and broken connections in their human partnerships as a commonplace experience: for other children in our society this need not be. I have argued that this is not a wholesale indictment of parents in poverty, rather that poverty robs a parent of the freedom to make the good choices and the wise choices on behalf of children.

A mother on welfare can be provided with all the useful information I have offered in this book on the importance of human attachments (she may know it without this book) and not be in a position to employ that knowledge to serve the best interests of her child. If AFDC policy requires her to work, or offers incentive to work, her own knowledge of what her child needs is practically irrelevant. If the additional income from her low-paid job provides her child with at least minimum adequate nutrition, she may have to weigh that fact against the psychological risks for her baby or young child. If her earnings at $2.00 or $2.50 per hour cannot obtain good substitute care for her child, she will have to settle for less. If the government-subsidized day-care center is regarded as "suitable" by AFDC and "unsuitable" by the mother herself, she may find it prudent to accept the day-care center. If she finds that her AFDC rental allowance gives her a rat-infested flat, she must settle for rats: she is unlikely to find something better. If her AFDC shelter provides her

---

periment conducted in New Jersey (families with a *male* head, the major group not now covered under cash assistance programs) analysis of data covering a three-year period showed no difference in the labor force participation between the experimental and the control group families. *Setting National Priorities,* p. 186.

with neighbors who are junkies and prostitutes, she is not likely to escape them through moving. If she teaches her kids to dodge the junkies and the street toughs, she will be lucky if one out of three will learn to dodge them successfully.

The bad choices are obligatory. And they are supported by public policy.

A rational public policy for children cannot coexist with poverty and our current welfare practices. Yet each of the income redistribution plans which has been proposed to date has created a storm. "Something for nothing!" "Astronomical costs!" "Inflationary!" In a year like 1976, for instance, in which our Defense budget was 114 billion dollars,[18] the phrase "astronomical costs" had a hollow ring.

The cost of maintaining children in poverty cannot be calculated in dollars and cents. For those who like to work out the figures, I would suggest some of the factors that need to go into the calculation. The lost and broken human connections which are the common lot of many young children in poverty are directly related to the social diseases of poverty. School failure, juvenile crime, mental instability are increased in any population in which the bonds between the children and his human partners are absent or eroded as in the circumstances of poverty. Malnutrition *in utero* and throughout the years of childhood is directly related to the high incidence of disease and early death in the families of poverty. The omnipresent neighborhood dangers and crime which every ghetto child experiences will infect a very large part of the child population and provide irresistible vocational models for the vulnerable. The climate of self-denigration and despair in the ghetto will do the rest. By the time the welfare child has reached the age of six, his net worth in cash and I.Q. will be calculated for him, and he will know it isn't much. If he survives to the age of marriage, he is likely, as the rest of us are, to reproduce the patterns of his child-rearing for his own children.

Someone else will have to go off to the library to get the statistics on the real cost of maintaining poverty for this nation. I think they will be "astronomical," as we say now. If we add these real costs to the dollar costs of our present welfare system, we might discover that a rational "income redistribution plan" is the best bargain of the century.

The ultimate benefits to the economy should also be weighed heavily in the calculation. My friend Harold Shapiro, chairman of the Department of Economics at the University of Michigan, points out that optimal development in childhood is related to future productivity in the labor market. The investment now in family support and the welfare of children could bring incalculable benefits to the economy in the future.

In dollars the costs of an income support program to bring a large segment of our nation out of extreme poverty will be very large: annually in the billions, we can expect.* Another such income proposal will certainly bring cries of agony from the taxpayer. On the other hand, the taxpayer shows a serene passivity in shelling out hundreds of billions for national defense. He can do this under the illusion that every billion is purchasing his security, and the more billions he invests in security the more security he will have.

The costs in billions of providing every child with the biological and psychological necessities for optimal development should not stir national outrage when they are placed beside the costs of insuring our national security. And I am assuming that the costs of a new income program for the poor would continue (like defense) for many years to come. Poverty and the social diseases bred by poverty cannot be

---

*One estimate by economists: The net Federal costs of an income support program to replace AFDC, food stamps, supplementary security income, etc., and provide an income guarantee of $4,800 for a family of four, would be about $15 billion, calculated in 1976 dollars. Such a program would include about a quarter of the U.S. population, the working poor as well as the dependent poor. *Setting National Priorities*, p. 204.

abolished in five years or ten years, perhaps not in fifty years. We can consult our history books and learn that massive social reform will not bring about "significant change" until generations have been affected by the minute increments of change which finally accrue as benefits to a population. For the cost accountants who will demand instant results from the national sacrifice to abolish poverty, there is a warning from us social scientists to put their computers to work on another program for the next forty years and leave the poverty budget to work on its humane mission without computing the cash value of children's lives.

The question, "Can we afford billions to abolish poverty and billions for defense?" falsifies the issues for the voter and the taxpayer. Our budget priorities have gone to defense because the generals have persuaded us that these billions will insure our survival as a people. It can be fairly argued that the highest priority for mankind is to save itself from extinction. However, it can also be argued that a society that neglects its children and robs them of their human potential can extinguish itself without an external enemy.

CHAPTER VI

The Tribal Guardians

THE LEGENDARY ANGELS and benevolent spirits who guide the fortunes of the newborn child are not invited to the christening of a very large number of American babies. In their place we send agents of the bureaucracy, immigration officers, insurance brokers, and cost accountants who examine the credentials of the baby for entering the human community. Now that he's here, should he be here at all? Can he pay his own way? If not, does he intend to live in decent poverty or does he intend to be dependent upon the taxpayers of this community? What are the moral credentials of his parents? Is he the right color for the human race? Has he in general chosen his genetic heritage, his parents, and his socioeconomic status in ways that conform to the high standards required for membership in our society?

It is not good for babies to have immigration officers, insurance brokers, and cost accountants to preside at the christening, and the babies cannot thrive.

To the credit of the celestial agents, they never ask these questions. They are sensible and, considering their habits, down to earth about these things. The baby is *here*, they say with commendable sense. He belongs to all of us. If misfortune has governed the circumstance of his birth, they appoint godparents, seers, sages, and even humble people to guide the fortunes of the baby. In my reading of legends, this kind of social action practiced by the angels has had a highly beneficial effect upon the babies. My analysis of outcome studies, widely dispersed in mythology and sacred texts, shows that the largest number of babies whose destinies have been guided by love and wisdom in a devoted human community have transcended circumstance and returned the gift.

Before I become hopelessly trapped in my allegories—and before I lose the certificate of mental health which is conferred upon me by my profession—I should set the record straight: I do not believe in these celestial spirits; I never believed in them even at an age when I should have. Like any observant child poring over the pictures in my illustrated Grimm's, I soon discovered that all those celestial celebrants at the christening had the same faces as the "real people" who appeared in other illustrations throughout the book. Beneath the wings and the crowns and the robes, and my own jelly smears, I could recognize every one of them. The celebrant in the blue robe and halo was the shoemaker who wore a leather apron and tiny spectacles when the elves visited him. The fellow with the tipsy crown and red robes was the baker who brought white loaves to a virtuous maiden who had been left to die of starvation. The radiant purple angel was the widow who had last seen her only son, a headstrong boy, when he ascended a bean stalk. They were the village folk in fancy dress. They had put aside their sorrows and just grievances with the world to celebrate the birth of a new baby and bring him gifts.

As I understand it now they were representatives of the village or the tribe who followed an ancient tradition in which the parents conferred life upon the child and the community united with the family to insure the human rights of the newborn.

The tradition survives in thousands of small communities throughout the world, including some in our own country. But as cities arise, the ancient bonds of community become tenuous, or are dissolved. The tribal guardians of the child are replaced by institutional guardians. In modern history the institutional guardians are agents of government in health, law, social welfare, and public accounting. Each of them is assigned a piece of the child and his family, and there is no one among them who is assigned the ancient role of celebrant at the birth and guardian of the human rights of the infant. The child and his family are anonymous, and will remain so unless misfortune brings them out of anonymity. There are also bureaus and agents in the department of misfortune.

It can be argued that the largest number of babies and families in megalopolis appear to survive without self-appointed guardians of the child's human rights and tribal celebrants at the birth. Those who do not fare well are victims, we say, of their own inadequacy. But, in fact, I can testify that nearly every young family faces great strain and extraordinary demands upon its internal resources when it brings a new baby into the world. Unaided by relatives and a devoted community, the young family is cast adrift to confer as best it can its own blessings upon the child and the store of its own wisdom. In favor of the ancient tradition, every baby and his family was embraced in the arms of the community, and the strength of the family was augmented a thousand-fold by the bonds of the community. It was a form of mental health insurance. It is conceivable that the community prevented breakdown in many families and thus insured the rights of infants. When it happened that all the blessings and sacred rites did not prevent trouble for a baby, the self-appointed guardians of the baby took their work seriously. They were not impeded by bureaucratic regulations. They brought the best of their wisdom to the endangered baby and his family with the love and authority that only a community can confer upon its members.

All this happens, even today, in a community when babies and their families are not anonymous. The baby belongs to his family, but he is also "our baby."

As a member of the mental health profession I am not suggesting the abolition of my profession in favor of celestial spirits, or paraprofessionals, for the guardianship of the mental health of infants. When a baby is in psychological peril, I would rather have his parents consult me than Great Aunt Sadie. I know more than she does about these things. But I welcome Aunt Sadie as a collaborator if she is the source of emotional sustenance for the family and if the baby is precious to her. We need each other. When, in fact, I am called in to see an imperiled baby in his home I will sometimes find the whole clan assembled there to look me over. They are not in the least interested in my university credentials. They take those for granted. Do I *care* about *their* baby? is what they want to know and they will put me to a rough test. For my part, I see the gathering of the clan, however quarrelsome and self-righteous this clan may be, as a good omen. I am counting on the baby, his parents, and the whole tribe to enable me to do my own work.

What I am saying, then, is that the institutional guardians of the baby's human rights—and I am one of those—can mend, repair, bring wisdom to the cause of babies but cannot take the place of tribal guardians of the baby. Neither can we all return to villages to revive the ancient practices. There must be ways in which a modern urban society can find measures to replace or reconstitute or rediscover the tribal guardians who insure the rights of infants.

Who is out there to take up the cause? Millions, I think. If the tribe is scattered and the guardians are scattered, the love of babies has not been extinguished. In work with needy children and their families, I have found that I have only to mention that something which is not immediately available is needed for a baby, and there may not be enough people to man the switchboard. If I write a piece in a popular magazine describing an unmet need of babies, our office will be snowed under as the letters of concern, the offers of help arrive, and continue to arrive, for weeks.

What I have seen is that when a baby and his family arise from anonymity because of need or danger, the sense of community is immediately aroused and we are transformed into a village in which every member of the tribe plays a traditional role. The purpose of this book has been to identify babies and their families and their needs and to make them visible. When this happens, the babies become *our* babies, the tribe rallies round, and intelligent solutions can be found.

A nation is a community, too. We are still new in the experiment of democracy and the ways in which our social institutions can respond to need on a vast scale. When the institutions do not serve these needs and may themselves be inventing new social diseases while we are working on the old ones, we spend much of our human energies in repairing and patching, or simply imploring the machine to work (a practice that I employ with my household appliances when they become obstinate). In the case of those institutions that serve children and their families, there is now a colossal apparatus which spans the country and consumes a fortune—and it doesn't work.

I think it doesn't work because there are no governing principles among these institutions, no ideas which give unity and purpose to their programs. They have lost "the human center," to use Erich Kahler's phrase.[1] And when that is lost, the programs themselves can do nothing more than perpetuate themselves, like those monstrous machines that have discovered the secret of self-duplication.

If we take seriously the psychological evidence that

emerges from the study of human infancy—and I think we must—there *is* a unifying principle which can govern the social programs which serve families and their children. The principle is found in the primacy of human attachments. If we translate this principle into a creed for the governance of these programs and the services provided by them it might be stated in these words: Every social program in medicine, law, education, and public welfare must commit itself to the protection of the human rights of children, the rights of enduring human partnerships, the right to be cherished by family and community, the right to fully realize their human potentials. The same principle provides useful guidelines for judging the performance of a program and revisions of programs. Thus, if medical practice exerts itself on behalf of the physical well-being of babies and their families but neglects the psychological needs of a child and his parents at birth and after birth, it has not fully protected the human rights of children and must answer to the community. If our laws and our court practices deprive children of their rights through obsolete beliefs and judgments, the laws and their executors must be called to public accounting for ignorance of the psychological needs of children. If our day-care programs and our educational programs ignore the psychological needs of children, or assault these needs through their practices, they must answer to an outraged citizenry. If our programs for families in poverty create conditions in which a child may be starved physically and psychologically, these programs must be abolished, and humane solutions must be found.

"Accountability," which most often today refers to cost accounting, must have the meaning of moral accountability to the public. And the public must itself be an informed public and a public that represents the children's cause.

In this sense we are all guardians of the children's rights. And if the village conditions which conferred tribal guardians upon the newborn and his family do not prevail in a complex society, we can reconstitute the mission of the tribal guardians for a complex society.

The children need spokesmen, advocates, and lobbyists, too, at every level of social and political organization in which public policy and law affect the development of the child and may impinge upon his human rights. On the highest levels of government we need powerful spokesmen for "the special interests" of children who can speak with authority and with the strength of numbers behind them.

The children's cause which is the subject of Gilbert Steiner's book of the same name has more often served other "causes" in Washington than those of the children.[2] As I read Steiner's book (which appeared as I was completing the first draft of this book) I found myself in another Looking Glass world. There have been, and are, many children's causes, nearly all transitory and issue oriented. The spokesmen for the children, also "issue oriented," have themselves been transitory since their mission was either accomplished or was not accomplished. School lunch programs, mandatory education of the handicapped, child abuse, day care, become issues that summon various factions to Washington, to speak for the children, to speak for themselves and *their* causes, to argue among themselves, to form temporary and often grudging coalitions, to disband after victory or defeat.

Thus, to use one example, subsidized day care has brought to Washington an assortment of bedfellows who, under ordinary circumstances, would decline to share an office suite together. There are career women who want subsidized day care as an instrument for their liberation from the home and children. There are welfare mothers who want quality day care for their children while they are working out of economic necessity. There are educators who see day care as an institution for enrichment of the lives of disadvantaged children. Unionists want an expansion of day-care programs for children in order to provide jobs for the large number of excess teachers on the market. Social activists see child development centers as a catalyst for community development and social change.

Since this is the way business is done in our democracy—and it has generally worked well for 200 years—why should one quarrel with this means of conducting business for the children? But self-interest and compromise, which work well for the allocation of funds for regional resources, government contracts, tax proposals, and other domestic issues do not work as well when children and human resources are at stake. In fact, as I have argued elsewhere in this book, self-interest and compromise have themselves been responsible for laws and public policies which have generated new problems for children and their families.

Thus, in the day-care coalition I have described, some of the issue-oriented lobbyists are speaking for their own special interests and some may be speaking out of altruistic motives and love of children, but none of them is asking the disinterested questions: "If the program is enacted will it serve the developmental needs of young children? Will the design of the program insure quality care for children? Does it define 'quality care' and specify how it will be obtained? Will it sustain and strengthen the vital human connections of children? When the compromises have been made by all the special interest groups, will the children be compromised?"

Each of the issue-oriented groups may be assuming that there is somebody else "out there" who will be looking out for those things. But there isn't anybody else out there. Except us.

The virtue of the tribal guardians, the ordinary citizens like ourselves, is that we are not encumbered by "self-interest," and the "issue" is the child himself. An informed citizenry, committed to the rights of children, can ask the difficult questions, read the fine print in the proposal, look for the guarantees of the children's rights and necessities, and refuse compromises if the children's rights are endangered. And each of us holds a ballot in his hands for the citizen who is too young to vote.

Those tribal guardians could be a formidable lobby once they got together.

NOTES

Chapter I

The literature on mother-infant attachments is vast and dispersed among a large number of journals and books in specialized fields of human and animal psychology. A good summary and discussion of the human and animal literatures will be found in John Bowlby's *Attachment and Loss*. René Spitz's work, *The First Year of Life*, is a valuable introduction to the central issues in the study of human attachment and brings a historical perspective to this study which only one of the great pioneers could provide. Studies of mother-infant bonding in the neonatal period are examined by Marshall Klaus and John Kennell, along with concise presentations of their own ground-breaking research in this area, in their book, *Maternal Infant Bonding*.

Konrad Lorenz's book, *On Aggression* (discussed at some length in Chapter II), is actually a fascinating study of the origins of love and the characteristics of mother-infant attachment in a wide range of species. Jane Van Lawick-Goodall touches upon infant-mother bonding among chimpanzees in "The Behavior of Free Living Chimpanzees in the Gombe Stream Reserve."

Cross-cultural practices in infant rearing which are touched upon in this chapter are still sparsely documented in the anthropological literature. Among the classics in the field which serve as good introductions to the subject are Beatrice Whiting's *Six Cultures: Studies of Child Rearing*, John Whiting and Irvin Child's *Child Training and Personality*, Oscar Lewis's *Life in a Mexican Village*, and Mary Ainsworth's *Infancy in Uganda*, which is devoted entirely to the issues of infant rearing.

1. On the "love language," see the following: Robson, K. S. (1967): "The Role of Eye-to-Eye Contact in Maternal-Infant Attach-

ment." *Journal of Child Psychology and Psychiatry* 8:13–25; Stern, D. (1974): "Mother and Infant at Play: The Dyadic Interaction Involving Facial, Vocal and Gaze Behavior." In Lewis, M., and Rosenblum, L. (eds.), *The Effect of the Infant on Its Caregiver.* New York: Wiley, pp. 187–215; Fraiberg, S. (1974): "Blind Infants and Their Mothers: An Examination of the Sign System," and also pp. 215–233; Spitz, R. A., and Wolf, K. M. (1946): "The Smiling Response: A Contribution to the Ontogenesis of Social Relations." *Genetic Psychology Monographs* 34: 57–125; Emde, R. N., and Koenig, K. L. (1969): "Neonatal Smiling, Frowning, and Rapid Eye Movement States: II, Sleep-Cycle Study." *Journal of the American Academy of Child Psychiatry* 8, 4:637–656.

2. U.S. infant mortality rates are now higher than sixteen other countries. Non-white Americans rank 31st. *America's Children 1976*. Washington: The National Council of Organizations for Children and Youth, p. 32.

3. Prescott, J. W. (1971): "Early Somatosensory Deprivation as an Ontogenetic Process in the Abnormal Development of the Brain and Behavior." In Goldsmith, I. E., and Moor-Jankowski, J. (eds.), *Medical Primatology 1970*. Basel: Karger, pp. 356–375; Korner, A. F., and Thoman, E. B. (1972): "The Relative Efficacy of Contact and Vestibular-Proprioceptive Stimulation in Soothing Neonates." *Child Development* 43: 443–453; Kulka, A., Fry, C., and Goldstein, F. (1960): "Kinesthetic Needs in Infancy." *American Journal of Orthopsychiatry* 3: 562–571; Frank, L. K. (1957): "Tactile Communication." *Genetic Psychology Monographs* 56: 209–225.

4. Van Lawick-Goodall, J. (1968): "The Behavior of Free-Living Chimpanzees in the Gombe Stream Reserve." In Cullen, J. M. and Beer, C. G. (eds.), *Animal Behavior Monographs* I, 3: 161–311.

5. Kaufman, I. C., and Rosenblum, L. A. (1967): "Depression in Infant Monkeys Separated from their Mothers." *Science* 155: 1030–1.

6. Harlow, H. F. (1959): "Love in Infant Monkeys." *Scientific American* 200: 68–74; Harlow, H. F., and Harlow, M. K. (1965): "The Affectional Systems." In Schrier, A. M., Harlow, H. F., and Stollnitz, F. (eds.): *Behavior of Nonhuman Primates, Vol. 2.* New York: Academic Press, pp. 293–298.

7. Here I am referring to the classic studies of Drs. John Kennell and Marshall Klaus at Case Western Reserve Medical School. They have amassed strong evidence for a "sensitive period" in mother-infant bonding which normally occurs in the first hours and days after birth. Grave disruptions in the conditions for bonding (and

hospital practices may constitute a major form of disruption) can impede the process of bonding. Klaus, M. H., and Kennell, J. H. (1976): *Maternal-Infant Bonding (The Impact of Early Separation or Loss on Family Development)*. Saint Louis: C. V. Mosby Company.

Chapter II

1. Lorenz, K. (1967): *On Aggression*. New York: Harcourt, Brace and World.

2. Harlow, H. F., and Harlow, M. K. (1965): "The Affectional Systems." In Schrier, A. M., Harlow, H. F., and Stollnitz, F. (eds.), *Behavior of Nonhuman Primates, Vol. 2*. New York: Academic Press.

3. Freud, Sigmund (1955): "Analysis of a Phobia in a Five-Year-Old Boy." Originally published in 1909, part of the Standard Edition of *The Complete Psychological Works of Sigmund Freud*. London: Hogarth.

4. Capote, Truman (1966): *In Cold Blood*. New York: Random House.

5. We should carefully distinguish this kind of group care from that provided babies and young children in a kibbutz. The kibbutz baby has a mother and is usually breast-fed by her. Studies show that the kibbutz baby is attached to his mother and that the mother remains central in his early development. The group care of the kibbutz does not deprive the baby of mothering, whereas such deprivation is the crucial point of the studies I cite in this essay.

6. Spitz, R. A. (1945): "Hospitalism: An Inquiry into the Genesis of Psychiatric Conditions in Early Childhood." *Psychoanalytic Study of the Child* 1:53–74.

7. Provence, S., and Lipton, R. (1962): *Infants in Institutions*. New York: International Universities Press.

8. Wolff, P. H. (1963): "Observations on the Early Development of Smiling." In Foss, B. M. (ed.), *Determinants of Infant Behavior II*. London: Methuen, pp. 113–138.

9. Spitz, R. A. (1965): *The First Year of Life*. New York: International Universities Press.

10. Freud, A., and Burlingham, D. (1944): *Infants Without Families*. New York: International Universities Press.

Chapter III

1. 23 *Buffalo Law Review* 1 (1972): "Adoption and Child Custody: Best Interests of the Child", pp. 1–16.
2. *Life*, 1 December, 1972.
3. *New York Times*, 23 February, 1972: " 'Low Moral Standards' Judge Ruled: A Case of Changing Mores" by Laurie Johnston, p. 36.
4. *Jet*, 23 March, 1972: "Black Infant Center" by Warren Brown, pp. 12–15.
5. *The Ann Arbor News*, 17 November, 1976: "Oft-Shifted Foster Child Sues." As I prepare the final notes on this chapter, a news report appears which is worthy of citation. A sixteen-year-old boy, Dennis Smith, has filed suit in Alameda County Superior Court, asking damages of $500,000 from the county social service agency and officials of the public school system there. In sixteen years he has lived in sixteen foster homes. "It's like a scar on your brain," he says. "I want people to realize what is happening to foster children." If he wins the suit, says Dennis, he will use most of the money to lobby for legislation to overhaul the foster parent system. In response to a question Dennis says that if adoptive parents offered him a home he would say no. "Because of what I've been through, I think I would take it out on them and I don't think it would be fair," he said.
6. DeCourcy, P., and DeCourcy, J. (1973): *A Silent Tragedy*. New York: Alfred Publishing Company.
7. Goldstein, J., Freud, A., and Solnit, A. (1973): *Beyond the Best Interests of the Child*. New York: The Free Press.

Chapter IV

For "day care as it is," see Mary Keyserling, *Windows on Day Care*. For day care "at its best," see Sally Provence, Audrey Naylor, and June Patterson, *The Challenge of Daycare*. For a digest of information on employment of mothers and child care facilities, see *America's*

Children 1976. Budget arithmetic is my own, worked out with consultation of experts.

1. All figures on day-care needs from Senate Finance Committee Child Care Data and Materials 1974, cited in *America's Children 1976* (1976). Washington: The National Council of Organizations for Children and Youth.

2. Provence, Sally, Naylor, Audrey, and Patterson, June (1977): *The Challenge of Daycare,* New Haven: Yale University Press, describes one such "ideal" center.

3. Keyserling, Mary D. (1972): *Windows on Day Care.* New York: National Council of Jewish Women.

4. Keyserling, Mary D. (1972): "The Magnitude of Day Care Need," in Van Loon, E. (ed.), *Inequality in Education 13,* Cambridge: Center for Law and Education, Harvard University, pp. 5–55.

5. "When everyone is taking care of their own children, none of this important activity is counted in GNP. When everyone is taking care of each other's children, it is all counted. This accounting convention makes it ppear as if something new, different and better is going on when in fact, the opposite might very well be the case." Harold Shapiro (personal communication).

"If American society recognized home making and child rearing as productive work to be included in the national economic accounts (as is the case in at least one other nation) the receipt of welfare might not imply dependency. But we don't. It may be hoped the women's movement of the present time will change this. But as of the time I write it had not." Moynihan, Daniel P. (1972): *The Politics of a Guaranteed Income.* New York: Vintage Books, p. 17.

6. For summaries and analyses of the WIN program, see Moynihan, Daniel P. (1972): *The Politics of a Guaranteed Income,* New York: Vintage Books, and Levitan, Sar, Rein, M., and Marwick, D. (1972): *Work and Welfare Go Together,* Baltimore: The Johns Hopkins University Press.

Chapter V

1. *America's Children 1976* (1976). Washington: The National Council of Organizations for Children and Youth, p. 32.

2. Ibid., p. 24.

3. Levitan, S., Rein, M., and Marwick, D. (1972): *Work and Welfare Go Together*, Baltimore: The Johns Hopkins University Press, p. 80.

4. Moynihan, D. P. (1972): *The Politics of a Guaranteed Income.* New York: Vintage Books, pp. 88–89.

5. Levitan, p. 49–50.

6. Moynihan, pp. 29, 35–39, 85.

7. Ibid., p. 8.

8. Levitan, p. 124.

9. Moynihan, pp. 87–88.

10. Levitan, p. 61.

11. Ibid., p. 19.

12. *New York Times*, 18 September, 1976.

13. *Newsweek*, 9 August, 1976.

14. Levitan, p. 8.

15. For the best reader's guide, I recommend Moynihan's *The Politics of a Guaranteed Income.* Since Moynihan was one of the architects of FAP and is one of the nation's authorities on the Looking Glass Economy of Welfare, I will leave the instruction to him and only summarize the birth, decline, and fall of FAP.

16. Levitan, p. 129.

17. *America's Children 1976*, p. 17.

18. *Newsweek*, 9 August, 1976.

Chapter VI

1. Kahler, E. (1957): *The Tower and the Abyss.* New York: George Braziller, Inc.

2. Steiner, G. Y. (1977): *The Children's Cause.* Washington, D.C.: The Brookings Institution.